Hot as Hell

Hot as Hell

HelenKay Dimon

BRAVA

KENSINGTON PUBLISHING CORP.

www.kensingtonbooks.com

BRAVA BOOKS are published by

Kensington Publishing Corp.
850 Third Avenue
New York, NY 10022

All Kensington titles, imprints, and distributed lines are available at special quantity discounts for bulk purchases for sales promotion, premiums, fundraising, educational, or institutional use.

Special book excerpts or customized printings can also be created to fit specific needs. For details, write or phone the office of the Kensington Special Sales Manager: Kensington Publishing Corp., 850 Third Avenue, New York, NY 10022. Attn. Special Sales Department. Phone: 1-800-221-2647.

Brava and the B logo are Reg. U.S. Pat. & TM Off.

ISBN-13: 978-0-7582-2225-1
ISBN-10: 0-7582-2225-4

First Kensington Trade Paperback Printing: November 2008

10 9 8 7 6 5 4 3 2 1

Printed in the United States of America

To Suzanne Jones Lugo for joining me on that memorable hiking spa vacation and for being a dear friend for two decades—yeah, it's been that long.

ACKNOWLEDGMENTS

About a thousand years ago I traveled to Southern Utah with my friend Suzanne to visit a hiking spa that no longer exists. It was called the National Institute of Fitness. It's called something else now and is a totally different type of place. Back before the spa got fancy, we endured a week of exercise, being weighed and measured, eating very green (and not very tasty) food . . . and had a fabulous time. The beauty of Utah with its clear sky and pure air was a lifetime away from my then life in Washington, D.C. I borrowed the scenery from my trip for HOT AS HELL, but everything else is pure fiction. At the "real" spa, the staff was exceptional and no one was murdered. Really. Not a dead body anywhere. So, if you ever get a chance to grab a friend and go away for a week without television where the focus solely is on you, your health and your friendship—take it!

Huge thanks to my fabulous editor, Kate Duffy. You continue to guide these books with a gentle hand. Don't worry; the reality of your tough-gal reputation is safe with me. Thanks also to everyone at Kensington who had a part in making this work. Again, Kristine Mills-Noble—you are a cover goddess.

My continued appreciation goes to Wendy Duren for reading the first draft while you were busy writing your Pushcart Prize–nominated short story—congrats!

As always, the biggest "thank you" goes to my husband James. You make it all possible and worthwhile.

Hot as Hell

Chapter One

"This is your idea of a vacation?" Noah Paxton asked the question with a practiced level of calm he did not actually feel. By the way Alexa Stuart—Lexy to him—jumped up and out of her pool lounge chair, he guessed the fake tone did not impress her, either.

Dark sunglasses hid her eyes, but her dropped jaw suggested he caught her off guard. "Noah?"

She remembered his name. That was something. "Miss me?"

She settled back in her seat and smoothed out the magazine she had just crumpled in her fists. "No."

"I'm going to take that as a compliment."

She flipped her sunglasses to the top of her head and squinted up at him with intense green eyes. "What are you doing here?"

Funny, but the woman did not look at all surprised to see him. Probably had something to do with the fact she ruined their relationship, screwed with his career, and then ran. She had to know he would track her down eventually.

"I could ask you the same question," he said.

"You already know the answer to that one. I'm on vacation."

"Uh-huh." That was all he could think to say while trying to ignore the size of her tiny pink bikini. The thing seemed to shrink more the longer he stared at it, but maybe that was wishful thinking.

With the burning southern Utah heat bouncing around and searing through his long-sleeved shirt, he understood her less-is-more theory of dressing. Still, there were other resort patrons hanging in the area. As far as Noah could tell, they all had eyes.

He scanned the pool deck to make sure none of those eyes belonged to men and none were staring at Lexy's incredible shrinking bikini. Only a few other people braved the beating sun on the pool deck. Most of them sat up to their necks in the water. All but one was female.

The male-female ratio qualified as the only positive Noah could find about the high-adventure hiking spa Lexy chose as her temporary playground. Not that he knew what the hell a high-adventure hiking spa even was. He read the description online three times before jumping on a plane to retrieve Lexy. Once he saw the price of the joint, he seriously considered changing careers from security analyst to spa owner.

He wondered how the folks who ran the place convinced otherwise competent people to shell out a couple grand a week to stay at a no-frills location in the middle of nowhere. The place in question consisted of a few single-story and two-story stucco buildings painted almost the same color as the towering red rocks ringing them.

Deep in a valley and about two hours from Las Vegas, the spa felt more like an isolated boot camp than an expensive resort. Clean with well-kept grounds, but no extras. A bit too much of a throwback to his military days for Noah's comfort.

"How did you pick this joint?" he asked.

"What's wrong with it?"

"Aren't we touchy?"

"Let's just say I'm waiting for you to tell me whatever it is you came the whole way here to say."

He ignored that and started with the most obvious problem with her choice of bathing location. "This place is forty miles from the nearest anything. Didn't see a restaurant or store anywhere close."

He tolerated the desert as much as the next guy, but why not enjoy it after a little gambling while looking down from a luxury room high above the Las Vegas Strip?

"That's why people stay here," she said.

"To starve?"

"For the seclusion. Red Valley Fitness is known for its intense exercise and nutrition packages."

"You sound like a walking advertisement." Not a surprise, since she was a marketing genius, but still.

She let out a little sigh. "No one asked you to come here."

Which explained why anger continued to spill through his veins at a rate that threatened to crack his spine. "I couldn't resist."

"But you *can* leave."

"What happened to you going to places close to the house to get your toes painted and body scrubbed..." Scrub. Bikini. Yeah, he needed to change conversation topics. "Or whatever that stuff you do is called."

"Toenails, not toes." She wiggled them as if to emphasize the distinction. "And I do not get body scrubs."

She seemed determined to kill him with visual reminders of what she hid under that skimpy bathing suit.

"We're getting off course here," he said in an effort to preserve his sanity.

"I'm not even sure what course we were on."

"I could say something obvious, but I'll let that one go."

She rested her magazine against her thighs with an exaggerated sigh. "To answer your previous question, people choose this spa for fitness."

"They don't have an outside at home where they pay a mortgage and get fresh air for free?"

"You can't get everything you need at home." Her eyebrows inched up with the provocative phrase.

"Don't remember hearing any complaints from you on that score before now."

"I'm not there now, am I?"

"Very funny." Not even a little funny, actually.

He was two seconds away from giving her a reminder of just how well they worked together on the home front. Probably would have if it were not so damn hot. And if she didn't look ready to kill him.

"I was talking about the exercise facilities," she said with a smile that suggested she liked his discomfort a bit too much. "Some people come here because they like the exercise classes and hiking."

He glanced around, expecting to see people passed out from dragging around backpacks in this heat. "Only an idiot would walk around out here in early September. It still hits a hundred degrees before noon."

"That's why the hikes start at six."

She had to be kidding. "In the morning?"

"Of course."

Not kidding. "Is the goal to steam clean your body from the inside out?"

She closed her eyes for a second. "I give up, Noah. What are you doing here?"

Now, there was a damn fine question. If she would throw on a towel he might be able to come up with a damn fine response. As it stood, only strings of babble filled his brain.

Times like these he wished he were an ass man. Lexy sat

on that particular and very impressive part of her anatomy. Her long, sexy legs . . . well, he had always been a leg man. Then his gaze skimmed over her to the tops of her breasts where they plumped over her skimpy suit. Okay, he was a bit of a breast man, too.

Who was he trying to kid? Eyes. Mouth. Shoulder-length, baby-soft brown hair, and the sexiest shade of green eyes ever. Hell, even knees. He loved all of Lexy's parts.

"Noah?"

"Huh?"

"Answer me."

Sure. Once he figured out what the question was.

She tapped on the magazine. "Why are you hovering over my chair?"

"I was in the neighborhood."

"You're about seven hundred miles from home."

"Dry heat makes you grumpy." He held up his hands. "I'm not judging. Just stating a fact."

"Yeah, the heat is the problem with my attitude." She added an eye roll as if he could not pick up on her sarcasm without it.

"I'm here looking for you." Because being the only person at the pool's edge dressed in a suit without a blazer in temperatures nearing one hundred did not make him look like enough of an idiot.

"Why?"

"You're not at the office."

"Believe it or not, that's not a crime."

"You never go on vacation."

"So?"

"We have a work emergency." He cleared his throat to make sure he had her attention. "Then there's the misunderstanding between us."

He took her wide-eyed "have-you-lost-your-mind?" stare

to mean she was not happy with his interpretation of the situation between them. "What's with the look?"

"We do not have a misunderstanding."

She said that a little too fast for his liking.

He sat down nice and slow on the chair next to her, so he didn't tip the thing over. Landing on the cement at her feet lacked a certain male appeal. Bad enough he had to run after Lexy. Crawling around at her feet stepped over the line.

"Don't sit," she ordered.

He faced her on the same level this time. "Too late."

She slapped her magazine against her bare legs. "The chair is taken."

"By?" He glanced around ready to beat the shit out of whatever poor loser tried to wrestle the seat away from him.

"Anyone who wants it except you."

"I'll get back up if I need to. That's one thing I still do just fine."

She let out a little huff before speaking. "Let's just get to it, okay?"

Sounded good to him. "Thought I'd have to wait longer for you to talk about this subject."

He had been waiting for four weeks for an explanation. The woman breaks it off, hands back the ring, ignores him, and then she races off to a place where people cooked in the sun for fun. Not her usual style. She had abandoned her stay-and-fight mentality in favor of hiding.

Something other than her being ticked off at him was happening here. He picked up on that clue when his computer password stopped working at the office. He fixed that easily enough. Finding the files Lexy stole was proving to be a bit harder.

"How did you find me?" she asked.

He dropped his shoulders, letting the tension ease out. "Of all the things we need to discuss, that's the subject you pick?"

"What else is there? Actually, forget that." She waved her hand in front of her face. "Instead, tell me how you figured out where I was."

Appeared she was not ready to open up about the most important topic—them. "I'm a security expert. Tracking you down was not all that difficult."

"You checked my financial records? Had me followed? What?" She seemed appalled at the idea.

Lucky for him, finding her turned out to be much easier than that. He simply asked her brother, who happened to be his friend and partner in Stuart Enterprises, Gray and Lexy's family's business. Gray had no idea why his sister ran off, why she tampered with office security before making her great escape, or where the client files disappeared to, but he did agree with Noah that Lexy was behind whatever was happening.

"Some information is privileged," Noah said.

She folded the top corner of the magazine page down and then flipped it back up. The back-and-forth went on as she spoke. "You're not a lawyer. You don't have some sort of confidential relationship with a client, so stop pretending you do."

"Is it my imagination or have you become obsessed with my career?" At this point, he would be happy with her showing an interest in anything about him. Since his career appeared to be in some jeopardy, he was happy to start there.

The chair creaked when he leaned forward to rest his elbows on his knees. Being a bit closer to her felt right. The chances of her belting him or shoving him increased, but he decided to take the risk.

She shifted to the side of the chair farthest away from him. Another inch or two and she would be sitting on the cement.

"Problem?" he asked.

"Other than you?" she asked in a tone best suited for a conversation with someone with a negative I.Q.

"You're much friendlier in San Diego." He pretended to think about that for a second. "Well, it's more accurate to say that you were up until four weeks ago. Are you ready to talk about that?"

"I'm going back to my vacation." She slid her glasses back down to hide those beautiful eyes behind tinted lenses. "We're done."

"Really?"

"Really."

He thought about pushing the subject. They could argue, fight . . . maybe even make up at some point. Her frown suggested that last part would not be happening soon. So he decided to pull back. If Lexy wanted to fight on Utah turf, he would comply. He needed a room, a shower, and a change of clothes.

"You win." He stood up and stared down at her.

The magazine shook in her hands. "I do?"

"Yep."

Her eyes narrowed to tiny slits. "What's the catch?

Smart lady. "Why would you think—"

"Experience."

He smiled. "Enjoy your sunbathing."

Chapter Two

Two hours later Lexy walked past the aerobics studio and started toward the main administration building. Exercise class started in thirty minutes, but jumping up and down on a little step was the last thing on her mind. No, she had other problems.

Two men. Two potential disasters. Two reasons to have a headache all the medications in the world could not fight.

She did not enjoy anything about the spa, the situation, or Noah's presence in the same state. Oh, she knew he would run after her. Decreasing his security clearance and blocking his access to work files guaranteed that. If she could have come up with a better way to ensure the confidentiality of her company's private information, even temporarily, she would have done that, too.

It was not as if she had a bunch of great options sitting out in front of her begging for attention. Noah and her brother ran the business. Noah was in a position of power. She took care of the public relations and marketing end, but a huge chunk of the day-to-day operations fell to Noah.

Noah enjoyed a great deal more trust and fewer restrictions than anyone else in the office. Seeing him appear in the middle of the desert brought it all back—the frustration, the humiliation. He lied to her from the beginning. And she bought every word.

Now she would get her revenge and reveal him to be the crook he was.

She had studied the comings and goings at the spa for the last few days. She knew the resort's security chief, Charlie Henderson, left his office at the same time every day, grabbed coffee or whatever else he carried around in that white cup, and headed to the weight room for a mid-afternoon work-out session

Today was not any different. As she rounded the corner of the terra-cotta-colored building, she saw Henderson jog down the building stairs.

Bingo.

The man would be gone for at least an hour. While he worked on his pecs, she'd figure out a way into his office to conduct her search. The details of how she was going to do all that were a bit murky.

Her previous visits taught her about the location of Henderson's office and the hours he kept. She knew the people who worked at the spa were not sit-at-a-desk types. Most spent little time in their offices. She was counting on that being the case today. With Noah at the resort, she no longer had the time to wait.

She ducked behind the building until Henderson took off. She waited another few seconds and then headed for the door of the administrative building. She barely got up the ten steps to the porch before she felt a presence behind her.

She turned around expecting to see Noah. She saw Henderson.

Even from the step below her, his six-foot-huge frame had him looming over her. Blondish gray hair gave him an older look than the forty-four years her private file on him indicated. Either way, up close the harsh angled lines of the guy's face gave him a scary look.

"Looking for something?" Henderson smiled, but there was no amusement in his voice.

Yeah, a good excuse for being exactly where she was not supposed to be. "I got turned around. I have an aerobics class in a few minutes and seem to be in the wrong place."

"You're nowhere near the studio."

Unease zapped through her at his sharp tone. "My mistake."

She tried to breeze past him. Stay calm, keep her head down, and get down the stairs before he could get a good look at her.

He was having none of it. "There's no need for you to rush off."

Something about his deep voice caused her head to snap up. This time she saw emotion swirl in his dark eyes. Something dark and knowing.

"I have a class," she said as her mind raced, trying to come up with a Plan B.

"Uh-huh."

There it was. The male grunt that meant something but failed to say anything. "If you'll just—"

He stepped in her path. "You were looking for me."

"What? No." She tried to step back, but her heel slammed smack against the stair.

"You were following me."

She snorted and hoped her voice sounded genuine. "Of course not. Why would I do that?"

"That's what I want to know."

Something about his demeanor and hovering sent a tiny tremor of alarm skipping through her. "I took a wrong turn. No big deal."

He leaned in until she could smell the peppermint gum on

his breath. "I've seen you around this building for two days now. You've been in the hall and asking questions."

So much for her investigative skills. Time to concentrate on her lying skills. Being with Noah taught her something about that subject. The man lied about everything, which was why she was stuck on the steps talking to Henderson.

She swallowed the nervous energy that threatened to drown her. "I've been thinking about using the resort for an office retreat and—"

"Questions about me."

"No, no. There's some confusion here." She tried again, figuring the more she talked, the more likely it was that someone would walk by and she could sneak away without a scene. "I really was just walking around the resort."

"You were conducting surveillance."

"I don't know what you're talking about." Okay, she did, but he did not need to know that.

Henderson rested his hands on his hips. The move emphasized just how big the guy was. Somehow his frame managed to block the sun.

"I know who you are," he said.

That's exactly what she was afraid of. "Of course you do. I'm staying at the resort."

"I know about your company. Your brother and your fiancé."

"Ex-fiancé." The correction slipped out.

"What?"

"Never mind."

"You followed me back from San Diego. I want to know why."

This guy had an ego big enough to match his truck-sized forearms. She thought about pointing it out, but he could snap her in half with one hand, so she let the comment go.

"You were in San Diego? Lovely, isn't it?"

"This is your last chance, lady." Those arms crossed in front of him this time. "Tell me what you want."

"Just some rest and exercise. See, I'm on vacation." She figured if she kept saying it, maybe someone would start believing it.

"Uh-huh."

The third time with this guy was not one ounce more charming than the first two. "Are you always this direct and difficult with patrons?"

"Just the nosy ones." He dropped his arms and took two steps until he stood above her. "You need directions back to the aerobics studio?"

"No."

"Good."

Noah leaned against the corner of the building and watched Lexy talk with a guy who looked like he should have bolts in his neck. Noah strained to hear, but was too far away. Whatever they were talking about made Lexy frown. By the end of the conversation, she was squirming hard enough to pop right out of her skin.

Rather than guess about the topic of conversation, Noah decided to ask. The guy walked off, leaving her alone on the steps. She owed him an explanation. Owed him more than that by his count, but he'd settle for very little at this point. Anything.

"New boyfriend?" he asked from the bottom of the staircase.

Lexy held her hand up to her eyes and squinted against the glaring sun. "I'm getting a little tired of men sneaking up on me."

"What does that mean?"

She stopped in front of him. "Why are you still here?"

"At the resort?"

"In Utah."

"Ah. As to that, I'm just looking around."

She shook her head. "Go home, Noah."

She tried to walk past him. He let her get about two feet before saying anything else. "I asked you a question. Who's the guy?"

She glanced over her shoulder. Whatever expression she saw on his face, whatever she perceived or imagined, made her stop running and face him. "No one."

"The talk looked pretty serious to me."

"You're wrong, and it's not the first time you've jumped to conclusions about me and other men, either."

She made him sound like the raving jealous type. Wrong. He was a practical guy. Having Lexy break off their engagement is what made him lose his control. He kept searching for reasonable answers to her unreasonable behavior. Four weeks later and he was not one inch closer to understanding what the hell happened.

"I assume you're talking about that limp wrist you've been going out with for the last two weeks."

She somehow sighed and glared at the same time. "That is not appropriate, and William is not gay."

"He's not manly. He owns a pink polo shirt, for Christ's sake." Noah gritted his teeth together at the thought of Lexy with any man. Any man. "He wore it with red pants to have lunch with Gray. Red pants, Lexy."

"How did you know about their lunch?"

Noah shrugged, pretending William's newfound coziness with the Stuart family did not matter, even though it did. "I hear things at the office."

"My life isn't your business—"

"Wrong."

"—and shouldn't be the subject of office gossip."

"Yell at your brother, not me."

"Oh, I intend to."

"All I'm saying is just because a guy has a cock, that doesn't make him a rooster, if you know what I mean."

She blinked a few times. "Actually, I have no idea what you're talking about. I rarely do."

"That is one of the problems in our relationship. A failure to communicate." The conclusion settled into his skin and felt right there.

"The bigger issue had to do with your lying."

The woman needed to find a new complaint. He had heard this one over and over. "Never said a thing that wasn't true."

"You rarely say anything that makes sense."

"Yet you heard me just fine when I proposed."

"We are not talking about that."

"Why?"

"Even though you seem to think I'm dating every man I know or meet or pass on the street, I'm not. I'm trying to enjoy my vacation."

"Fair enough." With that out of the way . . . "So, who's the guy?"

"Didn't we just cover this?"

"I can find out, you know. It would just be easier if you told me."

"Don't you have work to do?"

Now there was a subject as raw as an open wound. "About that. Any idea where my work files disappeared to?"

"Ask someone at the office."

Yeah, he'd tried that already. All roads led back to Lexy. "I'm talking to you about it."

"I'd love to work this all out with you, but I have an aerobics class." She pushed past him and called over her shoulder. "Enjoy your flight back to San Diego."

He did not know what was going on, but he did know he was not going anywhere without her. As much as he wanted to take Lexy back home and put that ring back on her finger, he had to wait.

If his fiancée—and that is exactly how he thought of her and would until she became his wife—wanted to spend some time in the desert, he would get used to the heat. Hell, he was used to cold showers, anyway.

Chapter Three

Lexy suspected Noah would be waiting when she came out of her aerobics class all hot, sweaty, and desperate for a shower. She waited until almost everyone else, including the instructor, filed out just to see if he'd hang around. With all the other disappointments he had given her over the last few weeks, this was not one of them.

"Have fun?" He asked the question while lounging against the side of the building, just outside the front door.

"Up until about two seconds ago, yes." She threw her bag over her shoulder. She thought about storming off, but two women from her class hung around and listened in without making any attempt to hide, so she refrained from causing a scene.

"Tell me about your relationship to Charlie Henderson."

She tried not to flinch. "I thought you didn't know him."

"I don't."

"But yet you know his name?"

"Is his name a secret?"

"You tell me."

"I don't know what you're talking about."

She scoffed. "Please. Give me a break. As if you just happened to guess his name."

He tapped on his temple. "Security expert, remember?"

"Since you're so brilliant, why not figure out who the guy is yourself? You shouldn't need me."

"I'd rather hear from you. I'll stand here and melt into a puddle while you explain it to me."

She tried to imagine how much time it would take to dissolve all 190 pounds off his six-foot-one frame. The result would be a water hole the size of Cleveland.

"When you put it that way, I'm thinking a vow of silence might be in order," she said.

"Doubt you could stay quiet for five minutes." He smiled. "But go ahead. This should be entertaining."

As the seconds ticked by, Noah said hello to their nosy audience. He engaged in a random bit of idle chitchat with a third woman who joined the group. All the while, sweat collected behind Lexy's knees and dripped off her neck.

Since he was wearing the same charcoal-gray dress pants and blue cotton shirt from earlier, she figured Noah had to be near the toasting point. The thought made her smile.

It disappeared when he smiled and that familiar tingle started down deep in her belly. It had been this way from the beginning. He walked into her family's business two years ago to interview for a job and knocked her over. Literally. He ran her right down in the hall with the force of a train. Came around the corner with his head down and slammed her into the wall.

Bruised and counting the butterflies winging around her head, she looked up, saw him, and never saw another man the same way again. She remembered every minute. Every detail. Black suit with a crisp white shirt and bold red tie. Dark brown hair clipped short and sexy. Melting chocolate-brown eyes. Lean, buff, muscled.

Any woman, concussion or not, would have fallen for him even if he were not the best damn kisser ever, which he was. She had not felt the same way about another man before or since. Even though she just turned thirty and had a lot of kissing in front of her, she doubted she ever would feel the same way about any other guy ever again.

Seeing Noah now should have been a huge shock. It wasn't. Despite all the anger and hurt, the pull between them tugged just as strong.

Noah laughed at something one of the women said before they stepped back. Neither lady left or wandered very far. No, they hovered around the weights and mats just inside the door, about fifteen feet away. Lexy decided to ignore them both and deal with Noah.

"Hot yet?" she asked hoping his internal temperature had spiked to crisis levels.

Noah made a scene of glancing down at his watch. "Three minutes."

"What?"

"That's about as long as I thought you could go without talking."

"Really? I'm wondering how well you could breathe with a hand weight stuffed up your nose."

"I've dealt with worse."

"Is that another secret from your past you've decided not to share?"

"I'm here now. Ready to talk. Shoot."

She considered doing just that. "I don't have anything new to say. You know why I gave the ring back."

"Actually, I don't."

Since they had an audience, she decided to play to it. "Let's start with the global issues, shall we?"

"I like international things. Go ahead."

From the way he stood up straighter and his gaze darkened, she knew his mind and body were on high alert. As usual.

"You were not honest with me." Quite an understatement,

but she figured the comment would get the ball rolling in the right direction.

"And?"

"*And*?" Her squeal of outrage made the eavesdropping ladies give up their pretense and openly stare.

"Uh, yeah."

"Dishonesty is a huge deal."

He frowned. "Is that really the only complaint you have about me?"

She seriously considered practicing some of those fancy kickboxing moves she had just learned on him. "It's more than enough for most people."

"Not sane people."

"You lied."

"To you?" he asked.

"To the guy who drives the airport shuttle." She threw up her hands. "Yes, of course to me. All the time and about almost everything."

His frown deepened at her assessment of his honesty skills, or lack of them. "Give me an example."

"I can give you fifty."

"Since it's not getting any cooler out here, let's start with one."

She homed in on the most obvious problem. "You failed to disclose important information about your past."

He scoffed. Actually, he made one of those male sounds that stood for "my woman is a nut job," then just stopped talking.

"You hid the facts from me." She held up a hand. "And if you make that noise again, I am going to test your theory about being able to breathe through a hand weight."

"Not sharing every irrelevant detail of my life is different from lying."

"It is not."

"See, I knew it. This is just a difference of opinion. We can work thought this. No problem." His head dipped to the side and he shot her one of his let's-go-to-bed stares.

No freaking way. No matter how he affected her, how fast her heartbeat galloped whenever she saw him, sex was not going to happen.

"About some subjects, I was the only one who didn't know . . ." The words caught in her throat. "Do you have any idea how it feels to practically live with a guy and not know anything about him?"

She had waited for months for him to tell her about his past. Months of ignoring the fury building inside her as his silence chipped away at her trust. Then she got the call from one of the company's business clients about a break-in that pointed to Noah. The evidence was shaky. The company had more of a suspicion than anything else, but Lexy knew the truth. Lying, stolen money . . . it all added up to getting scammed by an expert. One Noah Paxton.

The realization had nearly destroyed her. Loving someone so much only to have him screw her and her family made her throw up for days. Then she gave the ring back, locked down the business information she could, and followed every lead. That had taken her to Charlie Henderson and southern Utah, which was why she was sweating off pounds by the minute.

She had to find the evidence to prove Noah had participated in ripping off their client. Without that, he would sweet-talk his way out of it just as he did everything else.

"Your past never mattered so long as you were honest about it. You could have answered a question now and then, but no." She waved her hands in the air for effect. "Everything was a great big secret. *Everything.*"

He rolled up his sleeves. "What do you want to know? And make it quick, because my skin is turning to liquid."

He opened the door for the first time since she'd known him. She sensed a trap and refused to step in it. "Why the big change in attitude?"

"Okay, I'll start." He leaned in and lowered his voice out of eavesdropping range. "Are you upset about Mexico?"

"Mexico?"

His dark eyes searched her face for a second before his expression wiped clean again. "Never mind."

What the hell was he talking about? "As in the country?"

"Is there a Mexico in Kansas?"

"Being a smartass is not a good move when we are this close to the edge of a big desert where no one would find your body for months, possibly years, after I finished with it." She was just furious enough to do it.

"Good point."

"So," she blew out the anger clogging the back of her throat as she struggled to catch up with his side of the conversation. "Tell me about Mexico."

"Why?"

She scoffed just to see how he liked it. "How should I know? You're the one who brought it up."

"Only because I thought that was the reason you broke off the engagement. It wasn't, so it's not relevant."

Typical. She kept stacking the information he hid from her on a mental pile. The thing was within inches of toppling over and crushing them both.

"If it's not Mexico, then I'm thinking you must have found out about my time in jail and got pissed." He nodded. "I can see where that might be an issue for you."

"You were in prison?"

"Jail." He held up a finger. "And I can explain."

"I somehow doubt you will."

"Parts of the experience are fuzzy. A little alcohol and a parrot and things got crazy, but—"

"Parrot?"

"No big deal. The charges were dropped before trial."
He reached out and traced a thumb along her chin.

"Unless you want to lose a finger, now is not the time to
touch me." She brushed his hand away. "So, this parrot
issue is in addition to the time in prison?"

"Jail."

"What's the difference?"

"A trial and a conviction, and I didn't have either. And,
by the way, no harm came to the bird."

"You didn't tell me any of this, Noah. You still haven't,
really. We were engaged for two months. You never said a
word."

"That's what I don't get. If you didn't know about this
stuff, then how could it matter?"

"Being purposely obtuse is not helping your case."

She wanted to scream, but the women had edged closer
and no longer pretended not to listen in. No need to give
them more of a show or make it easier to eavesdrop.

"None of what happened to me before we met means
anything to us," he said as if he actually believed it.

Even if that was true, there was still the problem of the theft
of a client's money and trade secrets. "What about the part
where you forgot to tell me you were married?"

The older woman of the two gasped. For some reason the
idea of Noah being in prison did not warrant a sound, but
news of a wife did.

If Noah heard the noise, he ignored it. "Yeah, you yelled
a lot when you found out about Karen."

"Your wife."

"Ex." He smiled at the women he had charmed earlier.
"She conveniently forgot to mention the divorce."

One of the woman treated him to a tsk-tsk sound, then
started whispering to her companion.

"The existence of an ex-wife is not one of those things that just slips your mind," Lexy said.

"You shouldn't assume that. Karen is a pretty forgettable lady."

"Not to me."

"Because you never met her. If you had, you'd see a certain similarity between Karen and jail time."

"This isn't funny." It managed to be the exact opposite of funny as far as Lexy was concerned. Hearing him talk about another woman as his wife—the role Lexy at one time thought she would fill—made her wonder why she traveled to Utah instead of just turning him over to the police and letting them figure out his crimes.

But she knew the answer to why she stayed involved. Despite everything that happened, Lexy wanted to believe in him. To hear a simple and understandable explanation that would amount to something other than a string of nonsense and lies. Seeing him appear in Utah caused hope to flicker to life inside her.

But his words . . . well, nothing changed that she could see.

"Lexy, listen to me." Those dark eyes softened in a way guaranteed to crush her defenses against him.

"Don't call me that."

He rested his head back against the wall and made a strangled sound. "It's your name."

"My name is Alexa."

"Alexa Annabeth Stuart. We slept together for eighteen months, honey. I took the time to learn your full name."

"Then use it."

"Also figured out in the first hour the name didn't fit you."

"Meaning?"

"Alexa Annabeth is a stuck-up rich woman's name."

"Annabeth happens to be my mother's name."

He lifted his eyebrow. "Your point?"

"Sure, it's not as pretty as your *wife's* name." Lexy sneered over the word. "Karen. How lovely."

"Ex. We've been divorced for more than a decade."

"So you say."

"Back to your mother."

"What's wrong with her?" The dangerous question came out before Lexy could stop it.

"What kind of woman saddles her kids with names like Alexa Annabeth and Grayson Jameson but then calls her dogs George and Martha?"

"Mom wanted the corgis to be patriotic."

Noah's jaw dropped. "You know that's crazy, right?"

Lexy did. Over-the-edge nuts. That described her parents. They were successful to a shocking degree and smart, but that was all to the outside world. In the eyes of those who really knew them well, which was almost no one, they were utterly dysfunctional.

And the whole damn family adored Noah. Her brother Gray turned out to be Noah's biggest supporter. Gray whined almost daily about her decision to break off the engagement. Tried to talk her out of it about a hundred times. Her dad grumbled about Noah being a man who could handle her. Her mom, well, Noah charmed the woman right out of her expensive designer shoes.

Noah worked hard with Gray and refused to quit even after she dumped him. Since the entire family sided with him, Lexy got stuck with a reputation as an unreasonable outcast. Little did they know she was trying to save their collective butts.

"You know, if you had asked me about any of this before you stormed out, I would have told you. There was no reason to go to limp dick—"

She growled in frustration for the first time in her life. "William."

"You sleep with him yet?"

"That's not your business."

"We can debate that point if you really want to."

"I'm not playing this game." She tightened her hold on her bag.

"You missed me." The idea made Noah grin like a monkey on speed. "I can tell."

She did. Every single day. "I prefer grown-up men now."

That killed his stupid smile. "Limp ones."

She wondered if her head would explode from the back-and-forth. "There's nothing wrong with William."

"All of his body parts work? You've been to bed and he passes?"

"William is a friend and—"

"So you haven't slept with him." Noah nodded nice and slow, even shot the watching ladies a smile. "Good, don't you think?"

"I didn't say . . . what's so good about it?"

"Because you're not cheating on me."

"It would be hard to do since we broke up," she said in an attempt to point out the obvious.

"Semantics."

"It always is with you."

He sighed. "Seems to me we're still not communicating effectively."

"How's this? Get lost."

"Clearer, but not going to happen. See, I'm thinking I could use a vacation, too."

"You haven't taken a vacation since high school."

"Then I'm overdue." He nodded toward her bag. "Any chance you packed my bathing suit? Last I knew it was in your apartment."

"If so, a homeless guy has it, since I donated all of your leftovers to a shelter."

He let the shot whiz on past him. "Well, the gift store probably sells men's trunks. If not, we'll have to hope the spa has a liberal policy on skinny-dipping."

No way was she sticking around for that show. "I'm going to my room."

"See you at dinner." He winked at her.

That stopped her hasty exit. "You are not staying here."

"Yeah, babe, I am."

"I am not your babe."

"Whatever you want to call yourself, you can't hide from me."

Oh, she bet she could.

Chapter Four

Four hours and two ice-cold showers later, Noah sat in the oversized dining room nursing a beer and his fractured ego. He passed over the salad bar and trays of something called macrobiotic food in favor of the bottle he had smuggled into the joint.

"Not having dinner?" asked a tanned, trim, salad-eating guy as he sat in the chair across from Noah and started a full-fledged unwanted conversation.

"I prefer food." Noah hoped the guy would pick up on the cues and disinterest and move on.

"I assure you, all of our selections are very healthy."

"Whatever."

"The food has the optimum mix of fiber and protein." The man flashed a huge smile before swallowing a green glob off his fork.

"So does this." Noah took a long swig and kept his gaze locked on the white double doors in front of him.

People buzzed in and out. Some mingled near the entry. Others broke into groups and claimed big tables set up in the middle of the all-white room. All that heat and hiking made them chatty, which explained the sound of laughter bouncing around the room and why Noah picked the empty four-person table closest to the door.

He was not there to make new friends. He had friends. What he lacked at the moment was a fiancée.

But Lexy had to eat sometime. Since the place had one location to get food, or what passed for food, Noah figured she would wander in and across his path eventually. Probably eat some grasslike entrée and then run off again, but he would catch her first.

"Where did you get the beer?" the unwanted table guest asked.

"Brought it in."

"The rules forbid alcohol."

"So?" Noah took a nice long pull to emphasize his point.

"It's a pretty big violation of policy."

"Yeah, I got that the first time you said it. You gonna turn me in to the health police?"

"I'd have to report you to me. I'm afraid we haven't been introduced." The man extended his hand across the table. "I'm Tate Carr. I own and manage the place."

"Noah Paxton."

"Yes, of course. Our newest guest." Tate sat back after his too-long, too-squishy handshake and adjusted the collar of his green and white striped button-down shirt. "You were a tight fit."

Noah thought the phrasing of that sentence needed some work. "If you say so."

"I'm sure you will find everything satisfactory in your room."

Only if he found Lexy waiting on his bed. "It's fine."

"The one problem we have is that beer in your hand."

"It's not a problem for me." Noah clutched the bottle. Good luck to any moron who tried to pry it out of his hands.

"There are restrictions here."

Noah figured one of them required Tate to wear clothes that matched the color of the food. Why else would a grown man choose to look like a green bean?

"You know what they say about rules, Tate?"

Tate sent him a look of pity. "Not this one. See, the diet and nutrition concerns are reviewed quarterly for optimal fitness and output."

Everyone in the joint qualified as a walking, talking brochure. First Lexy. Now the green guy. "Why?"

"People enjoy exercise and good health. We aim to give them what they need and seek. We pride ourselves on producing results."

"I meant why not eat real food and drink whatever you want. Like a hamburger. That's a good source of protein, right?" Noah would trade the beer for any nonbark food at this point.

"Well, we can't . . ."

"Yeah?"

Tate adjusted his collar a second time. "It wouldn't be . . ."

Since he wanted the conversation over, Noah offered the guy an assist. "Nutritious?"

"Exactly. These vegetables are natural and better for you than the processed food most people eat."

Noah did not want a lecture. "If you say so."

"See, in a macrobiotic diet—"

"Don't explain."

"You're probably right." Tate reached out and rubbed his hand up and down Noah's bicep. "You look like you're in good shape without too many dietary changes. Nice and firm."

"Whoa." Noah jumped out of his chair.

This is what happened when he tried to have a conversation. He should have told this Tate dude to get the hell out the second he sat down. Now Noah had to get the guy to back off without killing him. "Look, man. I'm not interested."

"Excuse me?" Tate asked.

Noah tried words one more time. "I like women."

"I still don't—"

"I'm engaged. She should be here any minute."

The news chased the confused look off Tate's face. "Your fiancée is at the spa?"

As far as he was concerned they were still engaged, so yeah. "Lexy Stuart." And if she did not show up in the next three minutes, Noah vowed to hunt her down.

"Alexa?"

Hearing her full name made Noah's head pound. "That's her."

Tate nodded toward the back of the hall. "She slipped into the room a few minutes ago. Looks like she's grabbing something to take back to her room."

Noah spun around and watched the little sneak creep around the salad bar. Tough to miss her, since she wore a bright blue dress that tied around her neck and showed off her lean bare arms and fit back.

No way was he letting her get away with a graze-and-run. It took less than three steps to pin her against the salad bar. "Still hiding, dear?"

Lexy froze in the act of scooping her uncooked food into a bowl. "The name is Alexa, and I'm just getting something to eat."

"That's not food."

"If you don't like it, you could always try a restaurant back in San Diego."

He rested his palms on her shoulders, letting the heat of her skin soak into him. Touching her never got old. Never felt wrong. Hell, he had to fight off the urge to lean down and place a kiss on her exposed flesh.

"In the mood for cherries and squash?" He whispered the question into her ear.

"It's healthy."

"It's barely a snack. I tried to tell Tate over there before he . . ." Last thing Noah wanted to do was describe *that* moment in detail.

She peeked over her shoulder. "What?"

"Nothing."

She turned around until the edge of her plate stuck Noah in the stomach. "Oh, it's something. You look mad enough to hit someone."

"Finally noticed that, did you?"

Her face fell. "What did you do?"

"Why do you assume it was me?"

"Experience."

Noah frowned. "That's harsh."

"I left you alone for two hours—"

"Four."

"—and you got in trouble with the owner of the spa."

"He started it and was lucky it ended without bloodshed."

"Very mature."

As insults went that one was not too bad. She had called him much worse.

"Come sit with me," he said.

"Let me guess. You're the one with an illegal beer at his chair."

Noah glanced over his shoulder and saw the bottle. Watched Tate eye it. "The brochure did not mention anything about forbidding alcohol."

"It actually did."

She grabbed her plate and dodged around Noah to go over and greet Tate with a hug and cheek-kisses. Noah realized he got screwed on the hello kiss from Lexy. They should be at the makeup sex point by now, but Lexy proved more stubborn than he expected.

Leave out a few historical details here and there and the woman went nuts. Why she even cared about his past ticked him off. None of it mattered. That's why it was in the *past*. It was over. Since it sucked, it should stay buried and forgotten. She should trust him and move forward. Picking through history could only lead to trouble.

And Lexy qualified as a trouble magnet.

Her decision making made him wish for a less independent woman. Maybe one with fewer smarts and no inclination to take off on her own. Sounded better than the reality where she broke it off, handed over the reins of her private marketing firm to her partner, and ran two states away to sit around in a bikini without him.

For a woman who thrived on perpetual motion, ran her own company, and worked for the family business on the side, she was spending a lot of time sitting around doing nothing. The scenario did not make any sense.

Tate threw an arm around Lexy's shoulders and pulled her close. "Alexa, I didn't know you were engaged."

"I'm not."

"But, I thought . . ." Tate glanced at Noah. Whatever Tate saw convinced him to let go of Lexy and sit down.

Good choice. Two more seconds and Noah would have body blocked the guy into the wall. Gay or not, no man had the right to paw Lexy.

"We're having some trouble communicating at the moment, but we'll work it out," Noah said instead of hitting.

"Funny but you'd think the word 'good-bye' would have been clear," Lexy mumbled.

"As you can see, we're still working on those issues," Noah added.

Tate nodded. "That explains the two rooms."

"You keep track of the sleeping arrangements of all your guests?" As far as Noah was concerned, some things were private or damn well should be.

Noah pulled out the chair next to him for Lexy. When she refrained from stomping off or sitting at another table, he breathed easy again.

Tate kept right on nodding. "Of course."

Did not even deny it. "Kind of nosy, aren't you?"

"Noah." The warning tone in Lexy's tone came through loud and clear.

"Just having a conversation with our host Tate here."

"You were picking a fight." She opened her napkin with a snap. "Stop."

"Yes, ma'am."

"So, Noah, if you are not here for the food and exercise, then why are you here?" Tate picked up a glass of something burnt orange in front of him and took a long swallow.

As far as Noah was concerned, there was not enough beer in all of Utah to make up for drinking something that color. "For Lexy."

"I see." Tate forced out a small smile. "Alexa, how was the hike this morning?"

"Invigorating."

"Happy to hear it."

"You're both insane," Noah grumbled under his breath before finishing off his beer.

"Tomorrow's planned hike is even more strenuous." Tate made that pronouncement with an eager gleam in his blue eyes.

Noah had the opposite reaction. He stared into his bottle, hoping more beer would appear. Getting through a long hike on nothing more than alcohol fumes did not sound like his idea of a good time.

"Any hike that starts at six sounds pretty shi—"

Lexy tramped on Noah's foot before he could finish and then turned her attention to Tate. "What makes it so tough, Tate?"

"That hurt," Noah muttered.

"Good," she muttered right back.

Tate ignored the byplay and kept selling the hike. "It's all off-trail. There's some slick places and steep ledges. Inclines over red rock. That sort of thing."

The good news just kept coming. Noah cut to the important information before he said something that made Lexy take out his other foot. Hard to hike without feet.

"How long?" he asked.

Tate's eyebrows snapped together in a look of confusion. "Excuse me?"

"How many miles?"

"Well, I don't—"

"Round numbers are fine. Preferably lower ones."

"Noah," Lexy warned again.

He pulled his foot back before Lexy could take aim. "Don't even try it."

"Then stop badgering Tate."

"I asked a simple question about mileage."

"Eight," Tate said the number with a smile as if climbing uphill for hours was not a big deal.

"Wouldn't it be faster for you guys to run around the complex a few times and call it a day?" Noah asked.

Lexy skipped the next round of violence and went right to staring. Tate wore the same "what the hell?" expression.

"What?" Noah asked. "What did I say?"

Tate broke his glare to focus on Lexy. "I know you will want to rest this evening, but—"

Noah looked at his watch. "It's not even seven thirty."

"As I was saying, you'll probably want to go to bed early, but I'd stick around for a few minutes of fun if I were you."

Noah could think of fun things to do in the dark and none of them included Tate. "Why should she stay here with you?"

"We're going to have a social gathering on the porch. Throw open the doors and enjoy the lovely evening."

"It's about a hundred degrees on that patio."

"Noah." Each time Lexy said his name her voice grew a touch more menacing.

"We do not have streetlights and other intrusions here, so you can see the clear night sky. It is quite something," Tate said.

"We have sky in San Diego." Noah did a double take when Lexy started grumbling. "Well, we do."

"There will be music and dancing," Tate said.

"Sounds fabulous." Lexy lowered her foot to the top of Noah's as if waiting for the perfect opportunity to shove her heel through his leather sneaker.

Despite the potential attack, Noah spoke up. "That's not the word I would have used."

"Forget Noah. He hates to dance."

"No, I don't."

Lexy gave him full-on eye contact. "Since when?"

Since he figured out dancing might be the closest he could come to holding her for a few minutes. "Right now."

"That's what I thought."

"Of course, I seem to have picked up a foot injury over the last few minutes, so I'm not so sure how good I'll be at the moves."

"Be happy that's the only body part I went after."

"I'll leave you two alone." Tate picked up his orange beverage and green food, then stared at Lexy. "I hope to see you later, Alexa."

"You scared him," Lexy said once Tate moved on to

greet guests at another table. "And notice how he only mentioned me being invited to the party."

"Then my plan worked."

"Come on. Tate is friendly enough."

"He's annoying." Noah had a few other descriptions he wanted to use, but he kept them quiet.

"It's his job to sell the place. He's the—"

"Owner. Yeah, I know. He told me right before he made a pass."

Lexy spit out a piece of green apple on the stark white tablecloth. "What?"

"You okay?"

She coughed a few times as she cleaned up her mess with a napkin. "Stunned."

"I can get some help." Noah glanced around. "There are about twenty people staring at us. One of them probably has some third-grade medical training."

"Get back to Tate and the pass comment."

Noah rubbed a hand over his face. "Look, I know you told me not to act like an ass and get all up in someone's face over this sort of thing, but the guy came on strong. I don't care what people do in their bedrooms, but when they ask me to join in, that's a different story."

"How?"

Noah debated stopping the conversation right there. "There was some touching."

"By Tate?"

"Sure as hell not by me."

"Tate touched you?" She separated each word with a smile.

"Can we talk about something else?"

"But Tate isn't gay."

Noah let his hand fall against the table. "No offense, but

you're not the best judge of this sort of thing. After all, you refuse to believe limp-dick William is gay."

She rolled her eyes in the dramatic way that only Lexy could do. "William is not gay, either."

Noah refused to go down that road. One gay guy at a time was enough. "Why do you think Tate plays for my team?"

"Oh, now that's a very evolved way of putting it."

"Trust me. I used up all my restraint in the last five hours."

She smiled. "That's probably true."

"So? Did you give him some sort of woman quiz or what?"

"I know because Tate made a pass at me. Subtle, but he tested."

"*What*?" The rage hit Noah in the middle of the forehead and spread from there. He stood up so fast that he knocked his chair over backward and slammed it against the thin carpet with a boom.

"Sit down." She tugged on Noah's jeans to get his attention. "That's enough."

"I knew I should have squashed him into the floor."

She waved off a few of their fellow guests, who stared with alarm. "You're scaring people."

"Tate's the only one I want right now."

"It was no big deal."

Noah balled his hands into fists as the anger surged through him. "It will be when I break the guy's legs."

"You were angry two seconds ago because you thought he was making a play for you. Now you're mad because you think he wants *me*."

"That pretty much sums it up."

"Tate has one of those flirty personalities. Once I figured

out he was sleeping with the aerobics instructor, I wrote
him off as harmless and ignored the touching thing."

Just one punch. "He actually touched you?"

"You claim he touched you, too." She pulled Noah down
into his chair. "Sit down and cool off."

"I can catch him later, you know."

"Probably. Tate looks your age, but he's almost fifty-six.
He has that touch of gray hair around his temples, but
there's not a wrinkle on him."

"I didn't get close enough to tell."

"Either way, I'm betting he has a lifetime Botox pass."

"Sounds as if you've conducted an in-depth study on the
subject." And Noah was not sure he liked the idea.

"Tate is like an impressionist painting. Pretty from far
away, but all blurry and not so hot from close up."

"And you insist that I'm the one who says strange
things."

"You do."

"So Botox is why Tate looks about forty, which is older
than me by four years, by the way." And Tate would look
forty and injured after Noah smashed his face in.

"That's what clean living will do for you."

Noah pitched his voice out of eavesdropping range.
"Probably has more to do with banging the aerobics instructor."

"The *married* aerobics instructor."

"So much for your clean-living theory."

"Imagine my surprise when I walked into class early and
saw his hands all over her butt." Lexy took a turn at whispering. "Did I mention she's twenty-something?"

"Never wise to shit where you eat."

"What a lovely visual image."

"Would you rather I drown the guy in the pool?"

"Maybe another time." Lexy pushed her plate to the center of the table. "So, why are you still at the resort?"

"Because you are."

"I don't need a chaperone."

"Maybe I needed to see you." No maybes about it. Seeing her, touching her, making love to her—without all of it, the world began to grind to a dull halt.

"My experience is that you don't need anything from anyone."

"For a smart woman you can get things pretty damn wrong."

Her eyes softened along with her voice. "You know how to woo a woman."

"I'm trying."

The tension broke the minute the wide smile fell across her lips. "Seems we've reached an impasse on that point."

In his view, it was one they could breach if she would set aside her stubbornness for two seconds. "You know what you have to do when that happens."

"Fight to the death?"

"Dance."

"You have never danced with me."

He had not danced in a decade. Since the last time was with Karen, he skipped providing that piece of information. A tentative peace descended. He wanted to enjoy the calm for at least ten minutes before he gave Lexy a reason to start screaming again.

"Then I'm an idiot," he said and meant it.

"I should go to bed." The yearning in Lexy's voice sounded as if she wanted to do anything but leave.

"Dance with me first."

She hesitated. "This can only lead to trouble."

"I sure as hell hope so."

Chapter Five

"Are you sure you want to do this?" Lexy asked as she tried to ignore the warmth of Noah's firm hand on her lower back.

He steered her through the center of the dining room and past two tables of gawking spa-goers. She noticed more than a few appreciative female stares aimed his way. Hard to blame the women for taking a good long look. Noah Paxton wore faded blue jeans better than any man on the planet.

The way his navy blue polo stretched across his broad shoulders and over his muscled chest deserved attention. Had hers. Walking beside him, feeling the heat radiate off him, made her realize just how much she missed him.

"Afraid I'll embarrass you out there on the fake dance floor?" he asked.

Never that. Despite their very different backgrounds and his rough edges, she never felt anything but pride at being by his side. Which was one of the reasons his determined secrecy hurt so much. The more she opened up, the more closed off he became. She was raised with secrets. She did not need or want more of the same in her adult life.

Noah stopped in the middle of the floor. "Are these people made of Teflon?"

"Just skin and wheatgrass, I believe. Why?"

"Not to be redundant, but it is a hundred degrees out here and some moron set up a fire pit."

Exaggeration came with Noah's black-and-white personality, but the reaction still made her laugh. "It wasn't even a hundred this afternoon."

"Felt like twice that."

"Because you were wearing dress pants and a long-sleeved shirt." She stopped to let him open the door.

They stepped outside. Fading sunlight streaked across the sky, casting shadows and highlighting the stark contrast between the towering red rocks and the pale blue of the sky. From the stone patio, out beyond the fire pit and gathered chairs, she saw miles of open, awe-inducing land. No houses. No traffic. No pollution.

The harsh beauty made her wish she could stick around and try out an actual vacation. But she traveled to Utah for a much more practical reason: to figure out what Noah did and how to make him pay for it.

Being with him now made her memory of that goal fade. She kept repeating the reality in her head as a way of working up an immunity to him. Problem was, it wasn't working.

"It's about seventy degrees out here now. If people stare at you this time, it's the dancing and not because you're melting into a big puddle of Noah."

He waved to the women from the aerobics room. "In the span of five hours, some of these people have heard about my divorce, saw you spit food across the table, and watched me throw chairs around the dining room. Seeing me dance can only be a step up."

She gave him a thoughtful look. "It's hard to argue with that logic."

"I love when you're agreeable." His hand slid into hers.

Yanking her hand away would have been the smart thing to do. Continue to take the tough stance and not allow for any confusion about her position. No waffling. All business. Noah was the kind of man who interpreted signals without gray areas. Slapping him down was the answer.

But holding on tight felt better.

"Don't do anything to ruin my good mood," she whispered before saying hello to three women gathered by the door.

She sat with Noah on the stone bench closest to the fire. Music, a mixture of blues and jazz, filled the air from the outdoor speakers. About ten guests and a few scattered employees roamed around getting drinks and talking about how difficult the exercise classes were that day.

"Tell me something." Noah pressed her hand between his palms and rested it on his knee. "What's so special about this place?"

"Meaning?"

"Why are you happy here when you weren't at home?"

That was just it. She had been unhappy and unsettled at the resort until he arrived. Lonely even. Waiting for the right moment to hunt down the information she needed, only to have the man who was both so right and so wrong for her drop down next to her shocked the boredom right out of her.

"Look around you," she said. "It's peaceful. The perfect place to get in touch with your feelings and remember what's important."

"Air-conditioning?"

She shot him her best scowl. "You are killing my meaningful moment."

"Sorry." He kissed the back of her hand. "Go ahead."

She opened her mouth then smacked her lips together. "Actually, that's all I had."

"See, I don't get it. For me, being content isn't about things or a place."

"Apparently it's about finding cool air."

The smile that broke out on his mouth resonated down to her toes. "Not even close."

"Hunting down non-green food?"

"Well, yeah, there's that." He nuzzled his nose against her fingers.

A breath caught in her throat, would have come out as a sigh if she had not swallowed it back. "Then what brings you peace?"

"You."

Typical Noah. Nothing flashy or extravagant. Just a simple word that stole inside her and chipped away at her doubts.

To prevent her protective shield from falling to the ground, she fell back on humor. "If I didn't know better, I'd say you were trying to seduce me."

"Working?"

More than she wanted it to. After all of those weeks of swinging back and forth between emotions, of fighting off anger and tears, she convinced herself she had no feelings left for him except anger. A few touches and sweet smiles later and her heart tumbled all over again, which proved her theory. Seven hundred miles of space was not enough distance to insulate her from Noah or her own vulnerability.

"The days of us being together as a couple are gone, Noah."

"You are stubborn as a . . ." He rubbed her hand against the stubble on his cheek. "What's the most stubborn animal in existence?"

"You."

"Speaking of animal." Noah nodded toward the door. "The aerobics instructor, I presume?"

Lexy followed his gaze to Marie Parks. Big brown eyes and even bigger boobs. Somehow she had managed to jump up and down and lead a class that afternoon without tipping over forward.

Clear skin. Wavy blond hair. The tiniest waist ever. From the previous peek Lexy had gotten of the hand-to-hand wrestling with Tate, Marie's fresh-faced, wide-eyed innocent look was nothing more than an elaborate act. The way Tate and Noah locked eyes on the girl, her swish-and-giggle shtick was working.

"How did you know it was her?" Lexy asked as if the way Tate was drooling over her had not given it away.

"The fact she's wearing her black and pink . . . outfit thing." Noah waved his hand in Marie's direction.

"It's a leotard." An uncharacteristic wave of insecurity crashed over Lexy. "She's pretty."

Noah finally stopped staring at the young blonde. "Huh?"

"You're ten seconds away from panting, old man." And from getting his ass kicked.

Noah squeezed Lexy's hand. "She's not my type."

"You're not into pretty now?"

"I've never been into unfaithful chicks. Besides, I prefer the sassy, wrongly named, stubborn, brown-haired, naturally buxom type."

"Did you really just use the word 'buxom' in a sentence?"

"Yeah, and believe me when I say it wasn't easy to work that in."

"I'm still trying to figure out if you meant to compliment me or not."

"Definitely the former. If you don't like it, you shouldn't have worn that dress. Christ, woman. That's a concentration killer."

Lexy stared down her torso. She had picked the sundress to ward off the blazing heat. With the sun dipping below the horizon, the flowing material allowed for a bit too much air. Up the skirt, on her face, and across her shoulders. Everywhere.

And then there was the fact she looked good in it. Really good. It hugged her torso, nipped at the waist, then flared a bit from the waist. The dress hid her flaws and highlighted her best features, those being her high, firm breasts.

Seeing Noah made her want to dress up and enjoy a girly moment. She refused to analyze the need to entice and torture him, but she did appreciate the fact he took a few minutes to notice.

"There's nothing wrong with this dress," she pointed out.

"Damn straight." Noah's gaze moved between Lexy and Marie. "And you look like a woman."

"As opposed to?"

"A stick figure with plastic breasts."

He was doing a lot of noticing of Marie for a guy supposedly not interested in exercise classes. Talk about annoying.

"She's thin," Lexy said.

Noah stood up and tugged Lexy along with him. "I'd rather dance with you than talk about her."

"Fine, but this means nothing."

Noah pulled her up against his chest. "You keep telling yourself that."

She tried, but the smell of the soap on his skin and touch of his hands on the bare skin of her back kept breaking her concentration. When he hummed against her ear, the vibration traveled down to her flat shoes.

"You feel so good," he said in a deep voice.

Gentle but firm, he pressed her tight against his body. Hands gathered around her waist. His nose fell into her hair.

Before her common sense kicked in, her arms slid up his arms to wrap around his neck. "One dance."

"Mmmm." He buried his face in her naked shoulder. Licked his tongue against her waiting flesh.

Everything around her swayed, then disappeared until all she heard was the beat of the music and shuffling of their feet against the patio. No people. No talking. No laughing. Nothing registered in her unfocused mind. The world consisted only of his hands, his heat, and the rumble of his nonsense against her skin.

With every circle they danced, her resistance dropped. One more step and they would have to find a private red rock somewhere.

And that could not happen. "We should—"

"Go to your room."

His husky voice snapped her the rest of the way out of her haze. "No."

"Oh, woman." He growled the words into her shoulder.

"This is a mistake."

"But it feels so damn good."

Yeah, what he said. "That's the difference between being a kid and being an adult, Noah."

"Not getting laid?"

She tipped his head up so she could see his eyes. "We were dancing."

"It's called foreplay."

"You're such a guy."

"When exactly during this dance did you come to your senses and remember you hated me?"

If only it were that easy. Life broke into easy blocks for Noah. Everything was clear and clean. Her life functioned at a more frantic and less organized pace. Always had.

"I'm tired," she said.

"Sounds like a convenient way to get rid of me."

"It is, but six will be here in no time."

He groaned. "Sure I can't talk you out of that damn morning hike?"

"I'm here to exercise."

"We'll practice working out by walking you to your room."

"There's no—"

"Don't bother to push me away. I'm coming with you." He stared at something behind her. "Besides, I'm not up for a show."

The something amounted to Marie providing an impromptu aerobics lesson. Jumping up and down and laughing and otherwise entertaining the crowd. Including Tate. Mostly Tate.

Lexy said the first thing that popped into her head after the word "slut," which she kept to herself. "Yuck."

"I was thinking of something more profane," Noah said and actually sounded like he meant it.

"Let's go." Leading Noah away from this scene had some benefits.

Not that she was jealous.

Lexy repeated that mantra over and over in her head. Noah was a free man. He could date whomever he pleased. Just not in front of her. Not after he spent several moments touching her as if she were the only woman left in the world.

"You can come along, but you are not allowed in my room." She drew a line at the threshold. If he crossed it she would . . . well, surrender. Which was the number one reason he could not cross it.

"Whatever you say," he said in the least convincing way possible.

"This is just a friendly walk."

Noah held up his hands in mock surrender. "Okay. I get it."

For some reason, she could not unlock her limbs from around his neck. "No funny stuff."

"Only unfunny stuff. Right."

"I'm serious."

"I see that."

"Absolutely no sex."

The music and chatter picked that moment to fall silent. Once again all eyes turned to them. More than a few looked in sympathy at Noah.

"Thanks for announcing that part of our evening plans," he muttered.

"Sorry."

He looked over her head to the silent crowd. "Carry on with the dancing."

After a few beats, the music blared to life again. The whispering and strange looks continued, but most guests pretended to mind their own business.

"How about this. If you invite me, I'll come in." He brushed his fingers against her hair then let them drop. "Otherwise, I remain outside your door."

There was a trick in there somewhere. She could sense it. "You're not getting an invite. Not even one finger can come inside."

"Unless you ask. Got it."

"I won't."

"You know something?" He leaned in until his nose touched against hers. "Your not-interested act would be more persuasive if you would let go of me."

His arms hung loose at his sides.

Hers remained twisted around his neck.

"I was thinking about strangling you," she said while trying to think of an alternative logical explanation for holding him hostage against her.

"Now that I can believe."

Chapter Six

"You really don't need to walk me back to my room." Lexy made her pronouncement as they left the party and rounded the corner onto the well-lit stone path.

Then again when they passed the indoor pool.

And once more as her building came into view.

"Noah?"

"I heard you the first twelve times."

"So you're ignoring me."

"That pretty much sums it up."

They followed the trail from the public area to the dome-shaped buildings that housed the sleeping quarters. Lexy had a private room near the back of the resort and facing towering rock formations. Noah's key fit the door two rooms down.

Now that he had tracked her to Utah, no way was he venturing more than a few feet away from her. That probably meant he had a long hike ahead of him in the morning. Good thing he spent the afternoon in the gift shop dropping a month's salary on clothes and supplies he did not need in order to get up early and take a walk he would rather skip in favor of sleeping and engaging in other bedroom activities.

He also had about a thousand other things to do. Gray

wanted to expand Stuart Enterprises from corporate security to include personal security. Since Noah was the guy in the office who set up the protocols and devised the plans to protect information and professionals, the bulk of the workload relating to the new project fell to him. Would have been easier to get that work done if his files had not disappeared.

Then there was the blackmail problem. Noah needed to be in the office, working to save his ass, not trailing Lexy across the United States.

And he had to work in time to kill Gray. Some best friend Gray turned out to be. He could have helped, at least given some insight into Lexy's bizarre actions. Instead, Gray told him to take a few days off and track her down. Not exactly helpful advice.

Apparently developing a sales plan to protect rich people, dealing with a blackmail threat, and winning back a stubborn fiancée were not enough things for a guy to do. Now he had to add "choke the shit out of Gray" to his list.

"You ready to tell me why you're here?" he asked.

"Still here for a vacation. That hasn't changed." She walked with her arms behind her back and her fingers entwined.

Probably a way to keep him from holding her hand. "I'm still not buying it."

"I'm too tired to fight with you."

"Words every man waits to hear." He gave in and touched her. Resting a hand on her elbow did not qualify as the kind of caressing he wanted, but it was a connection of sorts.

They moved up the three steps to stand at her door. The last time he felt this awkward he was fifteen, totally green and hell-bent on convincing his seventeen-year-old neighbor to let him do more than touch her breasts. Worked then. Wasn't working now.

"This is my room," she said.

"Also fine words to hear from a woman."

"Then you'll love these." She reached around his hip and put her hand on the doorknob. "Good night."

He slammed his hand against the doorjamb like a human barricade to keep her from going one step farther. "I'll wait right here until you unlock the door."

"It's not locked."

He turned the knob. The door opened with a short squeak.

Her lazy way of watching out for her safety ticked him off. "Has the desert heat rotted your brain?"

"If this is your idea of a pass, it's worse than anything Tate tried."

She pivoted to Noah's side, but he moved to block the entire doorway. He knew he had to stand in her path or risk having her stalk inside and leave him on the porch.

"Anyone could wander in there," Noah said in the calmest voice he could muster.

"Do not yell at me."

So much for thinking he was in control of the situation. "You're lucky I'm not shaking some sense into you."

She snorted. "Oh, please."

As usual, she took his threat for what it was. Empty. Thanks to her stubborn streak, getting her attention usually resulted in putting her on the defensive. But he needed to make his point. If she planned to keep the door open for anyone to enter, then he would be awake on her floor instead of trying to sleep back in his room.

"Since your family runs a security firm and makes a living telling businesspeople how to protect their information and people, I would think something as simple as locking a door would be obvious to you."

"We're not in San Diego."

"What, there's no crime in Utah?"

"Look around you." She swept her arm across the quiet landscape. "There's nothing out here. Unless a coyote is in there taking a nap on the bed, I'm fine."

"Until it pounces on you and rips your throat out." The images running through his mind filled his stomach with an icy dread.

"Stop lecturing me."

He rubbed both hands over his face as he tried to figure out the best way to get through to her. "You are so frustrating."

"Whatever you say, *Mr. Charm.*"

"You lock your door at home in La Jolla despite the fact you live in a gated condo complex where there's barely any crime."

"Of course I do."

Her ready agreement made him nervous. With anyone else he would have thought he won the argument. Not with Lexy. She always moved one way when he expected her to move another.

"Then what's the problem here?" he asked.

"I forgot."

His mind went blank. "You . . . ?"

"Forgot to lock the door." She crossed her arms over her stomach. "Humans do forget things sometimes."

She had him to the point where he did not even know what they were arguing about anymore. "So you know you should lock the door?"

She peeked inside the dark room. "I'm not an idiot."

"Then why are you fighting me about this?"

"Couldn't help myself. You get bossy and my innate need to fight surfaces and takes over."

He blew out the breath he had been holding. "In other words, you didn't want to admit you made a mistake."

"That doesn't sound like me."

"Of course not." He grabbed her arm when she started to walk into the room.

"What's wrong now?" she asked.

"What do you think you're doing?"

"Going to bed." She brought her face to within inches of his. "Alone."

"Not until I check the room."

She nibbled on her bottom lip. "You promised to stay outside unless I invited you in."

"Implied in that promise was the condition you would act rational and lock your damn door. You didn't, so I'm coming in to check everything out."

"What are you going to do if you come face-to-face with that coyote?"

"Tell him to find another room."

She glanced into the dark room then looked at him. "All right. You have your invitation. Five minutes."

"This will take two."

"Because you're a recon expert now?"

While he did not find his past all that relevant to their future, after the divorce issue came up he had made a silent promise never to lie outright to Lexy. With his varied history and her snotty remarks, keeping that vow got harder each day.

"Sort of," he mumbled hoping she would not hear him. When all signs of amusement disappeared from her face, he knew she had. "You have got to be kidding."

"Technically recon is not the right term."

"Is there anything about your past I do know?"

"That I proposed, you accepted, then you got bitchy and broke it off."

"Do your room check before I kick you." She pointed at him. "And if I kick, I'm aiming for right below the waist."

"Not nice."

"Consider it part of my bitchy side."

He flicked on the light just inside the door. Rather than wait outside and otherwise not drive him insane, Lexy followed him. He crossed the threshold, she crossed the threshold. He took a step, she took a step. He stopped, she stopped.

To put an end to her shadowing, he made a quick move that sent her crashing into his back. "I can handle this on my own."

Tonight was not the first time he had walked into a situation and tried to assess the danger. After years in covert ops and working undercover, he did not need protection from someone wearing a dress.

"This is my room," she pointed out.

"And as soon as it's safe you can come in and do whatever you want."

"Too late. I'm already in." She cuddled closer.

Because he enjoyed the sensation of her body next to his and the light scent of flowers on her skin, he did not fight her. He also doubted danger waited just around the corner.

Standing just inside the entry with her plastered against his back, he scanned the oversized room. Light blue walls. Blue comforter and pillows. The brochure said something about the color being a reminder of the sea. Since the resort sat in the middle of the desert, the water image did not make a lot of sense in his view. If people wanted the beach, they should go to the damn beach.

The closet door stood open. Clothing littered the bed and stuck out from the drawers. All sorts of files were stacked on one corner of the desk. Bags took up position on the other.

"I like what you've done with the place," he said.

"It's fine."

"Looks like someone tossed it."

Noah recognized the disheveled state. Lexy's extra bedroom at home had the same boxes-stacked-on-boxes, clothes-

all-over-the-floor, crap-everywhere look that grew more se-
vere whenever she felt anxious or confused.

For an organized and meticulous woman, she decorated
the unused bedroom in a style only a burglar could appreciate. There was not so much as a pillow out of place in any
other room in her house, at her marketing business, or in
her car. But that bedroom resembled a high-school locker
room.

Not a surprise in light of how she grew up. Her parents
saved and stacked and piled papers, boxes, and anything
else they could find around the house until all that remained
was a thin strip of carpet leading from one room to another
on which to walk. Lexy called the condition hoarding. Noah
thought it was just plain nuts. How two healthy, smart, fi-
nancially well-off people could live in such cramped, dirty,
and odd conditions stunned Noah. And why Gray and Lexy
continued to run interference so the family secret remained
just that did not make any more sense to Noah.

"You trying to find something, or did you just think the
room looked better turned inside out?" he asked.

"Just had some trouble picking out the right outfit to
wear."

He had heard the excuse, even that defensive tone, before. After almost two years of knowing her, analyzing her
family, and talking with Gray about his parents' issues, Noah
knew better. This went deeper than simple messiness. This
was a sickness. One that edged up on Lexy now and then.

Noah wondered what had Lexy so anxious right now. He
hoped it had something to do with missing him.

"Let me guess, you needed something light to wear because it was *a hundred degrees* outside," he said trying to
ease the tense look on her face.

"For the fiftieth time, it was not that hot today."

"Then the clothing explosion must have something to do

with you wanting to find a dress to impress me. You did, by the way. The bright blue color is damn hot."

"I thought hot was a bad thing."

"Not in this case."

"You can go now."

Tough talk from a woman who refused to give him eye contact.

"In a minute. Have to finish the check first." And stall his exit as long as possible.

He stepped up to the bed with her right on his tail. On the opposite side of the bed sat a desk and chair. After that was a sliding glass door to the porch followed by nothing but red rock towers and the vast nothing beyond until you hit Las Vegas.

He walked over to check the locks on that back door. "Everything looks—"

The rest of his comment slammed against his throat. He blinked twice as his brain processed the scene in front of eyes. He expected a mess. He did not expect this much of a mess.

She bumped against him from behind again. "Is there a shoe out of place?"

"Call 911."

She rolled her eyes. "I know you think I have a sloppiness problem, but you don't have to get dramatic about it. No one trashed the room. I really did leave it looking like this when I went to dinner."

"Not in this condition."

Squashed between the double bed and the chair was a man and a whole lot of blood. Even Lexy's family, with all its eccentricities, did not keep dead people lying around.

"What is wrong with you?" She raised up on her tiptoes. At five-ten, seeing over his shoulder was not tough.

"Make the call." Noah hoped the firm voice would get

her moving because he needed a few more seconds to digest and analyze the facts and figure out what happened.

Her mouth fell open. "Is that . . . ?"

"Yeah."

"But he's—"

"A dead guy on your floor. Yeah."

Her mouth stayed open. Wide open. "Oh my God."

"It's okay."

"Not if he's dead!" She shook her head. Any harder and things would start rattling loose in there.

Having her see the blood and lose control helped spark him into action. Grabbing her shoulders, Noah walked her backward until the bed blocked her view of most of the body.

"Make the call, honey," Noah said in his most comforting tone.

"Are you sure he's dead?"

Noah had seen dead. He knew dead. This guy was definitely dead.

"I don't see a knife sticking out of his back, but yeah."

Lexy's eyes were big enough to take over her face. "Who . . . Why my room?"

"We'll figure that as soon as you call the police." He rubbed her arms for a few seconds to ward off the chill shaking through her.

"Where are you going?" she asked as she made a frantic grab for his hand when he tried to break away.

"To double check."

"You mean he might be alive?" She sounded more horrified at that possibility than at the thought of the guy being dead.

"No."

"Then leave him alone."

Noah pushed her in the general direction of the telephone. "You stay right over here."

Without disturbing anything, Noah crouched down and

pressed his fingers against the other man's neck. Nothing flowing or moving in this guy.

"Well?" she asked.

"The lack of a pulse pretty much confirms my diagnosis. He's dead."

"Oh my God." She paced around on the far side of the bed, taking turns peeking over the bedspread and breathing heavy into her hands. "Ohmigod. Ohmigod."

"Lexy." He said her name nice and firm to get her attention.

She stopped walking around and mumbling. "What?"

"The call."

"Right." She fumbled with the phone. Her hands shook so hard that she knocked the receiver onto the floor. "I just can't believe this."

Neither could Noah. Scaring the shit out of Lexy for making a bad safety decision fit in fine with his evening plans. He was prepared to lecture her, then call it a night. Go back and take his usual cold shower. Instead, waiting around for the coroner moved onto his schedule.

A dead guy on her floor qualified as a disaster. Noah had seen enough suffering to last a lifetime. He never wanted Lexy this close to violence. Hell, he traded in his old life for a desk job to avoid more violence, or at least deal with it in a new way.

After a quick look to make sure Lexy had started dialing, Noah sized up the situation on her floor. The fall smashed the dead man's face into the carpet and on top of a few of Lexy's precious folders. Noah could see blondish hair. The bigger question came with the guy's outfit. A black T-shirt and pants. Not exactly the best choice for hanging around a hot climate. The scene looked less like a case of Lexy's sloppiness and more like an issue of someone trying to steal something out of her room.

Noah had no idea what she could have that someone would want enough to die for. And if the dead guy was a bad guy, why the hell was he dead? Exactly how many bad guys were wandering around the desert?

After a few minutes of animated conversation with the 911 operator, Lexy hung up the phone. She sat down hard on the bed. "The police are on the way. So is Tate."

Half of that information amounted to good news. "How did Tate find out?"

"I called the front desk first and had someone track him down."

"Couldn't have been too hard, since he was at the party."

She raised her eyebrows. "Not."

"A private evening aerobics class, I assume."

"Something like that."

The entire resort and every law enforcement officer in the area would track through the room within the next hour. There would be questions and more questions. Seeing the dead guy's face might make a few of those easier to answer, but Noah knew not to touch the body. No matter how much he wanted to.

"What are we going to do?" she asked.

He forgot about the anxiety balled up inside of him. Seeing Lexy hurt knocked into him like a kick in the chest.

"We're going to wait for the police and then take it from there," he said in his calmest voice because he wanted her to stay calm.

"But, I—"

He slipped his hands into hers and lifted her off the bed. With his arms wrapped around her waist, he pulled her close and let his body warm her cold skin. "At least there's one positive here."

She stared up at him. "What in the world could that be?"

"Tomorrow's hike is probably canceled."

Chapter Seven

Lexy stayed anchored in her room's doorway while Tate, the detectives, and numerous medical personnel buzzed around. The chill racing through her finally slowed down to a jog when Noah got permission from the police to grab one of her sweaters. When Noah threw it around her shoulders, then left his arm resting there, she did not argue. His strength and self-assurance calmed her.

All the people, all the lights, all the noise from the conversations of her fellow guests standing on the stone path just outside her room, it all worked together to ease the fear churning in her stomach. Maybe there was something to the strength-in-numbers theory.

Being pinned to Noah's side helped, too. So did the two no-nonsense police detectives circling around the room with the guns strapped to their sides. They came in, pushed Tate around, and had been issuing orders ever since. Even Noah stayed out of their way, which was quite something because one of the officers, Detective Ellen Sommerville, was about twenty-five, all of five-foot-three, and a smidge over a hundred pounds.

But she could yell. Despite her slight stature and fresh-faced college co-ed look, she walked in and ordered the ambulance crew members here and Tate over there. Unfortunately, the "there" included letting him back in the room.

Detective Rob Lindsay was a good two decades older and one foot taller than his partner. He refrained from yelling, but his hand never left the top of his weapon.

Lexy liked both officers immediately. They qualified as the most sane people she had met at the resort since arriving.

"How can we keep this quiet?" Tate took turns rubbing his temples and talking at the speed of sound as he paced the small space between Lexy's bed and the bathroom door.

Lexy winced as his foot tangled in one of her discarded sweaters. She wanted to pick up the room before half of Utah showed up at her door. Noah insisted she leave everything right where it was. Something about her clothes being part of a crime scene.

She just wished they were hanging up or in a suitcase or something. Whenever her life jumped out of control, her living space went to hell. She hated the habit. Letting her belongings get to this point clashed with the vow she made at fifteen not to follow her parents' pathological pack-rat tendencies.

Noah was one of the few men she let into her family's secret mess. Now every law enforcement official in the area would get a peek at the private battle she fought.

"Mr. Carr, while I appreciate your desire to handle the PR here, a man is dead," Detective Sommerville said as her gaze locked on Marie.

Marie was hard to miss, since she stood in the bathroom entry wearing only a short silky robe. One that became see-through with the bathroom light glaring behind her.

"Call me Tate."

Detective Lindsay put a quick end to Tate's attempted

flirting with his partner. "What we need is for you and your lady friend—"

"She's my employee."

Detective Sommerville looked skeptical. "Whatever you call her, the two of you should leave the room."

"You can't talk to him that way." Marie shuffled into the middle of the conversation, boobs first. "He owns the place."

"Shut up." Detective Sommerville ended her comment with a dismissive look at Marie's wardrobe choice.

Noah bent down from his position in the doorway and whispered into Lexy's ear. "I like these detectives."

That made two of them. "Probably because they carry guns."

"They're pushy and they're pushing the right people around. Namely that Tate idiot."

"Tate's not that bad." Lexy said the words, but it was getting harder and harder to stick up for the guy. The fact that he wore only a white undershirt and boxers made it easier to file him in the loser horndog category.

"Tell that to Marie's husband." Noah tilted his head toward the even bigger mess than the room, this one human. "She's a classy one."

"Would it have killed Marie to put on some pants?" Lexy whispered back.

"I'm not convinced she owns a pair."

Someone on the police force walked around with a video camera. Another guy took photos.

"This is a circus," Lexy said.

Noah tightened his hold on her. "Everything has to be catalogued."

"It's just so disrespectful. A man is dead and everyone is traipsing in and out like it's no big deal."

"Tate certainly thinks it's a big deal." Noah nodded in

the other man's general direction. "He hasn't figured out that Sommerville is the bad cop of this duo."

Lexy watched Tate try to convince Detective Sommerville of something. She was not buying whatever he tried to sell.

Detective Lindsay broke away from Tate's raving and came toward Noah. The detective's wrinkled khakis and stained white oxford suggested the guy was busying doing something else when he got the call about the crime. His short salt-and-pepper hair looked combed, but only because he kept running his fingers through it.

"Okay, folks. What can you tell me?"

"Nothing more than what we said when you first got here," Noah said.

Detective Lindsay nodded. "Looks like the guy tossed the place before he got smashed in the head with the lamp."

Lexy refused to look at Noah. "No one messed up the room."

The detective tapped his pen against his pad. "What?"

"I did that," she said, swallowing more than a little pride. "All this?

"Yes."

From the detective's frown, Lexy guessed he missed the lost-pride thing. "You mean after you saw the body?"

And there went the last little bit of it. "When I was picking out an outfit to wear to dinner."

The detective laughed. When no one joined him, he sobered. "Seriously?"

"She got a little carried away," Noah explained.

Before Lexy could debate the wisdom of grabbing for the officer's gun and threatening both men with it, understanding dawned on the detective's face. He glanced at Noah with a man-to-man smile. "My wife is the same way."

"This bad?" Noah asked.

"Well, no." The detective's gaze roamed over the room. "It looks as if everything you brought is on the floor."

Lexy rushed to ask a few questions before Noah and the detective bonded over the eccentricities of women. "Did you say somebody hit the man with a lamp?"

"Smacked him right in the base of his skull. Cracked it wide open. Blood spurted—"

"Hey!" Noah shifted until his body shielded hers. "Tone it down."

Lexy normally would have protested Noah's overzealous protective streak. Not tonight. The evening's events stole most of her energy for fighting.

"I apologize for my partner's choice of words." Detective Sommerville joined the threesome. "We don't see a huge number of murders here."

"Still don't have to get so damn excited about it," Noah mumbled.

"Intrigued, not excited," said the younger detective as she tucked a stray strand of blond hair behind her ear.

The elder detective's gaze wandered to the other side of the room. "You handle this. I'll go check with the lady in the robe."

"Thought you might volunteer for that duty." Detective Sommerville watched her partner all but run for the half-naked chick in the bathroom.

"He should consider wearing armor," Noah suggested.

"He can handle her. He has one just like her at home." Detective Sommerville swallowed her growing smile. "So, is anything missing in the room?"

"How could you tell?" Noah asked.

The snide comment earned him an elbow in the stomach. Lexy would have done more if the cop were not standing there witnessing the whole scene. "I haven't had a chance to check."

The detective took out a flip pad and pen and started taking notes. "Did either of you know the victim?"

Noah shrugged. "No idea."

"What does that mean?" Detective Sommerville asked.

"Hard to tell his identity with his face pushed into the floor," Noah said.

"Just a sec." The detective stepped over the piles of clothes to the other side of the bed and whispered something to the ambulance guys as they lifted the victim onto the gurney.

"What is she doing?" Lexy asked without taking her eyes off the petite policewoman.

"Probably wants us to try to identify the body. We might know him."

She gave in to the frustration percolating inside her and threw her hands up in the air. "How is that possible? Every person I know in Utah is standing in this room."

"It's a formality." Noah massaged the back of her neck with a gentle touch.

He had always been this way. So reassuring and soothing. Under that gruff and guarded exterior lurked an understanding and acceptance of people's vulnerabilities. If only he could open up and let her know the rest of him.

"You seem to know a lot about this police procedure stuff," she said.

His gaze moved around the room, taking it all in and ignoring her. "Uh-huh."

The signs were all there. Enough time and arguments had taught her that a nonanswer about his past was her *real* answer. He was right in that when it came to his past, he never overtly lied. He just never volunteered the truth or one iota of information. The stealing was a different issue.

"Were you ever a policeman?" When he ignored the question, she pinched him.

"Hey!" He rubbed his arm. "What's with the nails?"

"Were you ever a cop?"

"No."

Funny, but she would have bet money on him saying yes to that one. "How about something policelike?"

"*Policelike* is not a real career."

"You know what I mean."

He pressed his lips together with a smack. "I actually don't."

Her arguments and questions died in her throat when the medical crew lifted the gurney up to waist height and rolled it over. A white sheet draped the body. Knowing a human lay under there made bile rush up the back of Lexy's throat.

"Mr. Carr. Ma'am." Detective Sommerville motioned for all of them to come over to the gurney. She did not even bother to use Marie's name, a fact that made Lexy smile despite the nervous energy attacking her insides.

"Again, call me Tate," he said as he walked over.

The female detective ignored his request a second time. "We need you all to look at the body. See if you can tell us who he is, or if you've seen him around."

Tate straightened to show off every inch of his six-foot frame. "He is no one affiliated with the spa, I assure you."

"How about we look at the guy before you make that kind of pronouncement, hmmm?" Detective Sommerville said with an authority that belied her size.

Tate did not give up the fight. "I doubt—"

Detective Somerville lifted the sheet back. "Well?"

Marie gasped.

Tate made a sound closer to a gurgle. "Charlie?"

Lexy had been trying not to look at the body, but Tate's comment captured her full attention. "Henderson?"

Noah studied the dead man's face before turning back to Lexy. "The guy from this afternoon?"

How was she going to get out of this? "Looks like him."

Because it was him. The guy accused her of stalking and then wound up dead on her floor. Any way she examined the time line, it did not look great for her.

Or for Noah.

"Sounded like you all agree this is Charlie Henderson." Detective Sommerville eyed Lexy, too. "Ms. Stuart? Anything you need to tell me."

Lexy swallowed hard. "No."

"Do you know him, ma'am?"

"I don't *know* him know him."

"Is that English?" The harsh edge returned to Noah's voice.

"He works here," Tate said.

"Wait a minute. We're going to go one at a time." Detective Sommerville pointed her pen at Tate. "Tell me what you know."

"He works security here. Well, I guess you would now say worked." Tate's gaze did not leave the dead man's face. "He walks the premises, checks on problems, that sort of thing."

"Does he have access to the inside of the rooms?" Detective Sommerville asked.

"Well, yeah, but only in emergencies," Tate said.

"Since he's dead, I'm thinking we have an emergency." Noah kept looking at the dead man's face as if trying to memorize it.

Lexy did not have to. She had seen Charlie Henderson's face every time she opened the file she dragged with her from home. She followed the guy to the spa, he confronted her, and now he was dead.

Detective Lindsay took over and grabbed Tate by his elbow. "Mr. Carr, come outside with me."

"Why?" A squeal replaced Tate's otherwise even nature.

"You and I need to talk, sir."

Tate tried to break free from Detective Lindsay's grip. "I didn't do anything."

"Stop moving."

"But I—"

"We need some privacy," Detective Lindsay said as he led Tate and Marie outside. "So does Ms. Stuart."

Yeah, Ms. Stuart needed something all right. Something like a drink or a few days in bed. Charlie Henderson dead in her room. Somewhere along the line they had ventured into nightmare territory.

She peeked at Noah out of the corner of her eye and noticed the locked jaw and cold eyes. No way was Noah going to let this subject go. And now they would both be suspects in Henderson's murder.

She hated this supposed spa.

"Ms. Stuart?"

Lexy was so stunned, her body so stiff with shock, that she almost missed Detective Somerville's questioning tone.

Noah did not wait for Lexy to regain her senses. "No more verbal games, Lexy. Who is he?"

Lexy bit down hard on her bottom lip. She tried to think of a way out of this situation. Like, maybe an earthquake could strike and save her from having to answer.

"Lexy?"

"Ms. Stuart?" Detective Sommerville said her name at the same time Noah tried to get her attention.

Lexy looked from the detective to Noah and back again. Yeah, no way to run from this part. She had to come clean.

At least a little clean.

"He's the reason I came to Utah."

Chapter Eight

D etective Sommerville's expression turned from concerned to something much more harsh. Her features sharpened and the small bit of openness she had treated Lexy to disappeared.

Noah knew the feeling. Finding out his fiancée was involved up to the tip-top of her pretty green eyes in a murder did not help his frustrated disposition one bit.

"You were at the spa with him?" Noah said the words nice and slow. Tasted them and nearly spit from the sour stench.

"It's not what you think." Lexy's voice shook as she spoke.

She should be scared. This went well beyond fun and games, so Noah did not try to keep the anger out of his voice. "Lexy, you have two seconds to start making sense."

"What I meant to say is that I saw the man around the spa. I ran into him today and said hello."

He had seen that conversation. Couldn't hear it, but watched her body language. Whatever the two of them said went on much longer than the time it took to give a simple greeting.

"That's not even close to what you said a second ago," Detective Sommerville pointed out.

"It's what I meant."

"Sounds as if you're changing your story, ma'am."

Lexy rubbed her forehead. "It's been a long night, detective. I'm sure you understand."

Noah agreed with that part. Everything else she said about this Henderson character was pure bunk. But he saw the fear in Lexy's eyes. She tried to cover it under a layer of bullshit, but he knew her well enough to know she was unraveling inside.

The way he saw it his only choice was to step in and try to keep Lexy from being taken away in handcuffs. He turned his attention to Detective Sommerville. "It's been a rough hour."

The detective scowled. "Ms. Stuart can speak for herself."

He agreed with that, too. Half the time the problem was in convincing Lexy to shut up. Her uncharacteristic struggle to form a sentence for the last few minutes had him slipping into his own form of panic. The angry kind.

"Ease up," he said to the petite detective.

Lexy rested her hand against his chest. "She's just doing her job, Noah."

He sighed. So much for trying to protect Lexy from herself.

The voices on the lawn outside Lexy's room had died down. More police officers arrived to rope off the scene and keep the other guests back.

"Ma'am, do you or do you not know Charlie Henderson?" Detective Sommerville asked.

"I know who he is."

"Meaning?"

"I've seen him around." When the detective stayed quiet, Lexy fumbled with more words. "That's it."

A few more minutes without serious intervention and Lexy would probably admit to killing the guy. Noah searched his mind for the quickest way to get her away from the police and alone. Then he would get some answers.

He damn well better.

Detective Sommerville pulled the sheet over the body and nodded to the ambulance crew to take the gurney away. "Did either of you have contact with Mr. Henderson today or anytime before today except for this 'hello' you referred to a second ago?"

"No." Lexy gave the response before the detective finished her question.

"Not me, either," Noah said at a more respectable pace.

"Just because homicide is not the leading source of crime in this county does not mean we don't take it seriously." The detective aimed her comments at Lexy. "Or that we don't know how to solve one."

"Of course," Lexy said.

"This is not a time to tell me only half a story, ma'am."

Despite the harsh circumstances, hearing someone lecture Lexy about telling the truth broke through his frustration. Usually Lexy gave that speech. From her frown, he guessed she did not appreciate being on the receiving end of the "you owe me the truth" diatribe.

"Maybe you need a reminder about how we ended up at this point, but the guy was on my floor," Lexy said with a bit more strength to her voice.

"If something happened like, maybe, you defended yourself from a burglar or someone who was trying to hurt you, then you should tell me. We can work this out nice and easy and without too much trouble. The prosecutor will understand."

Noah appreciated the detective's style. Didn't appreciate Lexy being the object of her police tactics. "Lexy was with me in the dining room and then on the patio when this happened."

"And how do you know when the murder occurred? You have some experience with murder, Mr. Paxton?"

The target circle just moved from Lexy's chest to his. Exactly how he wanted it. "I know enough."

He felt Lexy flinch at his side.

"Not that you would dream of lying to cover for Ms. Stuart," the detective said in a voice heavy with sarcasm.

"He's telling the truth. We were together," Lexy insisted.

In the background, Noah heard Tate talking to Detective Lindsay about relocating guests. Tate fought the idea with everything he had. Mentioned the cost and problem about lost profits several times. When a few of those lingering outside heard the detective's suggestions, they ganged up on Tate. Words like "refund" and "lawsuit" flew around the courtyard.

"I need you both to come to the station now," Detective Sommerville said as a statement, not a request.

Not going to happen. "No."

"Excuse me?" Detective Sommerville said at a near roar that would intimidate most men twice her size.

Not Noah. "I said no."

"You're refusing?" The disbelief in the detective's tone suggested that people did not deny her very often.

"Lexy has had a hard evening. We've both experienced a terrible shock. Now is not the time for this."

"You're a big man, Mr. Paxton. You don't strike me as someone who surprises easily."

"It's not often I see a dead guy on my fiancée's floor."

When Lexy refrained from denying the engagement, Noah knew she needed a few minutes to get her act together. Which was good, since he planned to give his assistance with or without her permission.

If Lexy had something to confess, and he guessed she did, she could do it to him. Only to him.

"Just a few questions and then you can come back to the spa and get a good night's sleep," Detective Sommerville said.

Lexy's eyes widened as she glanced around the disheveled room. "I'm not sleeping here."

"No, you're not. This is a crime scene and off-limits from here on," Detective Sommerville started writing something down on her notepad. "We'll find you another room."

"You can sleep in mine." An offer Noah planned to make before the dead body showed up anyway. This just assured Lexy's agreement. He would have preferred a willing bedmate to a scared and potentially homicidal one, but he decided not to be particular on this point.

"Where are you staying?" Lexy asked.

The detective's pen stopped. "You don't know where your fiancée's room is?"

Noah ignored the detective's curious look. "Two doors down."

"That's too close to this room." Lexy wrapped her arms around her stomach and shook her head. "I need one somewhere else. Maybe a place in Arizona."

The detective's amusement faded with that remark. "You may not leave the state."

"She was kidding," Noah said.

"No, I wasn't," Lexy insisted.

"So, what's this about separate rooms?" the detective asked.

Suddenly everyone in Utah gave a shit about his sex life, or the obvious lack of one. "You have a problem with chastity, officer?"

The detective's gaze traveled over Noah's shoulders and down his body. The scrutiny made Noah want to shift his weight. Hit the wall. Something. Instead, he stayed right where he was. No way some tiny woman holding a gun and a pen was going to make him flinch.

He did not need another woman trying to make his life hell. Lexy held that position and was excelling at the task, thank you.

"I don't see what our separate room arrangements have to do with a murder." Lexy made her comment loud enough to draw the attention of the stragglers and extra cops outside.

They all stared at Noah.

"We don't need to talk about this subject." Noah cleared his throat. "Again."

Lexy pointed at the female detective. "She's the one who mentioned it."

Noah thought he saw a smile tug on the corner of Detective Sommerville's mouth before she flattened her lips in a frown. "Ma'am, your bedroom activities are your business."

There was a subject he wanted to discuss only with Lexy. And he would as soon as they got this Henderson mess figured out.

"But, as an officer of the law, this murder scene is my business."

Somehow they circled back around to the same place. Noah's position had not changed. "I'll bring Lexy to the station tomorrow."

"I'm right here," Lexy mumbled.

"We aren't negotiating this point, Mr. Paxton."

"No, detective, we're not."

"So, you are refusing to come with me." Somehow Detective Sommerville managed to look about a foot taller when she said that. "Do I have that correct?"

Lexy tugged on his arm. "Uh, Noah. Maybe we should—"

"We'll be there tomorrow morning. We can come in early since our hike is canceled." He glanced at Lexy. "That's true, right?"

Lexy snorted. "I'm not going outside while there's a murderer on the loose."

A guest outside picked up on Lexy's comment and started bombarding the officers with questions about safety.

Noah turned back to Detective Sommerville. "So, I guess that means we're free to go."

She tucked her notepad in her pocket. "Ms. Stuart, I think you should reconsider your boyfriend's plans for your evening."

He hated that term. "Fiancée."

"I'm talking to Ms. Stuart."

"She's not coming with you."

Lexy's stubborn streak resurfaced. "*She* can speak for herself."

Detective Sommerville grabbed onto the opening. "If Mr. Paxton insists on staying here, I can drive you to the station and have another officer drive you back to join Mr. Paxton later."

After a brief beat of silence, Lexy answered. "No."

"Excuse me?" The detective said the words in her yelling voice.

"Noah's right. We'll be down in the morning."

Noah did not know he was holding his breath until Lexy sided with him. "That's set, then."

"I expect you both by eight." Detective Sommerville stared at Lexy and then focused on him. "You have a lot of explaining to do."

Noah shot Lexy a glance of his own. Yeah, one of them did.

Chapter Nine

A nother hour passed before the police finished collecting everyone's name and contact information, questioned those who agreed to be questioned, which was just about everyone, and issued the do-not-leave-the-premises warning. Lights blared to life around the resort. Guests filed into their rooms. Officers roamed the grounds.

And Lexy's biggest problem sat on the bed in front of her wearing a sexy pair of faded jeans and a grim expression.

She gave up her position at the window watching the police go in and out of her room in favor of watching Noah. He balanced his elbows on his knees and stared at the beige carpet. Had not uttered a word since he unlocked the door and all but shoved her inside his pristine room.

She knew the topic on his mind—Charlie Henderson. She should have been horrified about the man's death and worried about what this meant in terms of her little excursion to Utah. Henderson was her key to figuring out what was going on with Noah.

Someone broke right through the security plan Noah developed and installed. That same someone tampered with the passwords and protocols making it look like Noah, at best, dropped the ball and, at worst, was in on the crime. At the time Henderson was in San Diego and working out of their offices on some top-secret temporary assignment, from what she could tell.

Yeah, Charlie Henderson's death should have been her biggest concern because it ended her line of inquiry. She should be spending the minutes trying to come up with something to tell the detectives so that they did not connect her with Henderson. She should be calling her client and informing them that the information she promised to provide was now well out of her hands.

But she did not care a whit about any of that.

Only one thing—one person—hovered in her mind. Noah. Need whipped through her with an intensity that threatened to knock her backward. The craving and desire swamped all of her good sense, beat down her firm resolve to keep Noah at a distance, and replaced it with a burning need.

She wanted to blame the lust simmering inside her on the shot of adrenaline she experienced this evening. The mix of shock at seeing a dead body and terror over everything that came after.

She knew better.

Something horrible happened and all she wanted was to share the moment with Noah. To let him wipe away all of her fears and confusion. To lose herself in his arms, under his mouth. No matter what the cause, all she wanted to do was to ease the rumbling mass bouncing around inside of her.

Which was why she entered the room and then stood as far away from him as the small space would allow. She had hoped the passing minutes would kill the need she felt for Noah. But the longer she watched him turn his hands over and stare at the invisible spot on the floor, the more she wanted him focused on her. The more she wanted back a tiny piece of what they had before everything blew up in her face.

Breaking off their engagement destroyed a part of her. The aftermath was even worse. Cleaning Noah out of her head and her heart proved impossible. He lingered there, tugging at her and testing.

All she wanted in that moment was to detach her heart from her body and enjoy one, two, three, lovemaking sessions. They both needed the release. They were there, adults and still attracted.

"Are you done hiding?" His husky voice ripped to the very heart of her.

"I'm standing right here."

"Are you ready to talk about Henderson?"

Oh, she was ready for something. "No."

He sighed. "Of course not."

"I'm done talking about Henderson."

Noah glanced up at her with a blank expression. "Because you can't come up with a believable lie?"

"Because I don't want to talk."

This was going to happen. Her. Him. Them. Bed. She missed the feel of him, his touch and kiss. The way he made her feel inside and out as his hands toured her body and his mouth met hers.

She could keep it physical. Separate her need from everything permanent and good she ever hoped for them. This could be about a release.

"I want to help you," he said.

"Good." Because that is exactly what she needed him to do. Help her out of this dress and into the bed.

"You have to know that I don't care what you did or didn't do."

She believed him on that score. He did not pass judgment. Did not insist that everyone live by his code. He took people as they were.

She could not dwell on that. On the good parts of him. No, now it was time for him to just plain take her. She would regret and assess and recover later.

She closed the curtain. "That's very accommodating of you."

"To figure out the best plan of attack, you have to level with me." His dark eyes flashed with determination. So serious and worried. "What did you and this Henderson guy talk about? How do you know him?"

She could see his confusion in the wrinkles around his eyes. The controlled anger in the way he balled his hands into fists.

"There aren't any police here. Just tell me." He practically begged.

She ignored the caring. She had to if she wanted to keep this physical and divorce her heart from the process.

"I have a better idea," she said.

His eyes narrowed. "That's what I'm afraid of."

"Oh, I think you'll like this one."

"Hard to imagine how that's possible."

"Trust me." She walked over and stopped when her knees touched his.

The position forced him to lean back and gave her the superior power she wanted. Having him vulnerable to his needs and her wants. Hovering over him until he had to look up to see her face. Perfect.

"Lexy?"

"We could talk and talk, go over this until you figure out some grand plan, but you know what, Noah?"

"Uh, no."

She crouched down until they were face-to-face and placed her palms on his knees. "I'd rather sit on your lap."

"*What?*"

"Kiss you all over."

She felt him tense. Saw a flush creep over his skin. Watched every bone in his body snap to attention.

He blinked a few times. "You're saying—"

"Feel you slide inside me."

He grabbed the bedspread behind him with both hands. "I sure as hell hope you're talking about sex."

"Hot, sweaty, fantastic sex."

Heat replaced the confusion in his eyes. "With me?"

The idea of letting another man touch her left her cold. The idea of being with him made something inside her soar. Something she wanted to beat back and ignore.

Something that refused to die.

"Only you." And she meant that with every part of the heart she tried to close off to him.

"You didn't want me earlier."

"I do now." She whispered as she kneeled at his feet. "Want only you and all of you."

"If this is your way of getting out of a conversation about Henderson . . ."

"Yeah?" His words did not register. She was too busy sliding her hands up his thighs until her thumbs rested against his growing bulge.

"I'm all for it."

"I'm itchy and fidgety. It's as if I have all of this energy inside me fighting to get out."

"Adrenaline. It's your body's response to the shock." His hands flexed against the bed.

"Have any idea how I can work a bit of this off?"

"One or two."

"Very good."

He cleared his throat. "Several of them require you to stay on your knees."

She rubbed her thumb over his erection. "I have a few thoughts of my own."

"They involve those fingers?"

She shifted her hands to his belt. With a tug she unbuckled and slid the leather out of the holder. "To start."

"After that?" His stomach dipped when her knuckles brushed his navel.

"Thought I'd use my mouth."

Syncopated pants rushed out of him. "Let's try your way."

"Lean back," she ordered.

He slid his hands on the comforter and leaned back until he balanced his upper body on his elbows. "Better?"

"Let's see." She bent down and nuzzled him, nipping against the thick material of his jeans until his hips lifted off the bed. "Yeah, much better."

Feminine and in control, she reveled in the smell and feel of him. How fast he hardened for her. How a slight tremor shook his arms. Despite everything that passed between them and all that went unsaid, they had this. A deep desire for each other. An ability to weaken each other's will.

Rather than let her mind butt in and examine her true feelings, she grabbed his zipper tab in her teeth and pulled it down nice and slow.

A shudder rumbled through him. "Shit, Lexy, you're killing me."

"Wait until I get you out of these jeans."

To ease his trembling, she tucked one hand inside the opening of his jeans and cupped him over his briefs. At her touch, he stiffened and the flex to his hips became more pronounced.

"Damn, baby. It's been so long." The roughness of his voice sounded as if he forced the word out through a wall of pain.

"I know."

"I missed you."

I wanted to shrivel and blow away without you. She stopped the words before they left her mouth.

Pretty words were not the answer. Feeling. She needed to feel.

With her fingers surrounding him, she pressed, squeezing him until a grunt of air left his chest. "Yes . . ."

"Do you like this?" Her fingertips slid past the waistband and inside his briefs until she felt his smooth, hot skin against her palm. Stroking and caressing, she swept her hand up and down the length of him.

"*Yes.* Everything about you." The words punched out of him.

With increasing speed, she pumped her hand, bringing him fully erect. Waves of heat rolled off him, filling her with a quiet female satisfaction.

All that control and power at her mercy. She could grant him release or push him on. She decided. She was in charge of when and how he found his satisfaction.

It was not enough.

She wanted him on the edge and sweating. His nerve endings begging for to finish the job.

"How does that feel?" She whispered the question against his bare thigh.

"Your mouth."

She pressed a kiss against his leg, let her hair fall over his lower body until it covered her hand and brushed his erection.

"Tell me, Noah."

"Use. Your. Mouth."

"Where?"

His body shifted, his legs jumping as if his mind no longer controlled the muscles. "On me."

"You want a kiss?" As her hand continued to work up and down, her lips traced an outline on his inner thighs.

His upper body slid closer to the mattress as his arm muscles gave out. "Damn, baby."

She smiled at his loss of breath. The man was driven to the cliff and hanging on by his fingertips. Exactly as she wanted him to be.

Just as his hips began to pulse, she lifted her head and her hand. "I want to—"

"God . . . don't stop." The pleading in his voice matched the need mirrored in his eyes.

"I want you naked."

"Hell, yes." His body jackknifed as he reached down and tried to strip his clothes the rest of the way off.

She shoved his hands away to stop him. "Let me."

"Damn it, hon. I'm fading here." His fingers clenched against the top of his jeans where they bagged on his lower thighs.

She tried to tug them out of his death grip. "My way."

"Faster."

"So impatient."

"It's been a month, Lexy. I've wanted you and fantasized and . . ." His chest rose and fell with enough force to shake the bed.

"What?"

"Just hurry." He slid the rest of the way down until his back hit the bed again. He propped his head on the pillow to watch her.

"I love the feel of you," she said as she peeled his jeans and underwear off and threw them on the floor. "The pure, natural taste of you is indescribable."

His moan echoed through the room.

The desperate, aching sound won her over. She turned his body over to her hands without hesitation. Unable to wait a second longer, she fit her lips over his head and pulled him deep inside her wet mouth. Plunging down, then pulling back up, each stroke going deeper, she sucked and licked until a ragged sigh escaped his lips and his head fell back into the pillow.

With her mouth over him, her hands roamed over his bare stomach, tracing the subtle indent, then the firmness of his chest. The assault of her hands and mouth set his body shaking.

"I can't hold off." The words choked out of him as his shoulders lifted off the bed.

With one hand, she pushed him back into the mattress. Her hands and mouth never stopped enticing him. Loving him.

"Lexy, I can't—"

She wanted to tell him to let go. To lay back, feel, and react. But she did not want to break contact or give him any chance to take over. This moment was for him. For them.

Her rhythm increased. Harder, firmer, her mouth caressed him. Her fingernails trailed down his chest. Rather than push her away, his hands slid through her hair to hold her head in place. The thrusts of his hips sent him deeper inside her mouth. The sweep of her tongue over his wet tip broke him.

He bucked and tightened his hold on her hair. With a final shout of satisfaction, he emptied into her mouth. The pumps hit against the back of her throat as his body stiffened to the point of breaking.

His lower body continued to thrust long after he came, finally going lax as his hands fell against the bed. His chest rumbled from his harsh breathing and his body glistened with sweat. Through the waves of his climax, she laid her check against his thigh and caressed his testicles.

The smell of sex filled the room. She waited until silence descended before breaking the mood. "I told you I had a plan."

His hand brushed through her hair. "It was a damn fine plan."

"Anything to break the tension."

"Or to evade the issue on the table."

Her shoulders tensed before she could stop the reaction. "I don't know—"

"Honey, I may be slow, but I'm not stupid."

"I never said you were—"

"Not that I'm complaining, 'cause I'm not. Believe me."

She gazed up at him. Saw a look of supreme satisfaction flirting around his mouth, the lazy amusement in those deep brown eyes, even felt the residual energy pinging around the room.

The man bounced back fast.

"You're not going to ruin good sex by annoying me, are you?" she asked.

"It was *great*, and no." He folded his arms behind his head and propped his neck up even higher. "But we are at a point where we have two options."

"You might want to keep in mind where I'm sitting and how easy it would be to castrate you."

He glanced down. "I am fully aware."

Full, all right, and with the stamina of a college boy. His skills were endless. "Are you suggesting we go a second round?"

"Believe it or not, I'd prefer that to talking about Henderson."

Knocking Noah stupid with sex did not seem to work. But she was not ready to talk. Not done feeling. "Me, too."

Chapter Ten

Noah's grin bloomed into a full smile. "That saves me the trouble."

"Of begging?"

"Having to say Henderson over and over until you break down and throw yourself at me."

"Uh, yuck. The man is dead, after all."

"It's amazing what a woman will do to evade a conversation she doesn't want to have, isn't it?"

This time Lexy smiled. Little did Noah know the flood of happiness inside her came from him, not from avoiding a tough discussion. She could not stop the giddy feeling.

"That's your theory?" she asked.

"Consider it a proven fact at this point."

"Say it once and we'll see."

One of Noah's eyebrows shot up. "Really?"

"Test your theory and see if you get me to jump."

"A challenge."

"Up for it?"

He glanced at his lower half. "Henderson."

She crawled up the bed, up Noah's body, until she straddled his trim hips. If Noah thought this was a game or just some physical reaction on her part—good. He did not need to know her heart was as invested as her sensitive skin.

"It feels naughty to use a dead guy as an aphrodisiac," she said.

"Don't say it that way."

"Isn't that what we're doing?" She sort of needed Noah to say no to that one or the mood was sure to wither.

"I don't need anything but you." Noah's body picked that moment to stage a live demonstration. "No photos, movies, diagrams, or names."

"Let's see just how hard you can get." With her breasts pressed against his chest, she leaned down and kissed him.

And wondered what took her so long to get back into this position. It felt right. *He* felt right.

Their lips fused together as if their bodies had never been apart. Wet, warm, and so inviting, his mouth moved over hers in a kiss so deep it pulsed through her nervous system.

When she broke away, he wrapped his arms around her waist and held her close. "Not yet."

A second kiss followed the first. This one more desperate, harder, needier than the last. All the longing and frustration broke open and spilled through her—through him—as if her mind and heart had been waiting for this moment to burst to life again.

"Take your dress off." He whispered the order against her lips.

If she was going to cede control, she wanted to do it this way. Naked, in bed, having sex with Noah.

She sat up, deliberately pushing her lower body against his erection. "You sure?"

"Keep that up and I'll rip that thing off you," he growled out.

"I like this dress." She reached behind to the tie around her neck.

"I'd like it better off."

While she struggled with the knot, he tunneled his hands up her skirt to lay against her bare thighs. "What the hell?"

"Something you weren't expecting?"

He bunched the skirt in his fist and held it up near her waist to peek underneath. The move exposed her naked legs and most every other part of her lower body. "You're not wearing underwear."

"Sure I am. It's just small." She tried to kiss his chin, but he was too busy looking at the area between her legs.

"I don't see . . . ah, there it is." With his lips buried in her throat, his fingers slid up until they reached the tiny triangle of black lace that lay over the very heat of her.

"Told you." The dress ties loosened and fell down and across his shoulders.

"I want to see."

"My underwear?"

"Everything."

She felt a tug, heard the screech of her zipper, before the front half of her dress eased away from her body. Cool air blew across her, causing her bare skin to pucker.

"Like that sexy little tattoo." He peeled down the front of her dress and lifted her breasts out of the built-in bra.

"My underwear doesn't cover it."

"It's been a long time."

"Not *that* long."

"Speak for yourself."

His tongue swirled around her nipple, wetting and arousing until shivers convulsed her shoulders. While his mouth caressed her skin, his hands finished off the zipper and pushed the dress down to her waist.

She shifted her hips until the scrap of underwear rubbed against his cock. "I bet we could make love without taking off another piece of clothing."

"Have before."

Memories hit her from every direction. Making love in cars, on tables, in a restaurant bathroom, and in the conference room at work. She always had a healthy attitude about the more fundamental part of the relationship. With Noah she could experiment at will. He never balked. Never said no. Never judged or made her feel dirty.

"I want to see you," he said in a rough, sexy voice.

"You first."

He lifted his polo up and off. "Now your turn. I want all of you."

A thought floated through her mind. The one issue that could put a quick and not-so-satisfying ending to the evening. "I don't have anything."

He was too busy nibbling on her breasts, weighing them in his hands, to look up. "Uh-huh."

"Protection. Condoms." She tugged on a piece of his hair until he turned his face to hers.

"What?"

"I'm not taking anything. We can't—"

"Bathroom." He plunged his hands down the back of her open dress and over the skin exposed by her thong. "In my Dopp kit on the sink."

"Come prepared, did you?"

"Two months, Lexy." He held up fingers to emphasize his point. "A man will grab on to any possibility after two months of depending on his own hand for a little relief."

She cupped his face in her hands and treated him to another kiss. This one, in part, a thank-you for the resourceful side of him.

"You poor thing," she said with as much fake concern as she could muster over the thrill zinging around inside her.

He lifted her off him and patted her butt. "Get the condoms and take that dress off."

"Wow. One blow job and you get demanding."

"Or we could talk about why you're in Utah . . ." He let his voice trail off before he winked at her.

"You play dirty."

"Baby, I will do anything, say anything, to get inside you and be with you again."

That was all it took. A few words and her body grew all dewy and ready. Seeing his tan body sprawled on white sheets, naked with a full erection, only made her more wet and more willing.

To torture him, she shimmied out of her dress, shaking her hips from side to side as she slid the blue silk down to puddle on the floor. All that remained was a swath of see-through black lace and the tiny palm-tree tattoo right above the junction of her pelvis and thigh.

Noah did not hide his appreciation as his gaze wandered down her body and settled on her lower half. "Take it all off, Lexy."

She grabbed the condom box so fast she knocked the rest of his toiletries kit onto the floor. His toothpaste landed in the toilet.

"What was that splash?" he asked.

She dumped a packet on his stomach. "Did you really want me to take the time to find out?"

"I'll buy a new whatever it is."

She hooked her thumbs through the thin string of her underwear and pulled them off. The temptation to hide that had hit with her other men passed right on by when she was with Noah. When she straightened up, she stood open and ready.

This was Noah. He knew her, had cherished her body so many times that he knew it as well as she did.

"You are so damned beautiful." A mix of awe and lust thickened his voice.

He never failed to make her feel desired. And when his

body responded, when his attention focused solely on her, she wanted to believe in him. To give him time to open up and trust her. But this moment was not about forever. This was about sex and a release of tension.

She threw one leg over him, bringing her sex in direct contact with his. "Is this what you wanted?"

"It's a start." He traced his fingertip over her tattoo with a reverence that made her breath catch.

When his palm traveled to her center, then down and just inside her, smiling was the last thing on her mind. Tiny fire-bursts exploded behind her eyes as her head fell back and his finger circled her most sensitive area.

Mouth on her breasts. Hands between her legs. The combination sent her skin raging into a wild frenzy. It was as if every inch of her body came alive under his touching.

Two fingers dipped deeper inside her, stretching her, sending a gush of wetness over his hand. "Noah . . ."

"Tell me you want me."

Now was not the time for game playing, so she gave him the truth. "I want all of you."

"Ride me."

Exactly the position she had been thinking about ever since he sat down next to her and started babbling about her being missing. Her favorite position. Eye to eye, able to watch the punch of desire hit him. See his shoulders tense from the force of holding back the orgasm that threatened to rip through his body.

"Now, baby."

She could not agree more. "Now."

The urge rode her as hard as it did him. Rather than engage in flirty banter or seduce, she followed his command. Her hips lifted. His hands and gravity did the rest. Full to the point of bursting, she sank down. Hard. He expanded inside her, growing to the sharp edge of pain. To the point where every sensitized nerve ending screamed in awareness.

"Ride." His teeth scraped across her collarbone, making her jump, then sink down on him even deeper.

Part of her wanted to stay there with him buried inside. Not moving and no questions. No problems. Just the slap of desire combined with the drive to fulfill every fantasy.

But her body refused to wait. Without a message from her brain, her hips moved. She slid and retreated, pushed and pulled through the sucking pressure, until her body bucked on top of his.

His hands locked against the tops of her thighs. His tongue tickled her breasts. Every sensation and touch tingled until the clamping sensation made her gasp with pleasure.

She rode faster, clenching her thighs against his hips with all her strength. Anything to ease the spiraling pressure, to make her body explode into a thousand tiny pieces. As if sensing her need to break free, Noah rubbed his forefinger along her clitoris. Circled and pushed down against the slick nub. With his touch, the tightness holding her lower body hostage sprang free. She shuddered from shoulder to knee as a scream of satisfaction tore through the room.

She grabbed the headboard as she fell forward. It was either that or land against him with a hard smack. The position pushed him even deeper. His whole body shook from the force of the plunge, as the orgasm sped through him.

A shout still echoed in her ears moments later as she roused her satisfied body enough to slip off him and lay across his chest.

With her ear pressed against him, heavy breaths bounced around his lungs and vibrated against her ear. She fell asleep wondering how she would ever go another two hours, let alone two months, without him.

Chapter Eleven

Hours later Noah rolled over to check the time. After five and still dark. The world outside their door remained quiet except for the rustling of shrubs from the night breeze.

"Makeup sex is amazing," he said to the quiet room.

Lexy stiffened in his arms at the comment just as Noah mentally predicted she would. After three rounds of swallow-your-tongue fantastic sex started off by one of the best blow jobs in the history of oral sex, Lexy held on to this bizarre idea that their relationship ceased to exist.

"Problem?" he asked as if he didn't know.

"We are not back together."

He slid his hand down and pinched her bottom. "Feels like it."

She got her revenge by digging her nails into his chest.

"Ow!"

"That was just sex."

"You sound like a . . ."

"Man?"

"Maybe we do better when we don't talk."

"The sex was about burning off extra adrenaline," she insisted.

"Which time?"

When her hand hovered in chest-hair-attack mode, he

covered it with his. Best to keep her palm flattened against his chest and out of jabbing range.

"Everything caught up with me. Being scared and surprised. The detective's accusations." Lexy's voice picked up speed with each phrase. "That's it."

"Even when you were going down on me?"

"Do you have to be so crude?"

She seduced him and insisted he was the one out of control with lust. Uh-huh. Talk about denial. "What should I call it?"

"It's ... you could say ..." She sighed. "Okay, going down is fine."

"You sure? I have some other naughty terms we could use."

"Are you twelve?"

"Let's just say it had been awhile."

Too damn long. So long that he got light-headed when she had hit her knees in front of him. When his zipper came down, he had to grab on to the mattress to keep from throwing her on the bed and stripping her naked. And was he happy he did. Being on the receiving end of all that pent-up sexual need was a damn fine thing.

"You can stop acting like a boy who's just touched his first breast now," she said.

"You brought it up."

"And I am infinitely sorry for that." She laid her head back down on his chest. The move sent her silky hair falling over his bare skin.

"My original point was—"

"You had one?"

He tapped his fingers against her head and talked louder. "My point was that what I just experienced was not the lovemaking of a woman who just needed to get some."

"Sex." She batted his hand away from her hair. "And, stop doing that."

"Use whatever word you want, but I'm not wrong."

"It's about what you said earlier. About the time that's gone by. It had been awhile for both of us."

Thinking about her having sex made him think about William. And that made him furious. Noah forced his body to relax. "You better mean it had been awhile since the last day we made love which, unless my memory is fading, and it isn't, was the same day you gave the ring back and stormed out of my office."

"I walked."

"You mentioned something about Karen and staged a dramatic exit."

"I left the room."

"The office talked about it, and our screwed-up sex life, for weeks."

"Do you really want to have a discussion about your wife now?"

"Ex and never." He swallowed what little bit of his pride was left and asked the question that played in his head without end. "Speaking of other partners, how is William going to handle us getting back together?"

"We're not."

Focusing on the ceiling kept Noah from yelling. "You know what I'm asking."

She sighed long enough and loud enough to make him think she was going to evade the question. Again.

"I can spell it out if you want me to," he added.

"We work together," she said in a terse, clipped voice.

"You and William?"

"Yes."

"At your marketing firm?"

"You're even slower after sex."

"Hell, a few more times and I'll talk backwards."

The rich, warm sound of her laughter filled the early morning. "The things you say."

"Don't evade the topic."

"Noah, you've got it all wrong about William and my feelings for him. There's nothing romantic going on. I hired him to come aboard and take over some extra work for me."

"So you're not—"

"Extras like Stuart Enterprises."

Noah sat up and took her with him. "You handle the company's work."

"For now."

She wasn't just running away. She was getting lost from him forever. "No fucking way."

"That's why he was meeting with Gray. Someone needs to handle the marketing and PR for the expansion."

With his hands on her shoulders, Noah set her a few inches away from him. "Why didn't Gray tell me that?"

The sheet she held up to her breasts kept slipping. Most of it was tucked under him, and he had no intention of moving so she would have more for a cover-up.

"You can ask my brother that the next time you see him."

Damn right he would. "I'm in charge of the expansion."

"The business end. This is the other end."

The end he planned to share with Lexy. Which meant she was removing herself from everywhere he would be. Whatever was going on in her head had to do with more than an ex-wife and a few secrets.

"Why the hell are you turning family business over to a complete stranger?"

"My marketing firm has taken off. I have more business than I can handle."

Since she did not give him eye contact, he assumed she was only telling half of the story. The less annoying half. "But that's not the only reason. Me. I'm the problem with you continuing to work at the company."

She exhaled for what felt like forever. "Yes."

"For God sake's, Lexy. Why?"

"It's time to move on."

The woman would be the death of him. It was only a question of which would give out first, his mind or his body. "All of this is because I didn't explain that I was married ten years ago to a woman who ceased to matter long before you and I even met?"

She plucked at the sheet. "That's only a little piece."

Her continued refusal to look at him ratcheted his anger up a notch. He lifted her chin so he could see those big green eyes. "I didn't get it then. I don't get it now, Lexy."

"I know."

That was it. No further explanation. He kept trying and she kept cutting him off.

"What about us? We're good together."

"It's just sex."

She kept pushing and pushing. "Stop saying that."

"Fine, but the point is the same."

"Funny but what happened in this bed felt like more than just two people getting hot and sweaty." It sure as hell meant more to him.

"To you."

Her swings kept getting lower. "Then I guess you were just keeping me quiet."

That stubborn chin of hers inched up. "I don't know what you mean."

"So it's just a coincidence that when I brought up Henderson's name—a subject you wanted to avoid—you stuck your tongue in my mouth."

"There's no need to be vulgar."

"That's who I am. That's part of the past you're so damned determined to drag out and discuss."

She slapped her hand against the sheets. "Would it kill you to open up to me?"

"I could ask the same of you."

Her shoulders tensed. "I have no idea what you're talking about. As usual."

"Think back to last night. I walked into your room and found a dead guy in a puddle of blood on the floor. Turns out, you know this dead guy and had a tense chat with him just a few hours earlier. You even lie to the police about him."

"I didn't lie."

"You didn't tell the truth. You know Henderson as more than some guy you saw walking around the resort grounds." Noah leaned against the headboard. "Admit it, babe. You're hiding a few secrets of your own."

"You're badgering me."

"I'm trying to prove to you how you have one set of rules for me and another for yourself."

Nervous energy radiated from her. Hands in motion. Muttering. Every sign of her anxiety rose to the surface except for the one where she lost control and threw her clothes and belongings all over the room.

He reached out and folded her hand in his. "Just tell me what I need to know about Henderson. What I should know to keep you safe."

"I don't need—"

"Hell, even if you killed him, just tell me why so I can figure out how to get you out of it."

Surprise registered in her wary eyes. "You would accept it if I murdered someone?"

"I figure if you killed someone, they needed killing."

The logic made sense to him. You killed to protect and when ordered to do so. He learned that lesson a long time ago sitting in the muggy heat at Fort Benning, Georgia, while attending the Army Sniper School. He put those skills into action all over the world killing on command for his government.

"Have you ever killed anyone?" she asked in a voice so soft he almost did not hear her.

"Yes."

Lexy did not need to know the particulars. He made a promise to keep the filth of his past away from her. Despite her family's wealth, her life had not been easy. She lived with parents whose eccentric ways brought them in contact with the police and numerous mental health professionals on a regular basis.

She was the strong one in the family. The normal one. The one, along with Gray, who kept the public image of the Stuart family as clean as possible.

Noah wanted her to find the peace she craved. To not have to be in control all the time. He could not give her normal. He had no idea what that even was anymore, but he could give her stability. He just could not get her to take the offer to take him.

"Have you killed more than one person?" She squeezed his hand as she asked the question.

"Yes."

"Did those people need killing?"

Those clear eyes of hers held no judgment. Intelligence lingered there. Some residual desire. No disgust, even though Noah knew he deserved it.

"I believed so at the time, which is why they're dead."

He noticed the slight narrowing of her eyes.

"What do you think now?" she asked.

"I don't know."

The answer was as truthful as he could be. His world centered on a few simple principles. Things were right or wrong. This idea that life consisted only of shades of gray amounted to nothing more than a sad excuse, as far as he was concerned.

But killing on command long ago ceased to make sense to

him. He traded his fatigues for suits, traveling around the world for commuting to work, shooting for investigating. All of those changes made sense when Lexy stood by his side. Without her, everything shifted and the world he carefully crafted turned to ash.

"I take it this all happened while you were in the military," she said.

The way she phrased the comment put him in the position of having to lie to her. Rather than break that internal promise, he answered the question he needed her to ask.

"While I worked for the government, yes."

She stayed quiet for a few seconds. She stopped the fidgeting, but her concentrated stare did not let up.

Just when he thought he would have to do something drastic to break the silence, she talked. "Did you recognize Henderson?"

"From this afternoon?"

"From our office."

"You lost me."

She stared so long that he thought she was going to stop talking. Then she piped up again. "Henderson learned security from us."

The words did not make sense to Noah. Separately, yes. Together, no. "What?"

"Ron Dexter trained him in technology and computer investigations. Henderson attended our conferences and classes. He was in our offices. Any of this sound familiar?"

Along with Gray, Noah considered Dex his closest friend. They worked side by side developing programs and plans at work. Dex handled technology. Noah handled the hand combat stuff. Gray ran the business part. They made the perfect trio.

"Not even a little bit."

"Tell me the truth, Noah." She grabbed his arm with an

intensity that struck close to pleading. "You can evade and ignore the rest, but don't lie about this."

What the hell was going on? "I never met or even laid eyes on the guy before I saw him with you this afternoon. The only other time I saw him was facedown on your bedroom floor."

"Noah . . ." Her gaze searched his face.

"I promise."

Her grip on his arm lessened as the tension on her face eased. Finally, she nodded.

"What does any of that have to do with you being in Utah?" Noah asked.

Her gaze slid to the window. The sun would not come up for about an hour, but she appeared fascinated by the darkness.

"Lexy?"

"I recognized Henderson. I knew he had trained with Stuart Enterprises."

"And?"

"Nothing. That's it."

Another half-truth. "Lexy."

She pulled away from him. "You don't believe me."

"Picked up on that, did you?"

Her mouth dropped open in an almost comical look of exaggerated indignation. "Well, I . . ."

"Yeah?"

He waited for her to come up with something. A lie, an odd excuse. Anything.

"I refuse to dignify that comment with a response."

"Come on, Lexy. Dignify it."

She chose to punt instead.

"I'm going to shower." She started to get up.

The tackle stopped her. He caught her in mid-escape and threw her back on the bed. Under him with her hands pinned near her head, steam from her fury rose up to greet him.

"What do you think you're doing?" She shouted the question at him.

If talking did not work, he would try the one thing that always did. "We're going back to the plan you put into motion last night."

"Is this the plan where you're an overbearing jackass?"

"While that's fun for me, I was thinking more along the lines of the one where I make love to you."

"You think I'm going to—"

"Yeah. Many times."

She rolled her eyes, but her skin warmed beneath him at the suggestion. "Your ego is outrageous."

"It's either sex or stay in this position until you spill the rest of what you have on Henderson."

She flexed her hands under his. "You've lost your mind."

"Your choice, babe. But I'm thinking I can last longer than you can." Now there was a damn lie. If he grew any harder, his lower half might explode. "You know what you need to do."

"Call Detective Sommerville and have her lock you up?"

"What's the password?"

"I am not playing this game." Lexy turned her head to the side and stared at the curtains at the back door.

All an act. He could feel the excitement churn inside her. The pink flush to her skin gave her away.

He nipped at her exposed breast. "Say the word and we'll get back to business."

"You mean sex."

"Oh, I definitely mean sex." He caught her lips in a long, drawn-out sexy kiss.

"Well?"

She sighed. "You win."

"We both do."

Chapter Twelve

Noah dragged Lexy out of bed and down to the police station before eight the next morning as promised. Since Lexy could not go into her room to retrieve her clothes, she wore sweats, sneakers, and a T-shirt Noah grabbed from the spa's gift store after forcing Tate to open the place.

Noah knew her sizes. She was not surprised, since Noah seemed to know everything.

"For a small woman, Detective Sommerville sure does put away a lot of coffee," Lexy said in a whisper when the detective left the stale-smelling interrogation room for the second time in forty minutes.

He leaned on the back two legs of his chair. "She's not getting coffee."

"Then what is she doing?"

"Watching us from behind that shaded glass." Noah nodded in the general direction of the long wall across from him and to her left.

Lexy stopped fooling with the string holding up the waistband of her pants and followed his gaze. "Really?"

"Don't you ever watch television?" he asked.

"Sure. But rooms like this are for when the police are shaking down perps."

He lowered his chair back to the floor. "Let's agree that you'll never use that phrase again."

"You know what I mean."

"I'm still waiting for you to agree."

"I'm serious."

"So am I," he mumbled under his breath. "Look, in case you haven't noticed, you are the suspect in this scenario."

She squinted trying to see who was hovering on the other side of the dark glass before turning her attention back to Noah. "Me?"

"Why exactly do you think we're here?"

"Because we found a dead guy on the floor." She wanted to add "duh?" but refrained, since it sounded juvenile.

"A dead guy you just happen to know. You keep forgetting that condemning little fact."

Lexy lowered her voice just in case Detective Sommerville or any other detective was watching and listening. "I told you I saw Henderson at the spa."

"You can stop pretending now. Detective Sommerville isn't buying it. No one with a pulse would."

"You were much more pleasant before we . . ." She waved her hand in the air. "You know."

A smile inched across his lips. "I love when you do that."

"What?"

"Go from a wildcat in the bedroom to Little Miss Priss outside of it. Hell, you climbed all over—"

"I am not a priss." She used her least prissy voice to make her point.

"Whatever you say, Alexa Annabeth."

She refused to concede on this issue. She was not a prude or anything even close. She ran her own business, battled Noah on even turf without backing down, and enjoyed mountain biking and hiking. Right now she was running a covert investigation.

Sure, years before, her mother had sent her to ballet classes and etiquette classes and every other class regularly attended by wealthy little girls. Lexy had stomached her parents' country-club life until she turned thirteen and rebelled. Since her parents never bought into the trappings of their wealthy lifestyle, the rebellion fizzled. In its place formed a tacit family agreement to refrain from engaging in the outspend-the-neighbors philosophy that ran rampant on their street.

Then there was the part that had nothing to do with her upbringing. It dealt with the here and now. Chatting about her personal life while half the police officers of southern Utah listened in did not qualify as her idea of fun. Some private conversations were better suited to the bedroom. This counted as one of them.

The door opened again and Detective Sommerville walked in. From the stupid grin she was trying hard to swallow, Lexy figured she picked up on Noah's sex comments.

"Can we leave now?" Noah asked as he tipped his chair back again.

Detective Sommerville stopped smiling. "Not until the two of you start telling the truth."

"Think of how much less fun that would be for us."

"Noah." Lexy thought about kicking him as part of her warning, but feared she would knock his chair over. And they needed to be upright and on their game to deal with this detective.

"Listen to your girlfriend, Mr. Paxton."

"Fiancée."

Lexy decided she strayed enough the night before and tried to restake old ground. "He means ex-fiancée."

"No, I don't."

The detective sat down with two thick file folders stacked in front of her. "I've taken the opportunity to check into both of your backgrounds."

The detective opened the top folder and scanned whatever was in there. Even if Lexy could read upside down, which was not one of her skills, it would not have helped. The detective held up the tip of the folder so the contents stayed just out of view.

"All of that is about us?" Lexy asked.

"Of course."

Noah's eyebrow rose. "You've been busy. Must have been a slow night shift."

"Except for the murder, you mean."

Noah gave the detective a look of reluctant admiration. "Well, yeah."

Right or wrong, Lexy had enough of the death talk. "How is it possible you collected all of those documents in just a few hours when all you know is our names?"

Lexy suddenly regretted providing even that much information when she checked in at the resort. She had toyed with the idea of using an alias, but Tate seemed harmless and the idea struck her as a bit too television-drama for her taste.

Now she wondered about that decision. Next time she went on a mission to track down the truth about Noah's ass—something she vowed would never happen again—she'd pay in cash and use the name Natasha.

"Mr. Carr was kind enough to fill in some of the personal information we needed on both of you," the detective said.

"Hate that guy." The front legs of Noah's chair hit the cement floor with a crack.

"What did he give you?" The idea that Tate knew her personal business made Lexy want to take a long, cleansing shower. Then strangle the guy.

"Information and plenty of it," said the petite woman with the big gun strapped to her side.

Lexy refused to be intimidated. "Meaning?"

"Tate gave you our addresses, credit card numbers, and that sort of thing?" Noah waited until the detective nodded in agreement to glare at Lexy. "I told you Tate was a leaf-eating jackass."

A mix of shock and disgust slammed through her. "That information is private."

"Not to Utah's finest," Noah grumbled.

The detective scanned the pages and pages of notes in front of her. "Correct."

"Why do I feel the need to contact a lawyer?" A kick of satisfaction went through Lexy when she saw the other woman frown. "Or maybe my Congressman?"

The detective turned her attention to Noah. "Mr. Paxton, I see you're in the security business."

"Yes."

"You're familiar with guns and weapons."

"Since Henderson was killed with a lamp, I'm not sure why that's relevant to anything."

"It's a simple calculation. A man is dead and you know how to kill."

"Not with a lightbulb."

Deep down, Lexy knew Noah had seen the worst of the world. The only information he had provided about his military career was a brief description of Sniper School. Between the gun expertise and his comments about killing, she had an idea of his life before her.

It was whatever was happening in his head right now that was her bigger concern. In some respects, she saw him as a scam artist. Finding out about his ex-wife and his possible involvement in a felony in the same week drove that point home.

Then there was this other side of him. The loving side. The part of him that accepted her parents and brought her a comfort and happiness she had never known. She wanted to believe—no, *needed* to believe—all of that was real.

But now was not the time. Not with Detective Sommerville listening in and looking to close a case fast.

"How about I give you a scenario to consider? I'll tell you what I think and you tell me how close I am." Pages crumpled in the detective's fist as she spoke.

"Guess this means we can't leave yet," Noah said to Lexy.

The other woman cleared her throat and started spelling out her theory. "Your girlfriend—"

Noah slapped his hand against the desk with a smack. "Why does everyone in Utah have trouble with the word fiancée?"

Lexy snorted. "Yeah, I wonder."

"As I was saying." The detective talked louder, enunciating her words until they bounced off the cement walls. "You find out your girlfriend, fiancée, or whatever you want to call Ms. Stuart, is at a secluded spa with another man."

Lexy had no choice but to interfere. "Wait a second."

"You come here to drag her back home—"

"That doesn't sound like me," Noah said.

Lexy thought about rolling her eyes, but refrained since no one was looking at her anyway. "Oh, right. Sounds exactly like you."

The detective treated them both to a quick frown, but kept right on talking. "You find them together, decide Ms. Stuart has been cheating, or at least engaging in a serious flirtation, and you get furious."

Lexy was tired of being the loose woman in this scenario. "Did you miss the part where I said wait a second?"

"You have every reason to be angry with Ms. Stuart for betraying you. And, understandably, you're jealous of Tate Carr."

"Have you spent any time with Tate?" Noah asked.

The detective's jaw clenched hard enough to make her voice tight. "You're furious with Ms. Stuart for her behavior, but you're even angrier at this Henderson guy for daring to touch what's yours."

"Do I look angry to you, detective?" Noah asked in a voice as disinterested as his relaxed sprawl in his chair.

But the detective would not be deterred. "Maybe a fight starts. Something you'd expect from your background and the circumstances."

"What the hell is that supposed to mean?" Lexy asked, wondering if the detective managed to find out something worth knowing about Noah.

The detective ignored the tension moving around her. "But then everything gets out of control."

Noah tapped his keys against the table. "Kind of like this theory of yours?"

"You lose it and hit Mr. Henderson harder than you mean to. Maybe he comes at you so you don't have a choice but to fight back." The detective's small smile never reached her eyes. "It's an accident or self-defense. Either way, it's understandable and we can work with it."

"It's ridiculous." Lexy did not know everything about Noah, but she knew he did not kill a man and then go out for a light dinner and some dancing.

Noah compartmentalized his life, shutting off the terrible parts, but he was not cold and unfeeling. She just refused to believe that. Scammer or not, there was something under all that muscle.

And then there was the part where she was with him almost every second from the time she left her room the evening before. The only thing on her floor at that point was a carpet and a bunch of clothes.

"Is this something you're reading from a bad novel?" Noah leaned over as if trying to take a peek at the detective's notes.

The detective proved faster. She rolled the pages into her palm to hide whatever hid there. "If you tell me about the fight, about what really happened in Ms. Stuart's room last night, I can do something."

"Like what?" Noah asked.

As far as Lexy was concerned, now was not the time for Noah's odd sense of humor. "Don't encourage her."

"I might be able to help you, Mr. Paxton. But I can't do that if you don't level with me."

"That's nice of you."

"After all, no one could blame you for protecting your fiancée."

Noah shot Lexy a huge smile. "Notice how she used fiancée that time."

"Because she's trying to trick you." Either way, Lexy thought the semantics battle was misplaced at that moment. "And we are not arguing about our relationship status now."

He shrugged. "Seems like as good a time as any to me."

"Self-defense. Defense of Ms. Stuart here. Tell me the scenario. We'll see if we can make it work with the forensics." The detective clenched the papers even tighter as she butted back into the conversation.

"You want me to lie?" Noah asked.

"I want to understand what really happened. Why we found a man on Ms. Stuart's floor. Believe it or not, Mr. Paxton, I'm here to help."

Lexy knew a line of crap when she heard one. "You can't possibly think Noah did something to Henderson."

For the first time during the conversation, the detective looked directly at Lexy. Almost through her. "Give me another theory to explore. For instance, we could talk about the papers found in your room, Ms. Stuart. Would you like to hear my theory about those?"

Lexy had feared this moment would come. Despite her protests, Noah had not let her grab any personal items before the police arrived last night. She was not in the state of mind to plan ahead and sneak items out. Now she had an even bigger mess to hide.

"My papers are confidential."

"Some. Others struck me as more personal than work-related. And some of them are missing." Detective Sommerville glanced over at Noah. "Anything you want to say about that, Mr. Paxton?"

Noah did not even flinch. "No."

"You're blaming Noah for the fact your people lost my papers?" Lexy asked.

"We have photographs of the scene. You can see certain items in some shots and not in others."

"There were a lot of people in and out of the room last night," Noah said.

"But, interestingly enough, the documents in question disappeared right after you were allowed to go into the room and get a sweater for Ms. Stuart."

"Coincidence," Noah said in a clipped tone.

Lexy peeked over at Noah. If papers were taken from her room, that was news to her. And if Noah had them, he wasn't talking.

The mess just got messier.

"I'm still digging, but I warn you both that I'll figure out all of the connections. I'll get to the bottom of this situation." The detective's soft, even tone proved far more threatening than the yelling she'd engaged in the evening before.

"Maybe you should check into Henderson's past instead of mine," Lexy suggested.

"I plan to do both."

Now there was a case of "be careful what you wish for." Having the detective dig around at all spelled trouble. Lexy wanted to be the only person in the room poking around into Henderson's past.

"Are we done now?" Noah asked as he tapped out a familiar rhythm on the desk with a tip of his keys.

"Do you have somewhere better to be, Mr. Paxton?"

"As a matter of fact, yes."

"You are not permitted to leave the state," the detective snapped out.

Noah's keys kept clicking out that song playing in his head. "No plans to do that."

"Good."

"Yet."

"Suddenly you want to hang out here?" Lexy asked.

"Definitely not." Noah tossed the keys and caught them. "The real issue is that we need to head back to the spa to meet a guest."

The odd news kept on coming. "We do?"

"Yeah."

From his dismissive tone, Lexy knew Noah wanted her to drop the questions. But since when did she jump whenever he told her to jump? "Who's the guest?"

Noah shot her a frown. "Your brother."

"Gray is in town?"

"Do you have more than one brother?"

Typical Noah. He wanted to change the subject and pulled out a huge load of sarcasm to accomplish just that. "You're going to be a smartass when we're this close to all of these weapons? That's ballsy."

Noah's eyebrow lifted. "On second thought."

Lexy realized Noah had knocked her off topic, but she got right back on track. The idea of Gray in Utah did not make a lick of sense. "Why is he coming here?"

The detective clicked the end of her pen and started scribbling. "What is this brother's full name?"

Lexy wondered if the detective planned to investigate every man in her life. "Do not write down one more thing."

Something worked, because the detective stopped writing. "Excuse me?"

"Gray wasn't even in Utah at the time of the murder. He is not involved in this. Dig somewhere else."

Detective Sommerville leaned back in her chair. "I have to ask you something, Ms. Stuart."

Lexy's defenses rose. "You mean ask me something else."

"Do all the men in your life come running when you're in trouble?"

Lexy wondered why she ever liked this woman. "I see you don't understand anything about the men in my life. If you did, you'd know I spend half my time getting them out of trouble."

Lexy stood up. It was well past time to go.

"You mean trouble like murder?" the detective asked.

"You walked into that one," Noah mumbled under his breath.

Stumbled into it was more like it. "Nothing so advanced as murder, I assure you."

Noah's chair screeched against the hard floor as he pushed away from the table. "What Lexy is trying to say is that she doesn't find the men in her life smart enough to pull off something so advanced. Hell, I can't seem to get an engagement to stick."

"But yet you can make important paperwork disappear," the detective said.

"You give me too much credit."

The detective looked from Lexy to Noah. "The one thing I don't do is underestimate either one of you."

"Can I at least have my files back?" Lexy asked.

"No." The detective smiled. " 'Fraid you'll have to do your investigating without it."

Noah smiled at Lexy. "You had to know she was going to say that."

"A woman can hope, can't she?"

Chapter Thirteen

Lexy barely waited until they got out of the interrogation room to start unloading. "Were you lying in there?"

Noah had a few questions of his own, but held off until they were across the eavesdropping officers in the squad room and out of Detective Sommerville's line of sight before answering. "Be more specific."

"Only you would think that is an appropriate answer to a straightforward question."

He slipped his hand around her elbow and steered her down the steps and out of the building. "You're asking about the papers? Yeah, I took some out of your room."

"Where are they?"

"In *our* room."

"Why?"

He noticed she did not bother to correct his assessment of their sleeping arrangements. He took that as progress. "When a person has that many file folders along on vacation, you figure there's something important going on that's unrelated to sunbathing or hiking."

"Not necessarily."

"And then there's the part where some of my office papers were missing and somehow turned up in your vacation stash." His eyebrow lifted. "Care to explain that?"

He hoped to hell she would explain it. Seeing the documents sitting there on her bed cut off his breath. After the ambulance had carted Henderson away, Noah returned to his room ready to confront her and demand answers. Then she touched him and his concentration blew all to hell.

"I must have picked them up by accident."

"Off my desk."

"Things happen." She shrugged as if to prove her point. "You could have warned me you took them."

He stopped about ten feet from his car's parking spot. "Hard to do that when you refuse to tell me what you're working on, what really happened between you and Henderson, and what you were hiding in all of those other documents you're carrying around."

"I see you've given this scenario some thought."

"You could say that."

Hell, this situation with Lexy was all he thought about. Her secrecy annoyed him, but the how-dare-she reaction had given way to a more reasoned view about a half hour ago. Lexy was investigating something. Something related to him. He did not know what or why or the Henderson connection.

For a woman who claimed to want complete honesty between them, who ended their relationship to prove just that point, she sure was engaging in a lot of covert behavior lately. He thought about pointing out the hypocrisy but knew from experience that ticking Lexy off would not get him anywhere. Feisty Lexy was one thing. Pissed-off Lexy was another.

He had to tread carefully and let her come around to filling him in on her own. He just wished she'd move a bit faster. A man could only be so patient.

"So, was I right? Do these documents that aren't mine point to anything the good detective will use against you?"

He asked because being prepared always made more sense than being caught off guard.

"You haven't looked at them?"

Truth was he wanted her to just tell him about whatever was happening. He was tired of guessing and trying to read her. Why couldn't women just say whatever they had to say without all the other crap?

"I can control my impulses." Barely.

Lexy looked amused at the idea. "Since when?"

"In case you didn't notice, I've been pretty busy during the last few hours, what with the dead guy on your floor."

"That kept you from reading through my documents?"

"I also made love to you and got accused of murder. It's been an unusual twenty-four hours even for me."

"No one pointed a finger at you."

He noticed she skipped right over the sex. "You're right. Detective Sommerville is more convinced you're involved than I am."

"I'm not."

"Me either."

"I know."

He let out a breath he had not even realized he was holding. "Well, that's something at least."

The tension pulling across her cheeks eased. "What information did she find out about you?"

"How should I know?" He aimed his key chain at his car and heard it unlock with a chirp.

"You're not worried?" Lexy reached for the door handle.

He slipped his palm over her hand before she could open the door. "About?"

"You were willing to throw away our relationship in order to keep your secrets. God only knows what else you're involved in.

"What does that mean?"

"Silly me, but I figured the information was worth hiding."

That was his Lexy. Never missed an opportunity to dig for answers. She just did not understand she kept planting the shovel in the wrong dirt.

"The detective found what anyone else who bothered to look would find." He fought to keep the edge out of his voice.

He knew someone had been looking into his past for months. The investigation triggered an internal alarm at the Defense Intelligence Agency and resulted in a bunch of calls and many warnings. All of the protocols stayed in place and only the nonclassified information showed up for anyone to find, but the higher-ups at DIA where Noah once worked were not happy. A second investigation by the Utah police was not going to play any better.

"What information would someone find on you?" Lexy asked.

She acted as if she did not know. "That I served in the Army. That I worked for the government for a short time once I left the service. That I have a mortgage, pay my bills, don't gamble or drink to excess, and hold down a job."

She slipped her hand out from under his. "The basics."

"The only truly pertinent information."

Her gaze did not leave the red taillights of a police car as it left the lot. "But there's more to your background."

"What makes you think so?"

"Educated guess." She shook her head as if clearing her thoughts and then reached for the door again.

He held the door shut with his palm. Touching her now was not the answer. "Hold up."

Her gaze went from his hand to his face. "You want to lose those fingers?"

"Since I plan to use them later on you, no."

"There's wishful thinking." Her voice said no, but that smile she tried to hide said yes.

"We're not arguing about sleeping arrangements now."

"What are we arguing about?"

He was done fighting. He wanted an answer or two. "What did you find when you checked up on me?"

The question had been bouncing around in his head for months. He tried to push it out, to make her investigation of his background not matter, to never voice it. But there it was. The thought struck him and out the words came.

"What?" she asked with genuine confusion in her voice.

"Your background check on me." He fought to keep any sign of emotion out of his voice.

"Noah, I—"

"You looked into my life. Dug around in my history. Tried to get those damn answers you insisted you needed in order for us to stay together and get married."

Her face blanched white as she stepped back from the car. "I didn't."

Her denials pricked at him. "Lexy, just tell me the truth. It's too important."

She shifted until his back pressed against the car and she stood in front of him. "Listen to me. I've watched what you're doing now at the company, but did not try to investigate your past."

"You did."

"I wanted *you* to open up to me."

Sure. He got that part. "And when I didn't?"

"I handed back the ring." She exhaled long enough and heavy enough to grab his attention. "I needed you to want to share your life with me, the good and the bad, without me begging or hunting for any tiny morsel you were willing to give."

The tremor in her voice vibrated through him. Up until

her recent behavior in hiding the details of her hiking trip, he never questioned her honesty. She spoke her mind even when her comments played to her detriment. She was not one to sneak around, which was what made their current circumstances so frustrating.

Who she was, how she led her life and never ducked hard work in favor of claiming entitlement, proved rock solid the entire time he had known her. This time was no different. It just took him a few minutes of silence to realize that fact. From her stick-straight back and unblinking stare, he knew she was telling the truth.

Some of the bonds between them strained to the point of breaking, but not this. He still knew *her*, the deep-down real her. The woman she was before she started running and investigating and lying to the police and him.

Like that, so simple and fast, the anger seeped out of his blood, leaving behind only a stream of thick confusion. "If you didn't go looking into my past, then who the hell did?"

"I don't even know what you're talking about."

He pushed off from the car and stood up with only a foot separating them. His mind raced as questions hit him from every direction. "Someone has been poking around in my military record. There was a second investigation, this one less intrusive, into the rest of my life. Around the time you gave the ring back, someone started checking into my past. I figured it was you."

She blinked but stayed quiet.

"It was a logical assumption." He hesitated to bring up a sore subject, but he needed her to understand his position. "You were so pissed off about Karen."

"I wouldn't mention your wife right now. Not if you want to live." Lexy crossed her arms across her stomach.

The pleading look in her eyes had evaporated. Her usual spunk seemed firmly back in place.

"Ex. And that's the point. You turned rabid on me when you found out one thing about my life before you. You wouldn't let up."

"Excuse me for caring."

"When I didn't fill in all of the other blanks, I figured you went looking for the information you appeared to crave."

"You still don't get it."

He started to wonder if there was anything he did "get" in dealing with her. "What?"

"My questions about you did not have anything to do with your past or wanting to analyze your life before me. Not really."

"Sure seemed like it."

How the hell did they get so off track? He wanted to talk about who else was out there poking around in his life. She wanted to fight.

"My questions related to trust. I wanted you to trust me and to be able to trust you in return."

The ache did not return to her eyes, but he heard it in her voice. And she could not have shocked him more if she hit him. Here he thought they communicated well and understood each other. He had been pretty damn wrong on that score.

"Lexy, listen to me." He touched her then, rubbing his hands up and down her arms. "You have this all wrong."

"Oh, really?" She sounded as snotty and unbending as he had ever heard her, but she did not pull away.

"There is no one in this world I trust more than you." When her mouth turned down in a frown, he pressed on. "You are the only person who matters to me."

She stared at him. Did not move. Did not speak.

Her lack of a response scared the shit out of him. "If you told me you saw a wild coyote break into your room, pick up a lamp, and smack Henderson over the head with it, I would believe you."

"Then we'd both be insane."

He pulled her closer. "There is nothing you could do to push me away or make me not want to be with you. That's what I'm saying."

Her gaze searched his.

He inhaled, drawing as much air into his lungs as possible as he broke his cardinal rule. "Don't you get it? My life before you is something I want to forget. I need to forget if I want to survive in society."

"Noah."

His hands moved to cup her cheeks. "You are the only person or thing in this life that I've ever found to be worth remembering."

He waited for her to pull back or argue—something—as his head dipped lower and his mouth covered hers. Instead, she slipped her arms up and around his neck. As he pulled her in tighter against his chest, she deepened the kiss by slanting her lips over his again and again.

If not for the sound of a car horn, he may have bundled her into the backseat and put that condom in his wallet to good use. "What the . . . ?"

Detective Sommerville pulled up next to them in a dark nondescript sedan and rolled down the window. "You two may want to move along."

Lexy's eyes clouded in confusion as she continued to hold onto his shoulders. "What?"

"If you want to answer a few more questions, fine." The detective pointed at the small camera mounted by the door to the police station. The same one aimed right at where they were standing in the parking lot. "Otherwise you may want to know that you are the afternoon entertainment for every officer in the station. At least the male ones."

Noah tried to wrestle back some of that control he lost whenever Lexy stood in the vicinity. "Goes to show there's no crime in this town."

The detective shrugged. "You picked the location for the show."

This is what happened when a guy went too long without sex. His body now waited on alert every second. If Lexy looked at him sideways, he was up and ready to go, even if that meant flashing every cop in Utah.

"We are engaged, you know." Noah explained that fact for what felt like the fiftieth time.

The detective smiled at both of them. "I'm starting to think that's the truth."

Lexy finally snapped out of her stupor and dropped her arms to her sides. "And I'm starting to hate this town."

"That's a shame, since you're stuck here for now." The detective winked. "You have a nice day."

Chapter Fourteen

Two hours later, Lexy glanced around Noah's room and wondered what the space looked like before she claimed it as her own. Another trip to the gift shop had resulted in bags and receipts being strewn about . . . well, everywhere.

Clutter in the form of blankets, pillows, notepads, and other items she had collected in the last twenty-four hours sat in stacks on top of the desk. Her newly purchased collection of unneeded T-shirts, sweats, and sneakers took up just about every inch of available space on the bed and floor. She even pulled out two of Noah's polo shirts and added them to her pile of goodies.

If she could find a few years' worth of old newspapers and magazines, throw in some garbage and a bunch of vintage-store rejects, the place would resemble her parents' house. And the realization scared the hell out of her.

Her entire life had been a battle against this. She grew up never being able to have friends to the house out of a mix of embarrassment and parental pressure. Living with the constant worry that everything she owned was dirty or lost or at the bottom of some mess somewhere in the house plagued every single day of her life until she went off to college at age seventeen.

Her parents collected and piled, and the compulsion never ended. Not when a neighbor had peeked over the fence between the properties and saw the mountain of rusty furniture blocking the back door, then called the police to report the fire hazard. Not when Child Services paid a visit after a teacher expressed some concern about an essay Gray wrote in grade school about the state of his family's kitchen. Not when she and Gray got older, moved out, and begged their parents to get help.

While growing up, her parents simply moved to avoid neighborhood questions. Eventually they excelled at keeping their lifestyle private so that no one asked questions. They became secretive about what went on behind the front door, all while presenting an eccentric but otherwise relatively normal front to the world on the other side of the big gate separating them from everyone else.

Lexy never expected to repeat the pattern. Gray did not exhibit any of the same pathological issues, but she did. A few years of therapy taught her to control the excessive behavior. To keep the madness focused. Noah's support and refusal to judge either her or her parents about this problem helped as well.

Even with the breakup, she had her life somewhat under control and had a purpose. Then a dead guy showed up on her floor and everything unraveled. Now with her life spinning and her relationship with Noah all screwed up, that racing feeling deep down in her chest would not stop.

She managed to evade his questions about the recent search into his background. The one she had her private investigator run. That did not explain the previous, deeper check on him. She could not explain that one. Knowing Noah and how he led his life, she was not surprised to hear that people were digging into his life.

He had gone to the main gate to get Gray almost a half hour ago. With a crime scene on the resort property and a killer on the loose, only registered guests, the police, and resort employees were allowed in and out without an escort. That meant she had about two minutes to—

A key rattled in the lock just before the door opened and Noah filled the open space. "We're here."

With a duffel bag in his hand, Noah looked around the floor for a place to step. After a few seconds, he set the bag down on the small porch outside the room.

"Why are you putting my stuff ..." The laughter in Gray's voice died as he stepped from behind Noah and glanced around the chaotic room. "Are my mom and dad here?"

"That's not funny," Lexy grumbled.

Noah grabbed an empty plastic bag by his feet and crumpled it into a small ball. "I see you went shopping again."

"I needed a few things."

Noah looked poised to crack a joke, but then his lips fell. He chucked the bag into the garbage and kept his mouth closed.

Something about her face convinced him to shut up. Lexy just wished she knew what caused her to have that sort of power over Noah. If she could harness that gift of silence, they might have a shot at putting their relationship back together.

"Good to see you, sis." Gray dodged a pile of clothes with an exaggerated step and wrapped her in a tight bear hug. "You okay?"

"Except for the part where the police think I killed a guy, yeah." She hated to give up the security and step out of Gray's embrace, but she did.

Gray winked at her right before he massaged her shoulder. "I heard."

"If it's any consolation, I'm a suspect, too. Want to rub my shoulders?" Noah asked in a mocking voice.

"Never."

"Good choice."

"So, what's the supposed motive for you?" Gray asked Noah.

Noah picked up some of the items she discarded earlier and put them on a folded pile on her bed. "Jealousy. The detective thinks your sister was cheating on me."

Since Lexy would never be unfaithful, would never even think to be, and would have killed Noah if he had strayed while they were dating, the suggestion grated on her nerves. "Hard to sleep around on you since we're not together."

Gray made a hissing noise through his teeth. "Ouch."

"She's testing me," Noah said.

"I wouldn't joke about that one, sis. Engaged or not, I can't imagine what Noah would do to the poor sucker who tried to climb into your bed."

"Listen to your brother. The man talks sense." Noah wound the T-shirt he was holding into a tight ball.

Lexy considered pointing out how Noah had believed she was sleeping with someone else, namely William, but abandoned the idea when she saw a black haze move behind Noah's eyes.

Still, for some reason, she felt the need to explain and defend herself. "I'm just saying that we would have to be a couple for me to be unfaithful."

"We felt pretty coupled last night in that bed."

Gray stopped in the middle of sitting down on the bed in question and shot back up to a standing position again. "Aw, shit."

"Noah!"

"What?" Noah held his hands up with her blue dress hanging off his fingertips.

Memories of him stripping the dress off her assailed her. From the fake innocent expression on Noah's face, she knew he was doing some remembering of his own.

"You're being rude just to be rude," she said.

He folded the dress with a reverence that made her internal temperature spike. "Honey, as far as I'm concerned we are back together."

"Since I get a say about our relationship, we're not."

A huge grin lit up his face. "At least you finally admit we have a relationship again."

The man made her want to hit something.

"This sounds like a familiar argument." Gray pulled out the desk chair and pointed down at the seat. "Anything I should know before I use this?"

Was nothing private anymore? "No."

"Well, not from us," Noah said at the same time.

Gray's mouth twisted in distaste. Probably had something to do with his exaggerated fear of germs. "I'm beginning to hate Utah."

"Join the club." Noah motioned for Gray to take the chair while Noah sat on the edge of the bed. "At least there aren't a bunch of reporters at the gate anymore. Tate or the police must have chased them off."

"If a murder happened here, and reporters are here, tell me again why you two are still here."

"The police want us to stay in Utah." Lexy did not move from her position resting against the desk as she stared at Gray.

Instead of his usual dark suit, he wore khakis and a polo. But the only thing casual about him was his wardrobe choice. He joked with Noah as usual, but the deep lines around his mouth spoke of the tension running through him.

"But why this resort? Why not one without a murder rate?" Gray asked.

"Look around the area. There aren't many hotels here." Noah's voice grew rougher. "Besides that, I'm not leaving here until I know why someone chose to kill a guy on Lexy's floor."

Yeah, they all wanted to figure out that part. Lexy kept hoping for a logical explanation. One that did not involve Noah or the family company.

"Why are you here?" she asked Gray.

"A guy can't visit his sister?"

"Miles from home on a workday? No. What's going on?"

Gray glanced at Noah before answering. When Noah gave a small, almost imperceptible nod, Gray fessed up. "Noah called and told me about Henderson and his connection to the firm. I grabbed some paperwork, what little I could find, which is a topic I intend to discuss with you, and caught the first plane out this morning."

So this was business. Lexy could not help but smile. That was Gray. Always ready to step in and resolve a work crisis. "Worried about the business PR angle? That's supposed to be my job."

Gray frowned at her joke. "More like I'm worried my baby sister walked into something dangerous. I'm not a complete jackass, you know."

Noah nodded with mock seriousness. "Yeah, not *complete*."

"If I had known Utah was so dangerous . . ." Gray let his voice trail off.

The overprotective angle was sweet, but annoying. "What? You'd ground me?"

"The idea has some merit," Noah said, then tried act innocent when she scowled at him. "What did I say?"

"I'm not sure we can blame the entire state for the death of one guy," Lexy pointed out.

"And where the hell were you when all of this happened?" Gray leveled the question at Noah. "I thought you were the big, protective fiancé in this scenario. What were you doing?"

"Dancing with Lexy."

Enough people knew the intimate details of her love life. "That's not really relevant to anything."

Gray shook his head as if trying to believe what he was hearing. "A guy got killed and you went dancing?"

Noah nodded. "You're confused on the timing, but yeah."

"Unbelievable."

Lexy understood Gray's sentiment. The whole situation bordered on impossible. It was as if the world tilted and everything went off center for twenty-four hours.

"Isn't that why you sent me to find her, Gray? You wanted me to win Lexy back."

"Later," Gray muttered under his breath.

"Wasn't that the point of telling me you didn't know why Lexy changed the computer access and took my files? Of this entire travel exercise to Utah?" Noah asked the questions in a deceptively quiet voice, but the impact landed like a bomb in the middle of the room.

The words registered in Lexy's brain a half second before Gray reacted. "*What*?"

Gray's shoulders collapsed. "Damn it, Noah. I expected you to keep information to yourself."

Noah shrugged. "I tried. Your sister's not stupid."

"Wait a second." She yelled to get their attention. Once she had it, she unleashed her pent-up anger on her brother. "You sent Noah after me like some lame bodyguard?"

Noah made a face. "Lame?"

Lexy ignored Noah. "One idiot at a time" was her motto of the moment. "Is that what happened, Gray?"

All six feet of her brother squirmed in his chair. "Not exactly."

"That's exactly how it was." Noah leaned back with his palms against the bed.

Gray's face turned red. "Would you shut up before she kills me?"

Detective Sommerville was right. The two men in her life spent a lot of time trying to protect her from imaginary insults and threats. Shame they didn't know that most of the time what she needed help with was them.

"Don't blame Noah for this mess, Gray."

Noah beamed at her. "Thanks, honey."

"Don't you start. I'm dealing with Gray right now. Your turn will come." She glared the smile right off Noah's face then went back to mentally planning Gray's painful death. "I'm still waiting for an explanation from you."

Gray took a deep breath and visibly calmed down. "Look, Alexa. It isn't what you think."

"That you got Noah all fired up?"

Noah scoffed. "Oh, that part's true."

"I should kick your ass," Gray mumbled.

Noah's shoulders tensed. "You can try."

She knew the boasts amounted to nothing more than empty talk. Gray and Noah had a near-sibling relationship. Sometimes that included a strange male-bonding ritual where they threatened to beat the crap out of each other. Some days she was tempted to let them. Not today. Not when she had so many questions that needed answering.

"I came here to help with the Henderson situation," Gray said.

Noah nodded in agreement. "And I figured if we told her that we knew about her office games, then she'd tell us why she's really here."

That brought the fighting to a close. The men stopping sniping at each other and stared at her. Confusion knotted Gray's forehead. Satisfaction pounded off Noah.

The weight of the silence nearly knocked her over.

"Why are you here?" Gray asked.

A double team. She should have seen it coming. Noah rarely did anything without a backup plan. "Don't change the subject."

"That is the subject, Lexy." Something behind Noah's eyes softened.

The sweet, honest look of interest was enough to reel her in. Almost.

"Gray's interference is the subject," she insisted in a stall for time.

"Fine. Let's get that out of the way." Noah leaned down with his elbows against his knees. "Gray?"

Gray focused his attention on his friend and partner. "She's being stubborn about you and cutting off your access to get back at you."

"That's not true," she said but neither of them noticed.

"I thought if I made it sound as if I couldn't help and that you had to find her and figure it out for yourself, that you'd have an excuse to talk with her and, maybe, she'd stop being so damn stubborn."

"Excuse me?" Sounded like more heavy-handed male bullshit to her.

Noah saw it differently, since he nodded his head. "I can understand that."

"That makes one of us." What she saw was men-gone-nuts.

Gray reached out and took her hand. "Alexa, you love this idiot. I thought if I made you deal with each other, you might stop all of this insane and unnecessary worrying. It was as much for you two as it was for the business. I can't have you seeking revenge by cutting Noah off without explanation."

Gray had the entire scenario all wrong. She really could not blame him, since she never shared the problem with him. She believed she could resolve it and present it to Gray as a done deal. That doing so might make it easier to accept his best friend's criminal role.

"Only a guy could think something so lame could work," she said.

Noah shrugged. "It did work."

"It did not." Taking on one of them was bad enough. Two was proving impossible, so she centered her attention on the idiot who was biologically related to her. "And why do you think I'm worrying?"

Noah and Gray shared a she's-lost-her-mind-so-tread-carefully glance before Gray finally answered her. "Because you gave back the ring. If you're not worried, what's the problem?"

Noah rubbed his hands together. "Good question. Care to answer that, Lexy?"

"According to you, we still are getting married."

A smile broke across Noah's face. "Then we don't have a problem. We're in agreement and can set a date."

"In your dreams."

"Actually, yes."

The firm tone of his voice stopped her for a second. Noah never doubted her or them. Despite the arguments, the differences in their backgrounds, and the baggage she dragged behind her into a relationship, he did not waver. He was rock solid in that respect. If he hadn't been, she would have left the relationship long before she did.

Gray squeezed her hand. "Noah took off work, which is a miracle, and came here to find you. You're sharing a room—one that could use a round or two of maid service, by the way—and you obviously still love him. What's the problem?"

Obviously? She would trade her soul for the ability to act aloof and feel nothing for Noah.

"We're sleeping together. That's it."

Noah coughed over whatever he said next and Lexy did not ask for a repeat.

"I thought you were here on vacation," Gray said.

"I was. Am . . ."

"No, she's not. She's snooping and hiding something. She brought my stolen papers along for a reason."

"Stolen?" She let go of Gray's hand. "It's clear the sun has scorched Noah's brain."

"That's possible, but I'm still right about this." Noah got up and walked over to the open closet.

Gray watched with a blank look on his face. "What's he doing?"

"Who knows?" But she had an idea. She saw the room safe earlier. Even tried to pry the thing open with one of those free resort pens after several tries at guessing at the combination failed.

Noah faced them with a fistful of papers. "Want to talk now?"

Lexy made a grab for the stack of papers she knew were hers, but Noah held them out of her reach. "Not gonna happen, sunshine."

"What are those?" Gray asked.

"Private. Noah, hand them over."

Gray threw his hands up in the air. "I'm lost."

"Lexy came here on a project of her own. Something to do with Henderson." Noah never broke eye contact with her. "Am I right?"

"Why ask me when you think you know everything?"

"She made some connection between our business and Henderson. She thinks there's a connection with me as well." Noah talked over her when she tried to object.

"There is no way you and Henderson being here at the same time is a coincidence."

Gray's eyebrow lifted in question. "Is that true?"

"Ask your best friend here. He's the one with the papers."

"I haven't read them." Noah glanced down at the papers. "But I do wonder what we'll learn when we do."

There was no ability to hide anymore. Henderson was dead and she was no closer to figuring out Noah's role in the theft. And from the determined looks on Noah and Gray's faces, she knew they were not going to let the subject drop.

"Alexa?"

"I came here to investigate Noah."

Shock registered on Noah's face. "Me?"

"You're on the verge of being arrested." She sat on the desk this time. "Or, should I say, arrested again?"

Chapter Fifteen

Noah stood there, papers in hand, with his mind wiped clean of any rational comeback. He waited for Lexy's comment to make sense. When that failed, he tried yelling. "What the hell are you talking about?"

"Do not speak to me like that."

So that didn't work. Noah got the message. Hard not to, since the fury thrummed off her, and she was not making any attempt to hide it. Never did.

He inhaled, using all of his strength to grab on to his last strings of patience, and tried again. This time he aimed for a softer tone. One less likely to incur her wrath. "Tell me what you're saying."

"You've either done a very bad thing, or you're being framed. A few days ago I thought it was the former."

"Now?"

Her gaze darted around the room. Everywhere but at him. "I'm not so sure."

Her sudden turn threw him off stride. The explanation raised more questions and did not provide a single answer.

Noah glanced at Gray. "Do you know what she's talking about?"

"Is it because he has a near-perfect shot and a history of

hitting his targets?" Gray asked. "If so, I'd think someone would have come looking for him years ago."

"Can we get back to the subject?" Noah asked because he honestly did not know what else to say to usher in a moment of rational thinking.

Lexy rolled her eyes. "Noah's big gun is not the issue."

"Back up and explain why you think I have anything to do with Henderson's murder," Noah said.

She frowned. "I never said that."

"You did." Noah looked to Gray for confirmation. "Didn't she? Isn't that what we're talking about?"

Lexy answered before Gray could jump in. "This isn't about Henderson."

"Hell. Is someone else dead?" Gray shook his head.

"This isn't about murder. This is about stolen information and a security system that failed when it shouldn't have. I'll show you." She grabbed the papers out of Noah's hand.

Easy to do since he was stuck in a comatose state. Nothing she said made any sense. Stolen information. A dead guy. He knew the definitions of all of those words, but he could not make any of them fit together in a logical way.

"Look, here." She pointed at an e-mail message. "Our client, Scanlon Industries, was a victim of a break-in. A physical one, followed by a cyber one. Hundreds of thousands of dollars are missing."

Noah knew the name without being told. Scanlon was not just *a* client. It was one of the firm's biggest clients. Lots of money. Lots of prestige. All sorts of government contracts for mechanical parts needed by the military with security provided by Noah and his team.

"What does any of this have to do with Noah?" Gray asked.

Noah did not need a road map. He saw the answer right in front of him. "Someone set me up as the thief."

Lexy threw him a satisfied smile. "Or you are the thief."

"Why would I hurt a company of which I already own a substantial percentage?"

"Happens all the time in business," Gray said.

"Do me a favor and don't help."

"I have no idea why you do anything, Noah." She hesitated for a second. "Maybe if I knew more about your past I could answer that."

Her lack of faith stabbed at him. Jabbed him right in the dead center of his chest until he felt as if one of his lungs had deflated. "You think I'm a convicted felon now."

She waved him off. "I know you're not."

Of course not. She knew because she'd checked. His disappointment morphed into fury. "So you were the one who investigated my past. You lied to me."

Gray scowled. "What the hell is up with that, Alexa?"

"The recent check. The cursory one."

"Is that supposed to make it better?" Noah asked.

"I was trying to figure out if you were the one behind the stealing. It's serious business. I didn't have a choice."

She acted as if that made her behavior better. "But I'm the only one in the company you bothered to investigate."

"Getting past the intricate security system at Scanlon and into the building was nearly impossible. But someone did and then got a look at private financial paperwork and started moving funds around."

"What happened when the building's alarm went off?" Gray asked.

"It didn't," she said.

Noah experienced the first *ah-ha* moment of his life. Someone broke into his system, to one he took months to install, got around it, and the suspicion now fell on him. If he owned Scanlon, he'd place the blame on the security expert as well.

"I don't get any of this." Gray stood up and paced to the window. "Someone is blaming Noah for a break-in?"

Lexy slowly shook her head. "Noah is the most likely culprit. The system is one we insisted was impenetrable when we sold it. It's personally designed."

"By me," Noah said.

"Exactly."

Gray slammed his hand against the window ledge. "Blaming Noah is a fucking insult. He would never do something like this."

Noah appreciated the support. Good to know someone in the Stuart clan believed in him. Noah just always expected that person would be Lexy.

Despite the force of that emotional hit, he knew another one was coming. Her story felt unfinished. The police never contacted him. No one at Scanlon complained. Something deeper and more complex was at work here.

Lexy knew what was going on. Noah planned to know before the next all-green meal hit the dining hall table.

"And?" Noah heard his voice waver from the anger running through it.

"There's more?" Gray's voice raised a decibel.

"There's more," Lexy added in a soft tone.

This was one time Noah hated to be right. "You've gone this far. Don't stop now."

She shuffled through her papers until she came upon a computer printout. She held it out to him as if seeing the document explained everything. It didn't. Noah stared at the lines and lines of babble. He was computer savvy, but hardly an expert. He depended on Dex for help with that part of the systems.

"What exactly am I looking at?"

"The cyber footprint leads back to you. If that's not bad enough, one of the accounts into which the stolen funds were deposited is registered in your name. Well, in a bunch of fake names that eventually go back to you." She held the papers closer to his face. "See?"

Gray peeked over his sister's shoulder. Whatever he saw on the documents made his face tense with anger. "You can't possibly think Noah stole money."

Lexy tugged the papers back when Gray tried to take them. "Some proprietary information is missing as well. The Scanlon execs are most worried about that development. Since Scanlon deals in military components, the long-term implications are huge."

Noah understood how it all unfolded. Lexy's role remained unclear. "You didn't say whether or not you thought I did all of this."

"Of course she doesn't." Gray looked at both of them. "Right?"

"I did. This fell right as I learned about Karen." She turned to Noah. "When you refused to talk about anything."

Noah felt the emotional hit down to his feet. "So you decided that I hid something far worse than an ex-wife."

"Yes."

"You took it upon yourself to bring me down. It explains the access and document issues. You were pushing me out while you gathered the evidence." The words scraped against his throat. "Was the plan to hold a board meeting and present your findings? Make some big scene to get your female revenge for Karen?"

He could see it in her eyes. He got a few parts wrong, but he nailed most of it. She wanted to expose him. Ruin him.

She took a step toward him. "This was never about your wife."

"Ex," he said without thinking.

"And you didn't let me finish what I was saying."

He rubbed his temples in the hope of ending the knocking sound echoing in his brain. "I'm not sure how much more I can take."

"I did believe it because I was hurt and frustrated."

"Welcome to the fucking club," he muttered under his breath.

"Noah, I'm sure she didn't mean—"

"But I don't anymore," she whispered the last piece of information.

The invisible hammer pounding into the top of his head and nailing him in place eased up. "No?"

"No."

His raw nerves kept snapping. "Why the change?"

"You have a lot of issues—loads of them—" She snorted as if she thought her comment needed emphasis. "But stealing for the sake of the thrill of it is not one of them."

Not the most flattering defense, but it was something. "Okay."

But Lexy was not done. She kept talking as if she was realizing the truth of her statements as she said them. "After all, you have money. You're known in the community."

He did not want to hear anything else. He doubted her reasoning would make him very happy. "I said, okay."

For some reason, the subject made her chatty gene take over. "If you wanted to steal or needed to, you would be smart enough not to get caught and risk everything you've accomplished."

"You've made your point." She made it several minutes ago, but for some reason kept right on going.

"You certainly would not steal from a company and leave a direct line right back to your doorstep. You're not *that* dumb."

Even Gray was staring at her now.

"Feel free to stop defending me." Much more of this and Detective Sommerville would have more than a murder charge on her mind.

Lexy's mouth clamped shut . . . but only for a second. "I was being supportive."

"You were engaging in a case of overkill," Gray said. "I'm guessing that was guilt talking."

Noah was grateful that his friend stepped in. Lexy did not look as if she was in the mood for a lecture from a fiancé she pretended was an ex. And they had much more material to cover before he could let this subject drop. "How did you get involved in all of this?"

What Noah really wanted to know was why no one bothered to confront him with all of these suspicions. He dealt directly with Scanlon on the security project. He had the relationship. If someone there had a problem, he should have gone to the source and not crawled behind his back to his girl.

"The Scanlon VP, Frank Wallace, and I are friends," she said.

Jealous jumped up and bit Noah. He knew Frank. The guy was fifty-ish, savvy, and *married*. "What does that mean?"

Gray chuckled. "Down boy."

"Simple. It means we've known each other for years." She held up a hand. "Because of our history—and not that kind of history, so back off—he contacted me with the banking info and the tracing Scanlon's internal tech folks did."

"I still don't—"

"He knows our family and has been with the firm for years. Basically, he was looking for a reasonable explanation for what happened. At first, he hoped the whole thing was a fake security test."

Noah still did not like how the entire scenario unfolded. "So he contacted you and not me."

"Think with your head. Why would he call up the guy he thinks stole from him?" Gray asked.

Lexy nodded. "Right, and he asked me to investigate on my end and see if I could dig up anything. He was also concerned that I had hooked up with a professional con man."

A red-hot flush ripped through Noah's body. No one ever questioned his integrity. He never expected it, certainly not from the woman he intended to marry.

"So you investigated me."

"The only thing I looked into was your whereabouts at the time of the incident, some financial stuff to see if the money showed up anywhere, and all of our records on the Scanlon job. Nothing about your work history or background prior to coming to work for us. I had everyone else investigated on a lesser level as well."

"Everyone?" Noah stared at Gray when he asked the question.

"I think he's asking if you're including me in that pile of people." Gray smiled at the idea. Clearly he thought he was immune to suspicion.

Lexy smacked her lips together then answered. "Everyone."

Gray was not laughing now. "What?"

"Employees, trainees, and everyone working on any project, no matter how tangentially related. I looked into all of it, tracked down everyone's potential motives and actual locations."

The risk she took ticked Noah off. "Since when are you a member of the police?"

She was no more in the mood to back down now than she was at the beginning of the conversation. The ways her voice rose and cheeks puffed out proved that. "I had a fiduciary responsibility to the company."

But not to him. That was the unspoken fact zipping around the room.

Noah now understood why she did not have the time to work on the firm's PR project. Lexy had been a very busy lady. Unfortunately all of those projects put her close to danger.

"I would have thought at some point you would have confided in me. I think you owed me that." She owed him more than that. Apparently loyalty and trust meant nothing to her.

"Frank confided in me. Keeping you in the dark was part of the deal. Since we were no longer together—"

"You would be wise not to bring up that topic again."

"I was the perfect person to look into this."

Gray continued to glance back and forth between them like a guy watching a tennis match. "And?"

"And when I traced back all of the people involved with the firm or who had access to firm resources during that time, Henderson's name popped up."

"In what way?" Noah asked.

"He was at the firm for training. He stayed on to do some computer work and analysis with us. I came here to find him."

"I never saw him," Gray said.

"Me, either," Noah answered at the same time.

"What were you going to do when you came face-to-face with him? Knock him down and nag him until he confessed?" Gray asked with as much sarcasm in his voice as Noah had ever heard.

Good question. She acted as if she believed she was safe from violence. Finding a dead guy on her floor should have clued her in to the reality. Apparently not.

Lexy clenched the papers to her chest. "I planned to follow him, maybe check his room, and eventually confront him."

Noah did not know whether to hug or strangle her. "Damn it, Lexy. That's nuts."

"And dangerous." Gray hovered over her. "Did you ever think to call me in on this?"

"This was something I needed to do alone."

"Because you have a death wish?" Noah asked.

Her knuckles whitened from the strength of her grip on the edge of the desk. "Because I was walking away from the company and wanted to make sure everything was fine. I owed the family."

Gray pointed at her. "You owed Noah."

She shook her head. Shook it a bit too hard and fast for Noah's liking. "We were over."

"Stop saying that." Noah kept losing ground on this issue. He had hoped their night of lovemaking might soften her, or at least make her stop declaring the end of their relationship to everyone who would listen.

"It's true," she insisted.

"That's bullshit and you know it," Gray said, his anger obvious.

But it did not come close to matching Lexy's fury. "Excuse me?"

Gray's defense stunned Noah. Rather than jump in, he waited to see what Gray would say next.

"Alexa, who are you kidding here? You did all of this with Frank and Henderson and the investigation because of Noah. That's the same reason I backed off and made it easy for him to come find you."

Silence filled the small hotel room after Gray's pronouncement. Noah thought about clapping, but refrained for fear Lexy would smash the television over his head.

"The point is that Frank has not pressed charges out of respect for our past work association. He put his butt on the line. He has been monitoring the accounts and files for more activity, even set up a few traps, but everything stopped once Henderson left town."

"What did you talk to Henderson about yesterday?" Noah asked.

Gray's eyes grew wide. "You talked to the man?"

"I was going to search his office and he stopped me."

Noah took a calming breath. He wanted to yell, but he wanted answers more. "What exactly did he say?"

"That he knew you and Gray. That he figured out I was following him."

"Good job, sis."

"Obviously someone else at the resort has information on all of this." To Noah, the bigger issue was whether this entire episode could be traced back to the blackmail attempts against him.

Someone had been sending threats via e-mail. Someone claimed to know about his past and planned to disseminate bits of information along with some twisted facts, enough to ruin his reputation, or so the blackmailer thought. No one knew about the e-mails. Noah kept the information quiet as he tried to track down the perpetrator.

The blackmailer said he or she would be back in touch with his demands. Noah worked day and night trying to come up with a list of suspects. God knew he did not have a more interesting way to spend his evenings.

Then Lexy took off and his priorities changed. Let the blackmailer, whoever it was, try to ruin him. Noah was more concerned with making sure Lexy was safe and that their relationship was back on track. Interestingly enough, the blackmail messages stopped once he left town. Now he wondered if the attempts to frame him for theft and the threats to expose him pointed to one person. Hard to imagine there were two people out there who wanted to destroy him.

"No one else affiliated with Scanlon or our company is here." Lexy sighed. "Well, not that I can tell."

"It is possible someone was after Henderson for another reason. If he is involved in scams and thefts, he'd have enemies." Gray sat back down. The energy pounding off him a minute earlier had faded a bit.

"If his body turned up anywhere else on the resort grounds but Lexy's room, I'd agree." Noah knew in his gut the death had something to do with the theft. He never ignored that stabbing feeling in his gut. "No, this connects to Lexy somehow."

"Then she should leave here. It's not safe." Gray looked around as if wanting to pack her up and go.

Noah understood the protective feelings, but running away was not going to happen. Whoever was tracking Lexy would follow her back to San Diego. At least here in the middle of nowhere, with fewer people and a police mandate to stay put, he had a shot at narrowing the suspects. He planned to start with Tate.

"*She* can't," Lexy said. "The detectives want us in Utah."

"And I want us here where I can look into this and into everyone staying or working at the resort." Noah dreaded doing all of that work with Lexy around. He just knew she would insist on helping. More like bossing.

"She needs to have one of us with her at all times," Gray said.

"*She* is a big girl and has gotten this far by herself, so stop treating *her* like a child," she said.

"You've been lucky not to get hurt," Noah pointed out. "Now you're stuck with us."

"I'd rather take my chances with the killer."

"Never going to happen, babe."

Her shoulders slumped. "I'm starting to hate Utah."

Funny, but he was starting to appreciate the place.

Chapter Sixteen

"What is this? And don't say food." Gray hovered over the dinner options in the dining room with an empty plate.

"I wouldn't."

"It sure as hell isn't edible."

"You don't see me eating it, do you?" Noah stood next to his friend while drinking from the beer he smuggled into the resort after the morning trip to the police station.

Gray used a serving spoon to poke around in a bowl of vegetables, but did not take anything. "I refuse to believe people pay to eat like this."

"You'll notice no one else is in here." Noah glanced around. A half-hour into the two-hour lunchtime and they were alone in the large room. Quite a difference from the pre-murder packed-to-capacity crowd.

"I thought the dead guy was keeping them away." Gray let a blob of mashed something plop back into the bowl. "Now I'm not so sure."

"I stopped at a fast-food joint before you got here. Actually drove twenty miles out of my way, over your sister's protests, just to get my hands on a hamburger." And had to go back through the drive-through a second time when Lexy ate his food.

"Where is she?"

"Aerobics class."

"You let her go alone?"

"I walked her there."

"Bet she complained every step of the way."

"Nagged and complained. Your sister excels at that sort of thing." Noah shook his head at the memory. "But I'm convinced this isn't a case of a serial killer running around mad at the resort. The clues, what little there are, point to someone taking Henderson out for a specific reason. Lexy is safe, but I'm sticking close just in case."

"She better be."

"I'll make sure of it." And that was a promise he intended to keep. The only reason he wasn't hovering around outside the exercise studio right now was because Gray showed up.

"At the very least, I'm surprised you're not watching the aerobics class." Gray's eyebrows lifted as if he was contemplating the idea of a workout. "I'm kind of shocked *I'm* not in there. Ladies in tiny outfits. Sounds good to me."

Noah nodded in a moment of male understanding. Oh, he had tried to weasel his way in for a peek at Lexy in her workout shorts. Even sat on the mats and tried to blend into the background, but then that bouncy instructor Marie spotted him and kicked him out.

"The resort has some dumb-ass no-visitors rule about the classes. You think I'd miss an opportunity to see Lexy dance around otherwise?"

"Show some respect." Gray looked out the glass doors as a few women walked by.

"I respect every single part of your sister."

"Shame you couldn't convince her to take a two-week stay at a place that serves food." Gray strained so his gaze could follow a younger woman as she walked out of sight.

"I'd give every dime in my bank account for a hot dog about now."

"The owner insists that crap is good for you." Not that Noah ever planned to eat any of it.

"The hell with that." Gray dropped the spoon in the crystal bowl. The clanking sound echoed in the empty room.

"Blame your sister."

"Why should I? This is all your fault."

Noah coughed over a mouthful of beer. "How do you figure?"

"Stop being an ass and tell Alexa whatever she needs to know about your past." Plates crashed against each other as Gray set his empty one back on the stack.

"It's not that easy."

"Of course it is. You're just making it hard." Gray dragged out a chair and sat down at the nearest table. "You know what your problem is?"

"Lexy?"

Gray motioned to Noah to take a seat. "Your ego."

Noah thought about cracking his beer bottle over Gray's head, but decided that would be a waste of a perfectly good beverage. He only had four left, after all.

"How do you figure my head is the problem?"

"It's this cover thing you have going on."

Noah could not remember a time when Gray did not side with him on a personal issue. This was a first, and not a welcome one. "My background is irrelevant to my engagement to your sister."

"The one that's over?"

"It. Is. Not. Over." He was getting tired of pointing that fact out to everyone. Repetition must not be working because no one seemed to believe him.

"If your work and personal history are so unimportant, then there's no problem to talk with her about them."

"You're much more logical in San Diego." In Utah, Gray sounded like Lexy, which, in this case and by Noah's way of thinking, was not a good thing.

Gray leaned his elbows on the table and exhaled. "Look, I get that you're not proud of everything that came before her. About who you were in the past."

"There's an understatement."

"Get over it. You are who you are today."

Finally someone agreed with him. "That's my point. The man I am right now is what matters."

Gray laughed. "Don't try to talk in circles. I've known you too long to fall for that shit. This is a simple problem. You want my sister, then spill it. You want to lose her and sleep alone while someone else wins her over, keep with your current strategy."

A wave of pain washed over him. Every cell inside Noah fought against the idea of Lexy with someone else.

Disclosing the sordid details of his life did not sit well with him, either. He learned a long time ago to keep secrets. He grew up in a family where disagreements meant punches and broken bones. Where black eyes and his mother's tears were common. Lexy knew part of that. He had skipped over the worst when he had seen a mixture of sadness and pity in her eyes. He never wanted to see that look again.

The rest she knew only as lines from his résumé. His time in the military and later with DIA depended on his discretion and ability to separate his private persona from the one that carried a gun. He did not want to be that person or have any-one associate him with that person. Certainly not Lexy.

He could protect her, and would, but he packed the dangerous and violent side away a long time ago. Dragging all of that history out now could only cause trouble. Trouble for his former bosses and trouble for anyone who tried to care about him.

"I'll think about it," he mumbled.

"She just wants to feel included."

"I said okay."

"She's lived with secrets a long time. I don't think she wants more."

"Do you not know that you should shut up when you win an argument?" The deficiency appeared to run in the family.

The tension at the corners of Gray's mouth eased. "I was talking about my parents."

"Now there's an interesting duo." Many words described his future in-laws. Interesting was the least offensive. Despite that, he liked the older couple. They were smart and loved their kids, even though they saddled them with strange baggage.

"Scary is the word you're looking for." Gray stared at something on the other side of the door.

Noah wanted to turn around, but he refrained. "But harmless."

"Tell that to the squirrel my father chased around the golf course with a club a few years back."

Noah had heard the animal-stalking story more as a country-club rumor than as a fact. From what he could tell, the meds calmed some of his future father-in-law's rougher edges. If that ever wasn't the case, he would act then. Until that time, he did what he could to help with the family's hoarding issues and ignore the rest.

"About Lexy—"

Noah decided to end the man-to-man chat before one of them got killed. "Since when do you know so much about women?"

"Oh, hell." Gray dropped back in his chair. "I don't know a damn thing about women other than they're utterly indecipherable."

"Your sister is a woman, you know."

"Her I get." Gray's eyes narrowed. "And I'd like to get that one."

"Who?"

Gray hitched his chin toward the door. "The one at the door."

This time Noah did look. Part of him wanted to smile, but the other part—the part where he groaned in frustration—won out.

"That, is Detective Ellen Sommerville. Petite and scary as hell."

The detective picked that minute to look in the door. There was no hiding now. The woman was on the prowl and he looked like the target. Again.

Gray's mouth broke into a smile. "Cute."

"If you say so."

"I'm a fan of dark curly hair. And . . . well, I can't quite see what's under that uniform, but it looks promising."

The desert air had melted his friend's brain cells. Noah decided that was the only explanation. "She carries a gun."

"That's not a turnoff."

"A big gun."

"Keep talking. What else?"

The detective opened the door with enough force to make it bounce against the inside wall.

"Damn, she's hot," Gray said with more than a little awe in his voice.

"Did I mention that she knows how to use that weapon strapped to her side?"

"That's a bit more problematic, but still workable."

"And she thinks I killed a guy." Since the detective was only a few feet away, Noah whispered that last part.

Gray's smile faded. "Oh, that Detective Sommerville."

"Yes, that Detective Sommerville," she said. "That would be me."

Playing the role of the perfect gentleman, Gray rose to his feet and held out his hand. Even wore his best hunting-for-a-willing-woman smile. "I'm Gray. Alexa's brother."

The detective stared at the outstretched palm for a second before joining in the handshake. "I thought she went by Lexy."

Gray shrugged. "She answers to both."

"But Lexy fits her better," Noah said.

"I heard you were coming." The detective glanced around. "Isn't someone supposed to be with you."

"Dex. He'll be here in a few hours."

The detective reached for her notepad with her free hand. "Dex?"

"Is that why you're here? To interview more people who didn't have anything to do with the murder?" Noah asked without standing up. He figured he and the good detective had gotten past the false friendship stage.

"Actually, yes." She broke the contact with Gray. "I was hoping Mr. Stuart—"

"Call me Gray."

"—brought the missing documents with him."

Noah knew the exact moment Gray realized his flirting was not working. Happened about a second after the temperature in the room dropped and the smile froze on his face. The fact the detective's hand moved to the top of her gun played a role as well.

"Excuse me?" Gray asked.

"Documents mysteriously disappeared from the crime scene." The detective scowled at Noah before continuing. "I assumed you were running an extra set over for all of us to review."

Gray's mouth dropped open. "Do you not have fax machines in Utah?"

If the detective got the joke, she wasn't letting on. "Did you or did you not bring the documents, Mr. Stuart?"

"I didn't know I was supposed to bring anything."

"Because you weren't," Noah mumbled.

"I came here because I was worried about my sister. I heard she was being questioned by you. That's a new thing in her life."

The detective nodded. "It's my job to talk to everyone associated with Mr. Henderson's murder."

"I wanted to see if Alexa and Noah needed anything." Gray held up his hands. "That's it. Promise."

"They seem to be doing fine without you. Mr. Paxton has done quite a job of protecting your sister's interests."

Gray tried another smile. "Better not use those words around Alexa."

When his friend's flirting failed, Noah decided to turn the conversation away from Henderson and the paperwork, which was now in the safe in his room. "Where's your partner?"

"With your girlfriend."

That got Noah up and out of his chair. "Where?"

"Are you worried about Ms. Stuart being interviewed without you for some reason?"

Hell, yeah. "Lexy can take care of herself."

The detective smiled. "Interesting."

"What's so interesting?" Gray asked.

"You gentlemen. Never seen two guys go from flirting to angry so fast. Usually the gun turns men off. Seems to have had the opposite effect on your friend here." The detective nodded in Gray's general direction when she said that.

No way. Noah refused to agree. "I was not flirting."

"I'm naturally friendly," Gray muttered.

"I'm sure you are."

"Was there something you wanted, detective?" Noah asked.

"No, I have everything I need at the moment."

Noah guessed the detective was so satisfied because she and her partner managed to get Lexy alone. Something Noah vowed would not happen again.

"I'll leave you two to your meal." The detective left the room with a smile as wide as the doorway.

"Still think she's cute?" Noah asked once they were alone again.

"Cute, but dangerous."

"I'm not touching that."

"Think we should find Alexa?"

Noah exhaled as he stood up. "Yeah, with my luck she's convinced the other detective I killed Henderson by now."

Gray cuffed Noah on the shoulder. "You're the one who proposed."

"Marriage seemed like such a good idea a few months ago."

"If you say so."

Chapter Seventeen

"I did not know the man." Lexy explained her relationship to Henderson one more time for Detective Lindsay. Since there was no relationship, she thought the conversation would be short and she could move on to her postworkout shower without delay.

Detective Lindsay had other ideas.

He stood in the middle of the aerobics studio with his back to the locker-room door, blocking her access to her bag. The fact Marie hovered around, pretending to put away mats after the class, did not help the conversation go any faster. With her bright orange leotard and tight butt, she functioned like a bright flashing light to Detective Lindsay. He would ask a question, then his attention would wander to the annoying blonde.

"Maybe you'd prefer to question Marie for a few hours." Days, weeks, months. Whatever it took to get him away from her was fine with Lexy.

The detective stopped drooling and started frowning. "I need to talk about the papers we found in your room."

The workout sucked the stress right out of her. This guy rammed it all back in. "I thought the documents went missing."

"We'll get to those in a second."

That's what she was afraid of.

He tapped his pen against his notepad. "I'm talking about the ones that did not mysteriously disappear. The ones we picked up at the crime scene and have been reviewing."

The idea of Detectives Lindsay and Sommerville sitting in a room, reading over her private information, and chatting about the contents made all the nerves in her head swell and thump. "I'm going to need those back."

"No."

He could be a little less emphatic about it. "Excuse me?"

"I guess I should say that you shouldn't count on a return happening any time soon."

"That doesn't sound very promising."

"The problem is the content of those documents. Some of them reference Henderson." He did not bother to hide his smile. "Of course, you know that."

Well, damn. Noah stole her files. He just didn't steal *all* of the files. For the first time she regretted that he was not more thorough in his pick-and-grab.

She tried to search her memory and reconstruct every piece of information she brought with her to the resort. She knew, in general, what was missing from the load in Noah's safe. Some forms. Paperwork Henderson filled out for Dex's training program. Notes from her investigations into his background. Minor bio stuff. Nothing about the break-in or Scanlon or Noah's ties to either. At least she hoped that was true.

"Ms. Stuart?"

"Yes?"

"Do you have an explanation?"

Not one she felt comfortable sharing. "What exactly are you asking me?"

"I'm giving you an opportunity to explain why Mr. Henderson's name was all over the papers in your room."

"It is?"

"That surprises you?"

"I brought work with me from home. I didn't say I had the time to do any of it or to know what was in it."

"Sounds convenient."

In her view, nothing about Henderson had been convenient so far. The man had caused her only trouble since she first read his name on the list of potential suspects she developed. On one level, the idea of his death horrified her. She felt awful for him and for anyone who cared about him.

On another level, she wondered if Henderson's life choices made his death inevitable. She was convinced the Scanlon thefts tied back to him. If so, he put Noah in danger. For that reason, summoning up huge amounts of sympathy for Henderson was tough.

The detective cleared his throat to get her attention. "Did you have a personal relationship with the deceased, Ms. Stuart?"

A sharp crashing sound saved Lexy from answering. Marie swore as the hand weights she was holding rolled across the hardwood floor.

Detective Lindsay was by her side in a second. "Are you okay, ma'am?"

Marie waved a hand in front of her face. "I'm just a bit nervous, what with everything happening around the resort lately."

The other woman did not look the least bit frazzled in Lexy's opinion. Seemed more like a case of extreme overacting. But Lexy appreciated the show, since Marie's little scene took the attention off her documents and Henderson and Henderson's name in her documents.

Lexy gave the other woman credit. She had her wounded-girl act down. Lexy watched in the mirror behind Marie as the other woman curled her shoulders, actually made her body look smaller and more vulnerable. She morphed from attacking viper to wounded angel without any steps in between.

That men did not see through this silliness . . . well, it just proved women were the more intelligent sex. A pretty woman cried and an otherwise smart male turned all protective and gooey. It was kind of embarrassing, really.

"Our security guard was killed in her room." Marie stole a quick peek at Lexy, then went back to her fake trembling. *This woman was good.*

Lexy noticed how the other woman managed to point the blame even as she worked up some tears. Now that was an impressive skill. For whatever reason, Marie's agenda included making Lexy the bad guy. But Lexy saw right through her. She added liar to Marie's list of roles. Right up there with aerobics instructor, adulterer, and skank.

"You're standing in a room with a guy with a gun," Lexy said in an effort to point out the obvious. "What are you supposed to be afraid of right now?"

The detective shot Lexy a chilling scowl as he huddled closer to Marie's shrinking form.

Marie's look was more telling. Her carefully crafted pretty-girl face crumbled, leaving behind only nastiness. Not a surprise to Lexy. She knew whatever lurked behind all that silicone and Lycra was not good. Not good at all.

Lexy almost felt sorry for Tate and certainly pitied Marie's clueless husband. There were probably more unsuspecting male victims spread all across Utah. Lexy just hoped they didn't show up at the resort. The drama quotient was already too high.

"I did not mean to interrupt your interrogation of Ms. Stuart." Marie made the statement through a sudden onset of the sniffles. "Go ahead."

No. Thank. You. "We were just talking. We're done."

The detective practically stood on top of Marie. He did not wrap an arm around her petite shoulders, but Lexy would have bet money that he was tempted.

Lexy toyed with the idea of executing a dramatic eye roll. God knew the gesture fit.

"I'm sure it's hard for you." The detective put his notebook in his pocket and smiled down at Marie. Despite the fact his interest in her seemed anything but paternal, he gave her one of those concerned fatherly looks.

"You should keep questioning the guest. I'm fine."

Lexy wondered when she went from "Ms. Stuart" to "guest" in Marie's conniving brain. "Actually, he was talking and I was listening. And we're done."

She probably could have admitted to killing Henderson right then and no one would have noticed. Marie sucked up all the attention in the room. Most of the air, too.

"I don't know how you managed to teach a class," he said.

Marie shrugged her slim shoulders. "I have to work."

"You only had three people in here with you."

"The guests are scared. Many have left. Only a few remain, and they demand certain services, like exercise classes." Marie aimed her last remark at Lexy.

Lexy assumed the other woman would rather have some time off. Well, Lexy would rather be home, so she figured they were even on the disappointment scale.

"It's understandable you're upset, ma'am. After all, you were close to Henderson." The detective talked to Marie as if she might break in half if he raised his voice.

Lexy thought the compassion thing was a bit overdone. Then again, so was Marie's fake crying.

"You guys worked together," the detective pointed out.

Marie's sniffles immediately dried up. "Who?"

The discussion went from annoying to interesting just

that fast. Lexy ignored her need for a shower in favor of seeing where this was going. Watching Marie squirm was just an added bonus.

"I'm talking about you and Mr. Henderson," the detective said.

"Well, no." Marie's glance darted around the room before focusing on the detective again. "I mean, I didn't really know him."

Uh-huh, sure. Lexy wanted to make the comment out loud but kept it to herself.

"No?" The detective shifted away from Marie. Left just enough space between them to send an unspoken signal to Marie that support time was over.

Lexy respected the maneuver. Anyone who could throw Marie off the scent of a willing male was okay with Lexy.

"I barely knew him," Marie insisted.

"I see."

Marie's eyes filled with tears. "You have to understand me. I really don't."

Lexy thought the pleading added a nice touch, but she doubted a word this woman said was true. Marie seemed to know every man at the resort—guests and employees. Probably even the guy who worked at the fast-food joint in town. She got around. The only mystery was how she kept them all straight.

"Really, I thought . . ." The detective's eyebrow's lifted in question, then fell again just as quickly. "Never mind."

That got Marie's attention. Anger replaced sadness on her face. Lexy watched the scene from ten feet away, but she could see Marie's mood shift. Her back straightened and her tone went from weepy to defensive.

"I should really leave you two alone. You need to speak with our guest about her relationship with Henderson." Marie's words came out in a rush.

The more desperate Marie sounded, the calmer Lexy felt. "Actually, he was asking about *your* relationship with Mr. Henderson."

"Nonsense. I'll let you get back to your work." Marie used her foot to roll the hand weights out of the way of her escape route to the door.

"You can stay." Lexy figured that was the only time in her life she would say that sentence to Marie.

Detective Lindsay did not wait for an opening. He took over, all business and serious, and with his attention centered on Marie. Not on those breasts of hers, either.

"Why don't we go to your office and discuss Henderson?" He used his size and refusal to move out of the way to push Marie in the direction he wanted her to go. In three steps, they were headed out of the aerobics studio and toward Marie's office.

Lexy appreciated getting out of a discussion about her documents. She just wished she owed someone other than Marie for that favor.

Chapter Eighteen

"Where have you been?" Noah asked Lexy the question the second she stepped into their room with three more shopping bags in one hand and her gym bag over her shoulder.

She nodded to him, which was her way of signaling her anger with him. Without saying a word, she dropped the bags on the bed and started rustling through the plastic searching for some new item.

"I asked you a question," he said.

"And I ignored it."

Okay, wrong Lexy strategy. He knew bossing her around rarely worked. Gave him some satisfaction, but just made her angry. Still, the exercise class ended almost forty minutes ago and Detective Lindsay was out there on the grounds somewhere looking for her. Never mind the fact a murderer could be lurking anywhere.

She needed a keeper.

Instead of falling back on his usual I'm-the-man-tell-me-what-I-want-to-know routine to get an answer, he tried something lighter. "Been shopping again?"

"I needed a few things."

Now there was a lie. She did not need a thing. Unless she planned to wear six T-shirts a day, she had more than enough to get her through the rest of their stay. However long that might be, and he hoped the answer was not long.

"Like what?"

"Just some shirts." She dumped the contents of the bags on the bed. Brochures, shirts, papers—you name it, she purchased it.

This was Lexy in full-on obsession mode. He did not understand whatever went through her mind at these times, but he knew he had to bring it to her attention and get her to deal with it.

"I'll throw these out." He reached for the loose papers, thinking at least they could take those out of the equation. No need to clutter up the bed with more junk.

He hoped to use that particular piece of furniture for much more interesting activities later. Suffocating in a pile of cotton shirts did not fit into his plans anywhere.

"No." Her hand covered his. "I want to look at those."

He glanced at the items in his fist. The receipt. Hiking pamphlets. A short book about the resort's diet. Yeah, no reason he could see to read through that. One thing that would not follow them back to San Diego was the resort's menu.

He dropped everything and put his hands on her shoulders. With a gentle tug, he shifted her body until she faced him. He wanted to see her eyes. Try to figure out what had her going wild on the inside while on the outside she functioned as normal. Without regard for her safety, but normal.

"What's going on with you?" he asked.

"What do you mean?"

He glanced around the room, taking it in nice and slow so she could follow his visual tour. Clothes here. Sneakers and other shoes there. Bags and books and papers of every sort everywhere. In a short time, she had taken his clean tidy room and turned it into a fraternity game room after an all-night party.

"You're having trouble with something." He knew the signs. He had gone to her old therapist a few times to see how he could help when the rough times hit.

Not that she fell apart often. She never crumbled, though he knew she had the right to do so. That's the part that worried him the most. When her parents did something odd or needed someone to cover for them so they could preserve as normal a public image as possible, Lexy stepped in without question. Her life revolved around hiding their embarrassing secrets.

All he wanted was for the Stuarts to get help. They preferred to let Lexy do all the dirty work.

"I can see it on your face, honey. You're feeling anxious. Have the need to organize your possessions." From the way her eyes grew wide, he knew he read the signs correctly.

"I'm fine," she said, sounding anything but fine.

"Look around you."

She peeked over his shoulder. "You make it sound like I'm crazy or something."

This always happened. It was a trained response. He tried to talk about the growing problem before it exploded into a full-blown mess, and she responded by going into hyperbole mode. It was her way of getting the subject off her and onto a fight that would go nowhere.

He did not feel like playing that game today. Or ever, but especially not today. "I did not make a diagnosis. I asked a simple question."

She tried to move out of his hold. He did not fight her. He loosened his already gentle grip to see if she would step back, put some distance between them.

She stayed right there. Right in his arms.

A rush of satisfaction pumped through him. Lexy had

been running for weeks. He wanted her home, safe and beside him. He had to hope that their room sharing would help to make that happen. Maybe he finally made some progress.

"You're shopping and gathering," he said.

"All of my stuff was part of a . . ."

"Crime scene?"

"I hate that word, but yes."

"I get that. What I don't get is what's going on in that head of yours."

"A guy did die in my room, you know."

Still feisty, but still not pulling away from him. Noah took that as a good sign. "I know."

"A guy I was following."

Noah did not need a reminder of that dangerous nightmare. "Yeah."

She moved closer into the welcoming circle of his arms and rested her palms against his chest. "My papers mentioned him."

"They're in the safe."

"Not all of them."

He did not see that bit of news coming. "What?"

"According to Detective Lindsay, he can tie me to Henderson through the stuff they found in my room."

Damn if the police did not pull off a divide-and-conquer routine. Well played.

Noah realized Detective Somerville was right about one thing. He had not appreciated the investigative skills of the police in this part of Utah. He would not make that mistake a second time.

"You saw the detective?" Noah knew the answer but wanted to be sure.

"He showed up at my class. Walked in, waited in the back, and talked to me after."

"I thought Marie had some rule about visitors in her sessions."

Lexy dipped her hand into the open collar of his polo shirt. If she was trying to distract him, it was working. He had a bunch of questions, but all he could think about was her hands on his skin. Their clothes on the floor. His mind and head and body filled only with her.

Yeah, that one night of lovemaking had only removed the hard edge of his need. He had a whole pile stored up and waiting for her.

Lexy kissed his chin. "Since there were only a few of us in the class, I guess she made an exception for the police."

"That hardly seems fair."

"Complain to her." Lexy smiled one of those seductive take-me-to-bed smiles. "Of course, you'll have to wait in line if you want her attention."

He did not know what they were even talking about anymore. "Should I know what that means?"

"The detective stopped questioning me and started talking with Marie. I was grateful for the reprieve, but I do wonder if the detective knows what he's getting into with that one."

The way she said the words stayed with Noah. She was saying something. He just wasn't picking up on the message. "You think they're talking or doing something else?"

"You know, at first I thought the detective was experiencing a typical dumb male attraction."

Now there was a line of thinking he needed her to abandon. A discussion about the weaknesses of men was not what he had in mind for the rest of the day. "Not all men suck, you know."

"If you say so." She shrugged as she unbuttoned the last of the three buttons at the top of his shirt and slipped her hand inside. "But in this case you might be right."

"That would be a nice change."

"Wouldn't it?"

He wrapped his arms around her waist. "Keep talking."

"Well, it's just that I got the impression Detective Lindsay played good cop, trying to reel Marie in, but that it was all an act to win her over. When they left the aerobics studio, then he had moved on to some more pointed questions about Marie's relationship with Henderson. She did not like the turn in the conversation one bit."

"Really? Sounds as if Detective Lindsay knows what he's doing."

"It was something to see."

The clouds cleared from Noah's head for a second. "Does Marie have some sort of thing with Henderson?"

"The correct word would be *had* since he's dead, and I don't know. Where the hell would she find the time to service another guy?"

"Service?"

"Seemed appropriate under the circumstances."

His fingers plunged under the elastic waistband of her sweats to settle on the soft cotton of her panties. "Good point."

"I think Marie was just upset that batting her eyes and making those sad little crying sounds at a male—any male— did not work."

"Anything else happen while you were gone?" He hoped the answer was "no," because he was ready to move on to a more personal discussion.

"I jumped around for an hour."

A much better conversation topic. "Wanna show me?"

"You wouldn't be interested in seeing me kick my legs up in the air."

"Are you trying to tempt me?"

"You can't tell by the sexy ensemble I put on for you?"

She looked down at her slim white tee and baggy pants and laughed.

On any other woman, the outfit would not work. Too shapeless and casual. On Lexy, it was damn hot.

"Do you have your exercise outfit on under here." He lifted her T-shirt and pretended to check.

She slapped his hand down. "It's in my bag. I showered after class."

"That's a shame. I was hoping we could do that together."

"Don't you need to pick up Dex?"

The woman underestimated his ingenuity and sense of timing. "I sent your brother."

"That was very enterprising of you."

"I thought so."

She moved those knowing hands to his neck. "Then I guess you're free for a few hours."

"Got any ideas on how we can use the time?"

She started nibbling on his neck. "A few."

"Me, too." He lifted her up off the floor and felt a rush of need flow through him when she wrapped her legs around his waist.

"Care to share your ideas?"

"Well, all of them require you to be naked."

"I like the way you think, Mr. Paxton."

"And I love it when you call me Mr. Paxton right before I ravish you."

Chapter Nineteen

"How bad is this situation?" Dex threw his suitcase on the bed and flicked on the light to the bathroom.

Gray did not venture past the closed door. He had a room at the resort. He knew the layout because his was right next door. Nothing new to see.

He also knew he would rather anywhere but at this resort. "A guy is dead, so I'd say pretty damn bad."

"There is that."

Gray leaned back against the door. His casual pose hid the frustration he felt at being away from the office and in the middle of a situation that did not make a lick of sense.

Once they solved the mysteries behind the Scanlon theft and Henderson's death, he planned to talk to Lexy about her decision to go off on her own and not include him in her plans. It was not her usual way of operating and Gray was determined to prevent it from happening again.

When the business was in trouble, he needed to know. He was the damn president, after all. She could put aside her personal problems and share news of something as big as a major theft at a client's business that could result in his firm losing its stellar reputation and going under.

For now he focused on the biggest problem. "What have

you found out about this Henderson guy's connection to our company?"

Dex looked around the bathroom then shut the light off again. "Nothing new."

"What about on the Scanlon break-in?"

Dex sat on the bed. Bounced up and down a few times, as if testing the mattress.

"Would you like to be alone? I can come back when you're done doing whatever it is you're doing." Gray made the comment in a voice loaded with sarcasm.

"I was just—"

"Tell me about Scanlon."

Dex rubbed his neck before leaning down and letting his hands hang between his legs. "Someone planted the computer trail back to Noah. It's a pretty sophisticated setup. There are all kinds of dead ends, but eventually you find Noah at the end of all the subterfuge."

"Didn't we already know that?"

"We hoped that was the case. I had to make sure all that fancy computer work was a ruse." Dex stared down at his hands. "It is and now we can prove it. At first the trail looked like Noah was trying to hide his tracks. More digging, and the discovery of a few false turns, showed that someone other than Noah pulled the strings and got the money."

"What did you do exactly?"

"Followed every computer path I could think of. Dug into the bank account information. Checked Noah's alibi for the day of the theft. He's clean."

"Of course he is."

Dex's fingers threaded together as he looked up. "Look, I didn't believe Noah did anything wrong or illegal, either, but I had to check out the possibility of his involvement.

There's too much at stake not to be thorough and just blindly defend him."

"Did you poke around for you to be satisfied or for you to collect proof to hand someone else?"

"The latter. Noah doesn't need to earn my loyalty. He has it."

Gray glanced at Dex's laptop case. "So now what?"

"Depends on what we know about Henderson on this end."

"You're asking me? If so, that's easy. Almost nothing."

"There has to be something."

This sort of thing fell well outside Gray's area of business expertise, so he said what he knew. "He had a room here. That's part of the employment package the resort provides."

"Not a bad deal."

Gray remembered lunch and scoffed. "Wait until you try the food. You'll think otherwise."

"That bad?"

"The worst."

"Doesn't sound like Noah's thing. He likes his food. Guess we have your sister to thank for the dining and accommodations." Dex massaged his neck again.

"What's wrong with you?"

"Bad flight." Dex's dark features grew more intense. Six-four, with black hair and a square jaw, Dex could intimidate even the toughest critic. Lexy once commented that Dex's bright blue eyes softened his otherwise harsh features and drove the ladies wild.

Gray did not care about either of those things. "Want to take a break?"

"Am I wearing a dress?"

The image made them both laugh.

"So, anyone look through Henderson's place since his murder?" Dex asked.

"You mean anyone other than the police?"

"They could have missed something and not realized it."

"Like?"

Whatever happened on that flight became a distant memory, because the serious grimace on Dex's face disappeared and a smile took its place. "We won't know until we check."

"You mean break in? We're businessmen."

"A break-in to solve a break-in." Dex made a face as if he was tasting the words. "I like it. There's some justice there, don't you think?"

The idea sounded good. Get out of the room, do a little business, find some answers. "I'm in. We can head out at dark."

"You're like a bad television show."

"What?"

"Why would we go at night and risk having someone see a light on in a room where no one should be? No." Dex shook his head. "It makes more sense to sneak in now. Less obvious."

"You're the expert. I'll call Noah and have him meet us at the room." Gray grabbed the cell phone out of his pocket.

"You said he's with Alexa?"

"Yeah."

"Now?"

"Sure. I passed her going back to the room right before I came to get you." Gray stopped in the middle of hitting speed dial and looked up. "Why"

"It's just that Noah might not want to be disturbed, if you know what I mean."

He did, and tried never to think about that. "You know we're talking about my sister, right?"

"Knowing Noah, he's not letting an opportunity for a reunion to pass." Dex stood up. "Besides, it will be easier for two of us to come up with a plan and get in without being seen."

"And if we get caught, someone will need to bail us out. Noah can have that job."

"If Alexa finds out we're doing this, she might not let him rescue us."

"Then the good news is that I've met the policewoman in charge of the case and she is not bad to look at. If we're caught, we'll go behind bars with a nice memory."

Dex did a double take. "You're attracted to a woman who carries a gun?"

"Surprised me, too."

Chapter Twenty

L exy lost the ability to breathe.

Naked, with her fingers wrapped around the bottom of the headboard and nails digging into the wood, she fought to fill her lungs with air. She had been in this position for twenty minutes. With her hips balanced on a pillow in the middle of the bed, her knees raised, her body was laid out for Noah's pleasure.

And pleasuring her he was.

It took less than five minutes for them to go from fully dressed and seducing, to clothes on the floor and stretched across the bed. She preferred the second option to the first. Even when she wanted to strangle Noah—which was all the time lately—she wanted him. The need went beyond sex. This grew out of the rush of satisfaction followed by the sense of calm she experienced after making love with him.

Never dull.

Always satisfying.

Today was no different. His body rested between her thighs. His hands and mouth traveled over her breasts. Every touch caught her skin on fire. Each brush against her nipple, or lick against her skin, sent a clutching need up her chest to lodge in her throat.

Her fingernails scraped against the headboard. "Noah, I'm never going to make it."

"Just a few more minutes."

He had said that a few minutes ago when his tongue left her stomach and moved up to tease her breasts. As he drew her nipple into his mouth, his palm traveled over her hip to graze along her upper thigh. Her nerve endings jumped in reaction to his soft touch.

Despite the caress, she needed more. She wanted his hand lower, until he rubbed against her and ventured inside. Those fingers were magic. His tongue. His lips. Every part of him set her blood racing through her body until her heart leapt and shuddered from the impact.

"Noah, please."

"Are you restless, baby?" His question rumbled against her skin.

"Yes."

He tongued her nipple, then blew a warm breath over her dampened spot. "We need to work on your control."

"Not now."

"No?" The back of his hand swept over her. The heat of his skin covered her soft wetness and made her body twitch in anticipation.

"Noah." His name left her lips as a soft plea.

"Tell me."

"Stop playing."

"But, I love to play with your body." He dragged his mouth down and kissed the sensitive skin of her belly button.

"*Yes.*"

"Love the feel of how you react to my touch. How my body aches as it slides over yours."

The images he put into her head added to her frustration. She did not want talk or chat. She wanted action.

His shoulders slipped lower until his head rested against her inner thigh. "I missed this."

A laugh burst out of her chest. "That part of me?"

He dragged a finger through her wetness. "This and every other."

Now they were getting somewhere. His fingers rested right where she wanted them. Hot breath blew against her. Her insides pulsed with the need to feel him inside her. Wheels of excitement spun around inside her stomach and her small internal muscles clenched under his hand. She was ready. Past ready. She was a woman on the edge.

And she wanted him to push her over.

She used her hands to make the point. Rather than hold on to the headboard, she grabbed on to him. Palms brushed across his broad sweaty shoulders. Her knees squeezed against him in a subtle signal that her lower half was more than ready to close over him.

With two fingers, he opened her. The room's cool air blew over her sensitive insides as her hips pulsed against the sheets.

Enough foreplay. Kissing him counted as one of her favorite things. But not now.

"Noah, now or I'll . . ." The threat died in her throat when his tongue flicked inside her.

This man was a genius when it came to pleasuring a woman with his mouth. He knew how much pressure to use. When to concentrate on his hands and when to switch to his mouth. How to use them together for maximum seduction. How to make her body jump up off the bed as a shot of desire ripped through her.

His tongue swirled and his mouth sucked. For a few minutes, she got lost in a haze of testing fingers and moving lips. It was not until her thighs pressed hard against his head that she knew she had lost the last ties to her sanity.

Just as her insides began to pulse and clench, he slid back up her body. His chest rested against hers and his body balanced on his elbows and over. "You ready for me, baby?"

Always. "Yes."

She watched his face, studied the dark ecstasy that moved into his gaze when she arched her lower half against his erection. She celebrated her feminine power. Pleasure washed through her until the feel of him against her stomach forced her eyes shut.

"Protection." She whispered the word right before she lost all common sense.

She went off the pill as part of her plan to put Noah out of her head. Being with him again, they needed the safety of not becoming accidental parents. Enough was happening without that added surprise.

But he was a step ahead of her. He grabbed something off the nightstand. The wrapper opened with a rip and his hand disappeared between their bodies.

To speed the process along, she reached down and slipped the condom over him. Then she took an extra second to slide her palm around him and give him a squeeze.

"Lexy, hon. That sort of thing is going to make this go too fast." The words punched out of him as if speaking were difficult.

She knew it was impossible for her. The time for words had come and gone, and would come again. But for now, action was the point. And lots and lots of moving. She needed him to do a lot of that.

His hands wrapped around her thighs, bringing her knees to rest on the small of his back. "That's it."

Coaxing was lost on her. No need for encouragement here.

"Now, Noah."

Before he listened and obeyed, he kissed her. Planted a

hard, possessive kiss on her mouth. One that promised a future of kisses. She did not examine or analyze it. She gave in. Let herself fall into the kiss and glory in the memory of all the kisses that came before.

While his mouth teased and tormented, his lower body went to work. Without warning, he pushed deep inside her. A long, steady plunge that lodged his body deep inside hers. No hesitation. No time to adjust. Just a rush of friction followed by a rumbling groan in her chest.

"Time to move." He whispered his direction just before his teeth bit down on her earlobe. Not hard or rough, but with enough pressure to shoot a splash of adrenaline through her system and spark every resting cell to life.

"*Yes*. Noah, yes."

He retreated and then rocked into her with that one long press again. Soon going slow and steady became impossible. He began to move. Over and over, each time going a little deeper and faster. The rhythm picked up until the steady beat echoed in her brain in time with each plunge inside her.

The sound of their labored breathing filled the room. The smell of their lovemaking wrapped around her head.

His hands pulled her legs in tighter and his body continued to move in and out of hers. Anticipation mixed with pleasure to form a ball of swirling need in her stomach. Her body pressed against his to try to stop all that churning.

Her insides grabbed him. When need sent her back off the mattress and her heels pressing into his back, she knew she was close. Her control hovered by a thread just waiting for one more second to let go.

When Noah continued to press and retreat, then press again, the tightness inside her broke free. With the spinning inside her growing wild and out of control, her mind went blank. A scream played on her lips. She did not think or try to form words. She just opened her mind and allowed the feelings to rush in.

Pleasure, security, love. It was all there. All wrapped up and handed to her when she wasn't even expecting it.

Even after the pounding of her orgasm faded, her muscles continued to pulse. Her bones turned to liquid and melted into the bed.

She felt a tremor ripple across his shoulders. With a muffled shout into her shoulder, his body shook and his hips fell still against her.

Neither one of them said anything for a few minutes. Noah lay on top of her, crushing her into the mattress. His harsh breathing blew against her ear as his body grew more lax. She should have asked him to move or at least shift positions. His weight actually made it hard to breathe.

But she wanted him right there. The warmth and sweet smell of his skin gave her comfort. Being wrapped in his arms, having his body shift against hers, felt familiar. Right.

She did not know if she had fallen in love with him again, or if she never really stopped in the first place. All she knew was that lying there in that room, under him, with her legs around him made everything else seem unimportant. They fought and argued. Heaven knew she did not understand him. But she loved him.

Her doubts about him fell away. She believed in him and trusted him even though the evidence pointed to another outcome.

She had no idea how to live with him or make him understand what she needed, but she knew there was a bedrock of love that did not fade during their time apart. Building on that was the key.

Making him understand that she needed more was an absolute necessity

*   *   *

Noah could almost hear her thinking.

She did not say anything. Her fingers combed through his hair. She hummed a low, almost soundless tune. He doubted she knew any of that.

"What's going on in that pretty head of yours?" he asked when he could not stand another minute of near silence.

"Nothing."

"Something."

She continued to run her fingers through his hair. "I just think it's strange that we keep falling into bed after all that's happened."

Yeah, not the kind of thinking he wanted her to have ten seconds after being together. Hell, his body had not yet cooled. "It was inevitable."

"Probably."

"Damn straight."

A few seconds of silence ticked by. Noah thought about jumping into the quiet, but he knew from experience that Lexy was just warming up to launch into a new discussion. So he waited.

And she did not disappoint.

"I mean, it's strange we fell back into this pattern without any hesitation, don't you think?"

"No."

"You came here. We're sharing a room and now we're sleeping together."

He lifted his head and shifted his body, so he wasn't squashing her into the sheets. "Nothing strange about any of that."

She pinched his shoulder. "You know what I mean."

"Ow."

"You're fine."

"I did not plot for Henderson to die as a way of luring

you into my room, if that's your concern." He let his frustrated tone speak to what he thought of the idea.

"You're good, but not that good."

Not exactly what he meant, but close enough. "If you say so."

"Think this is just a matter of the right circumstances—bad as they may be—the desert air and proximity? That we are traveling down this road because it's convenient?" She traced his mouth with her forefinger.

"No."

"What is it, then?"

She could not be this clueless. "You know why."

"Humor me."

He caught her finger and pressed it against his lips. "We love each other."

The tension pulling across her forehead eased. "This is about love?"

How the hell had they gotten on this conversation? "Isn't it?"

"I'm not so sure."

If she had punched him in the stomach, it would have stung less. Her flippant comment shot right to his chest and laid there like a heavy weight.

"I do love you," he whispered.

"I know."

He sighed with enough force to make her hair move on her cheek. "Then what the hell is the problem?"

"You are the only guy I know who can make a declaration of love and yell while doing it."

"The yelling came after," he grumbled because grumbling was all he could manage.

"You loved me when I left you."

A fact that drove him to his knees. She knew what they had and how they felt, and she walked away anyway. He just did not understand how she could do so and do it so easily.

"I need more, Noah."

"Love along with what we do for each other in bed isn't enough?"

He expected a tart reply or another lecture on how he blew it. Instead she smiled.

"Hmmmm." That was all she said.

"What does that mean, Lexy?"

"It means I'm thinking."

"Sounds dangerous."

The mood in the room shifted. All talk of serious subjects seemed to stop. That flirty look on her lips said something else.

"That kind of talk is not going to help you win your point, big boy."

Yep. Sassy, sexy Lexy was back. No more relationship discussion. "Seems to me you're overthinking this."

"This?"

"Our relationship."

"All I'm thinking about right now is sex."

He appreciated her thought process, but for the first time in his life, sex was not enough. He wanted this issue settled. Every second spent worrying about what she was thinking and what her future plans for him might be stole something from him in terms of internal peace and satisfaction.

He tried again. "I'm talking about something deeper."

Shoving against his shoulder, she pushed him over until he rolled onto his back. When she climbed on top of him, letting her hair hang down and brush against his cooling skin, something inside him ignited again.

He fought off the need driving him. Refused to be controlled by impulses. "Lexy—"

"I don't know what we have or what we are." She leaned down and kissed him.

"I do."

"But I know we have this." The second kiss was not her usual coaxing start of something bigger. No. This was a knock-your-socks-off kind of kiss. One that had him gulping for air and hoping his body broke all-time speed records in getting ready for a second round of action.

Conversation could wait. A smart resolution would come one way or another, but not right now. Now she was making a move, and he was not about to deny her.

"Why Alexa Annabeth. If I didn't know better, I'd say you were trying to control me in the bedroom."

"Two hours from now, you can tell me if it worked."

Chapter Twenty-one

The small employee apartments sat on the far edge of the resort property and backed up against a red rock formation that scaled at least a hundred feet into the air. Like the guest quarters, the natural color of the buildings blended into the landscape. Eight domed structures positioned in a semicircle with two apartments per building. No landscaping, just a short walkway leading from a central parking lot to the double doors of each building.

On the late afternoon weekday during the span between lunch and dinner, no one was around. It appeared that everyone who should be at work was, and anyone who should be here wasn't.

It was the perfect opportunity for two well-known businessmen with impeccable reputations to do something stupid. At least that's how Gray chose to look at the situation.

"Tell me again why we're doing this," Gray said as he stepped onto the small concrete patio in front of Henderson's apartment door.

"Hell if I know."

"That's comforting."

Dex sized up the outside of the apartment with a frown. "I'm a computer guy."

"You're not making me feel better."

"We need more information on this Henderson character."

"Uh-huh."

"Getting it this way seemed like a good idea an hour ago." Dex peeked in the window to the shadowed room beyond the thin curtains.

"Not really."

Dex flashed a smile. "You turning into a girl on me?"

"I'm thinking that I sit behind a desk all day. That I went my entire life without breaking and entering." Gray scanned the other buildings, looking for any movement, animal or human. "Another streak broken."

Dex reached for the doorknob then stopped. "We're sure this is the right apartment?"

"Yeah, Mr. Computer Genius. There's police tape on the door. I'm positive."

"Just checking.

"Get on with it."

"Sure thing. Make yourself useful and keep watch."

Gray was not one to toy with the law. He grew up with parents who attracted attention. The upbringing made Gray very private. He took risks in business, but never with his reputation. "This isn't exactly my regular day."

"What, the one where you talk on the phone all day?"

"Someone has to run the office and keep an eye on the money."

"And some of us do the fun part."

Gray ran the place. He left the hands-on work to Dex and Noah. One man had a secretive past. The other spent hours lost in computer work. Gray thought of Noah and Dex as the same type of men—driven, smart, and focused. Then Noah hooked up with his sister and proved to be much deeper, much more solid and level-headed than Gray at first suspected. They had been best friends ever since.

Dex tested the knob. "It's locked."

"So?"

"So I'm assuming you don't want me to kick the door in."

"Not unless you're intrigued by the idea of spending the night in jail. I'm not, in case you're wondering."

"What's wrong with you?" Dex took out his wallet and a small tool with flip-out parts.

"Call it an attack of common sense." Gray nodded in the direction of the small metal item in Dex's hands. "What's that?"

"I got Noah to teach me some of his tricks because sometimes security is about getting into things, not out."

"We should make that our company motto."

"I'll leave that to you and the board of directors," Dex said.

"That's all me."

"That's my point." Dex fiddled with the lock. After a few seconds of trying, it clicked open. "And if you're so against this idea, why did you agree to tag along?"

"Boredom."

Dex appeared to think about the answer for a second, then nodded. "Fair enough."

"Let's get inside before someone comes by." Gray pushed against Dex's shoulder and shoved him in the room.

Even with the bright sunshine outside, the room remained dark. They agreed not to use lights, but they did not need them.

"What the hell?" Dex beat Gray to the question by two seconds.

"It looks like a hotel room in here." An empty hotel room. An empty hotel room that had never been used.

The bed had been made, but the place looked ready for a new occupant. Beige and boring, not a personal item anywhere. Gray opened the dresser drawers, and found them empty.

Dex stepped back out of the bathroom. "There's nothing here. Not even towels or soap."

Opening the cabinets, Gray searched the small kitchenette for any signs of life. Nothing in the fridge or anywhere else that would indicate anyone had been living there for months.

Dex stood in the middle of the room with his hands on his hips. "The guy lived here?"

"That's what I was told."

"Someone cleaned the place out."

"The police?"

"Not to this extent. They'd bag up whatever they needed for testing and leave the rest behind." Dex shook his head. "No, this is about something else."

"It's only been two days."

"Guess the man didn't have much in the way of personal effects. Whatever he did have is gone."

"But where?"

They heard the squeak at the same time. Dex turned to face the entrance to the room right as Gray checked around for a weapon. The door opened fast. Gray jumped back and out of the way to keep the thing from slamming into his gut.

The gun barrel poked around the door first. Next came the guy who got both men their rooms at the resort. Gray could not remember his name, but he did know this was not a guy who should be holding a gun.

"Stop!" The older man shouted his order.

"Calm down." With his hands in the air, Gray tried to calm the other man down.

"What are you two doing in here?" The gun shook in the man's hand.

"Don't you own this place?" Dex asked. "Tate Carr, right?"

"Answer me."

"Okay." Gray continued to hold up his hands, but lowered them from chest-level to waist-level. "We can explain."

"Do it now."

Gray glanced at Dex. He thought about making up some story, but decided to go with the truth to be safe. "We're just trying to find out a little bit about this Henderson guy."

The gun stopped wavering back and forth. "Why?"

"Because he was in my sister's room when he died. I'm trying to figure out what's going on and if she's safe."

"All of the guests are safe. The resort is perfectly secure."

"Of course."

"You're trespassing."

Gray decided to appeal to the guy's sense of decency. He just hoped he had one. "We're sorry about that, but you know how it is. She's my baby sister. I want to make sure she's okay and see if I can find an answer to what happened, so she can stop worrying."

Tate lowered the gun. "This is about Alexa?"

Relief swelled in Gray's chest. "Exactly."

The gun now pointed at the floor. "She's been a very good guest."

"She likes the resort." Gray had no idea if that was true or not.

"We should contact her. See what she has to say about all of this."

Dex groaned.

Gray understood why. Calling Alexa meant hearing her complain and lecture. Worse, it meant talking to Noah. They would both be furious. If the call interrupted anything interesting, Noah would beat the shit out of him.

Gray doubted either one of them would let him forget

this scene. Of course, the chances of Gray forgetting one minute in this forsaken killing ground wasn't likely, either.

"Why don't we just forget this happened? We're sorry about the inconvenience. It won't happen again." Gray tested Tate by putting his hands in his pockets. When Tate didn't shoot anyone, Gray relaxed his shoulders. "We promise."

Tate pointed the gun at the phone. "Call her."

"Damn," Dex mumbled.

And here Gray thought the visit to Utah could not get worse.

Wrong.

Chapter Twenty-two

Noah and Lexy showed up in Henderson's doorway fifteen minutes later. Fresh from another bout of lovemaking and not at all happy about being disturbed, Noah walked in on the surreal scene with Lexy by his side.

Gray and Dex sat on the edge of the bed. Tate stood over them with a gun. There were so many things wrong with the picture. Noah did not know whether to beat the hell out of Dex and Gray for dragging him out of bed or laugh his ass off at the grim looks on his friends' faces.

"What the hell is going on?" Lexy asked.

Yeah, what she said.

"We have a problem." Tate acted as if that fact was not obvious.

"Looks like a whole lot of stupid is happening in here." Noah glanced over at Gray. "A huge amount."

"I am well within my rights here," Tate insisted.

By Noah's thinking, there was nothing worse than a morally indignant man with a gun. "Why don't you skip the legalese and tell me what you were doing?"

"I am merely defending my resort." Tate lifted his nose in the air with a touch of superiority that highlighted his usual clueless manner.

At least he wasn't wearing green. That saved Noah from having to shoot him just for that. "From what, the guests?"

"They should not be in here." Tate used his gun to point at Dex and Gray.

And got a bit too close to Noah's head. "Whoa. One of the ground rules to this discussion is that no one shoots me. Put that down."

"Maybe we should let him shoot Gray and Dex instead," Lexy suggested.

"I'm thinking about it." Noah scowled at his friends. "Believe me."

Noah saw Gray's jaw clench. Dex's face remained blank. Noah thought about knocking their heads together.

"That's enough on that topic. We get it. You're pissed." Gray ground out between clenched teeth.

Lexy upped the outburst with one of her own. "Picking up on that?"

"Oh, we'll get back to your genius in a second." Instead of launching into a lecture, Noah turned to Tate and handled the scariest and most obvious problem. "Where did you get a gun?"

Tate glanced at the weapon in his hand as if it materialized out of thin air. "I bought it this morning."

"Where?" Because Noah wanted to go to the place and warn the seller never to do something so reckless again.

"At a store."

"Aren't there any gun laws in this state?" Lexy asked.

Tate must have thought it was a serious question, because he answered. "Well, no, not really."

Lexy rolled her eyes. "Just what a situation like this needs. Bullets."

"I wish I had a gun right about now," Gray mumbled.

Lexy aimed an angry finger in her brother's direction. "You should know better."

They all should. And the idea of the leaf-eating moron holding a weapon chilled the last of the sexual fantasies playing in Noah's head. "I'm all for the right to bear arms, but there's something wrong with a system that would allow you to walk out with a gun."

"You go in and buy it." Tate shrugged. "It's not a big deal."

"No background check or anything?" Lexy asked.

Tate stared at the gun and then back at Noah again. "Well, no, but I needed it following the incident."

Lexy tried to step around Noah to get to Tate. Noah considered letting her. She would probably rip the weapon out of his hand and beat him over the head with it.

Lexy settled for yelling. The woman certainly could yell. "For the record, dropping a glass is an incident. What happened at *your* resort and on *your* watch was a murder."

Tate's casual manner lapsed into anger. "You can't possibly hold me responsible for something like that. I'm a businessman, not a policeman."

"Is he kidding?" Gray started to rise, but Lexy's scowl had him sitting back down.

If he heard much more, Noah knew he would lose what was left of his mind. "Do you even know how to shoot that thing, Tate?"

"Not yet."

"What?" Gray's shock was obvious by his wide-open mouth and bug-eyed look of horror.

Tate ignored their collective groans and gasps. "I plan to take a class."

"A class? Give me that before you shoot someone." Noah grabbed the gun out of Tate's hand. "Detective Sommerville would blame me if you took your foot off. The lady thinks everything around here is my fault."

"I'll hold it," Lexy said.

"As if I'm going to give you a loaded weapon." Noah snorted. "Right."

"Can we go?" Dex asked.

"No, no, no." Tate emphasized his denial with a head shake as if no one understood the word. "Not until I get an explanation."

Gray stood up. "We gave you one."

"Which was?" Lexy blocked the doorway. "And don't even think about trying to go around me. You're not moving."

Tate reached out to grab Noah's arm. Noah shrugged away. He was not in the mood to have any hands on him except Lexy's.

The near miss did not stop Tate. He kept right on explaining. "They said they were in here because they were worried about Alexa."

That made about as much sense as . . . well, nothing. "Okay."

"We want to know more about the guy who died on her floor." Now Dex rose to his feet.

The Stuart Enterprise crowd overwhelmed Tate in number and height, but he kept up his PR campaign. "It was an isolated event. This is not a reflection on the safety of the resort."

"You sure have a problem using the word 'murder,' " Noah said.

"The *incident* was not related to the resort, its employees, or the clientele."

Noah had no idea how to respond to that bit of wisdom, considering one of the employees got murdered at the resort, so he pretended Tate never said anything. It was time to get some information from Gray, anyway. "Find anything?"

Tate made the arm-grab again. "That's not the point."

"It is to me." Noah did not bother to look at Tate while he said it.

"We have a problem with trespassing. My inclination is to call the police."

Lexy shot Noah a do-not-move look as she walked around him. In three steps she stood in front of Tate with a sweet smile on her face. "You don't want to do that."

"I don't?"

"More police cars stacked up at the front gate? Imagine what the press will do with that. They still sit out there waiting for a photo of something juicy." She placed her palm on Tate's forearm. "We can work this out without involving reporters and causing more trouble for the resort."

"That's true."

"If not, reservations will go down, and that's not good for anyone."

Noah admired the strategy.

Hated the touching that went along with it.

But Tate was buying into it. He covered her hand with his. "That's a good point."

"Clearly my brother is an idiot." Lexy glanced over her shoulder and shot Gray a look that let him know she believed what she was saying.

When Gray looked as if he was about to jump in and call his sister a name or two, Noah spoke up. "She's not wrong."

"But he meant well." Lexy's tone was a combination of pleading and flirting.

Tate finally tried to speak up. "He shouldn't have—"

"True. There was a better way for him to handle this. But he chose this route. We'll talk to him. Right, Noah?"

"If you let me keep the gun, I'll shoot him for you."

Gray grumbled something unintelligible under his breath.

"I missed that. What did you say?" Noah asked.

"I wondered why I ever tried to help out with your messed-up relationship with Alexa."

Lexy pulled Tate to a corner of the room. Away from the other men and their arguing. "I would consider this a personal favor, Tate. Since I'm thinking about using your resort for corporate retreats, I would hope you could overlook this show of brotherly affection and move on."

"You are?" Gray sounded horrified by the idea.

Noah had to side with Gray in this fight. He did not plan to ever step foot on the resort grounds again. Once the murder was solved and he won back Lexy, they could all leave and never look back. Tasks he feared would take months instead of days.

Tate nodded in understanding. "I think I see what happened here. They were misguided."

"That's a nice way of putting it," Noah said.

Both Tate and Lexy were smiling and nodding and otherwise chatting in their own world. One where any of this seemed rational, which was not this world.

"I think I could be convinced to overlook this incident and forget it ever happened," Tate said.

Dex let out a loud exhale. "More incidents."

"I appreciate your courtesy. Thank you." Lexy looped her arm through Tate's and brought him back to the group. The move was subtle and the steps small, but their conversation went from intimate to open to everyone in the room.

Which was the only reason Noah was not aiming the gun.

"Now are we done?" Dex asked.

"Of course." Lexy patted Tate on the arm before letting go. "Tate needs to get back to work. And the rest of us need to talk."

*   *   *

Dex, Gray, and Noah all crowded into the small room Lexy shared with Noah. She sat cross-legged on the desk and scanned their pathetic male faces. Gray by the window. Dex hanging in the doorway to the bathroom. Noah lounging on the bed as if nothing was out of the norm in his life.

Well, two pathetic faces. Noah was too busy being amused to wear the same dour frowns as his friends.

"A burglary, gentlemen?"

Gray rested his hand on the window ledge. "I'm getting tired of being lectured to."

"You could try acting your age." She still could not believe they took the risk and broke into Henderson's room.

"Right now I'm thinking about catching the next plane back to San Diego," Gray said.

"No one is going anywhere until this is straightened out." Noah laid back against the stacked pillows with his arms folded behind his head.

From his smoky gaze Lexy knew Noah was thinking about their afternoon lovemaking session. His body language spoke of his relaxed state. The heat behind his eyes said something else. Something private that she was not prepared to deal with at that moment.

She had other issues to resolve first. "What were you two thinking? Are you trying to get Noah arrested?"

Gray's head snapped back. "What are you talking about?"

"The detectives think he killed Henderson."

"Technically, I think Sommerville believes you killed the man," Noah said.

"The point is that bringing more attention to us and risking another call to the police was not smart." She thought two college-educated and savvy men would know that on instinct.

"What were you looking for?" Noah asked.

"Anything that would give us some insight into Henderson." When voices sounded outside the window, Gray stared out.

From the way he pulled back the curtain and concentrated, she knew the voices came from attractive women. Gray had a weakness for those.

"Any luck?" Noah asked.

Dex pushed away from the door frame and sat on the edge of the bed. "Did you see that room? Kind of tidy for someone's home. Didn't make any sense."

And with that she lost all control over the conversation. Her stern lecture on common sense turned into a strategy session. She considered yelling until they paid attention to her. If she thought it would have worked, she may have tried it. As it was, they were determined to do the stubborn male thing and ignore ever reasonable thing she said.

And Noah was not helping.

Sure he started out angry. Getting that call from Gray right after he opened another condom wrapper caused more swearing than Lexy had heard from Noah in a year. Once he heard the reason for the call, the profanity just got worse. But now an air of calm hovered around him.

The heavy-lidded gaze gave him away. The rubbing of his hand over the comforter, back and forth, suggested he had some interesting things on his mind. None of them related to solving a murder. With the crisis behind them, his mind had moved on to another topic. Her.

"We know only what I found out before I came here. The guy was forty-something, single, no family except a grandmother with dementia who lives in an assisted-living facility in Arizona, and no debts to speak of." Dex read off the list with all the enthusiasm of a man reciting a grocery list.

"How did he find us?" Noah asked.

Dex warmed to the subject, ticking off whatever he knew that might help. "He came to our company for some training and showed potential, so he stayed on for longer than originally intended."

"Did Tate send him to us for training?" Noah asked.

"No. It looked like Henderson took this on himself. Probably trying to find a more lucrative position than security at this resort."

"Can't blame him for that," she said.

"Probably wanted somewhere that served better food," Noah pointed out for the hundredth time.

"Unless we intend to go around in circles, we need a new plan." Dex threaded his fingers together and waited.

"Maybe he had a locker or a car we could check," Gray said.

Lexy thought about calling the police and saving Tate the trouble. "I see you learned your lesson."

Everyone started talking at once. Dex and Gray argued about other places to find Henderson's belongings. Lexy tried to talk them out of the insanity.

"I, for one, am sick of all the secretive stuff. No more slinking around or breaking into rooms. If you have a theory or avenue you think we should try, just say it. Don't go off on your lonesome and try to be a hero."

"She's talking to you," Noah said to Gray in a voice with more than a little edge to it.

"Are you sure?" Gray fired back.

"Stop!" That time she did yell. It felt good to let some of the rage building inside her find a release. "Fighting annoys me as much as the sneaking around."

"There might be an easier way to go about this." Noah's deep voice rose above the bickering and caught their attention. They went from thinking and scheming to listening.

Lexy envied the skill. "Care to clue us in?"

"My thought is that we try a plan that won't result in us having to raise bail money. It's not as sexy as breaking and entering, sure, but we need something more effective. Besides that, it's so simple that we should have done it sooner." Noah shifted and leaned up on his elbows.

"Is this the part where we get on a plane and leave?" Dex asked in a tone that suggested he was only half joking.

"Follow me here." Noah sat the whole way up. The lazy sensuality that weighed him down disappeared in a flash. He was wide awake and in full business mode.

She loved him this way. Well, any way, but especially when he went after a task with a determination that did not allow for failure. It was just a shame he did not use that same skill on her.

"The evening of the murder, we were all in the dining hall then out on the patio for a party. That means—"

She understood where he was going and thought it was brilliant. "Who wasn't there?"

"Exactly." Noah swiped a small resort-provided notepad off the nightstand. "We figure out who isn't accounted for and start there."

Gray loosened his grip on the window. "Guess that makes you two innocent."

Noah winked at her. "Innocent might not be the right word to describe us."

"At least we didn't kill anyone," Lexy pointed out.

Noah just smiled. "There are hours left in the day. Give us time."

Chapter Twenty-three

Two hours later they had reviewed all of the resort employee information in the brochure stuck in the desk and pieced the rest together by using Dex's laptop and the spa's website. With the help of a hiking schedule that listed every guest's progress, they had a list of everyone else on the grounds.

That was the easy part. Putting names with faces took much longer. Now they had to go through the pages of information and account for each person's whereabouts during a short span of time when Noah was too busy ignoring the resort's menu and Tate's annoying presence to concentrate on the company.

Dex and Gray left earlier with a promise to stay out of trouble and jail. They were on the lookout for a fast-food fix, leaving Noah alone with Lexy.

They sat next to each other on the bed with their backs balanced against the headboard. The documents he had recovered from her room the night of the murder were spread out over her legs. The only thing Noah saw wrong with the arrangement was the fact they both still had clothes on. Then there was the part where Lexy focused only on the written lists in front of her.

He could have his jeans and T-shirt off in a second. Taking off the slim new cotton dress Lexy threw on before going to rescue Gray would not be much of a bother, either. Noah had been there when she scurried around the room trying to find something to throw on to get to her brother fast. He knew how little she had on under the bright blue dress. A tiny pair of white cotton undies. Nothing else, which is exactly what he could think about. Nothing else.

But all of her earlier talk of secrets and sneaking around clicked a switch on in his brain, one he could not turn back off no matter how many times he shut his eyes and tried. He knew the tenuous peace he now shared with Lexy could break apart into a thousand little pieces the minute he refused to fess up to some stupid detail about his past. If she got mad, he was sleeping alone. Possibly forever.

For a guy who prided himself on fast thinking, he had been slow to accept the inevitable. If he wanted to keep her—and he absolutely did—he had to open up the parts of his life he wanted to close off forever. He had to feed this insatiable need she possessed. The same one that washed over her at the most inconvenient times. Not that there were many convenient times, but she did have a habit of picking the worst.

He thought about the blackmail threats. The e-mails appeared to have no relationship to the murder, but Noah knew better. Coincidences, while fine in movies, happened rarely in real life. Putting the pieces together in a way that made sense would take longer.

That was a project for another time. There was no need to worry Lexy with that problem. Not when they had a murder to solve.

Work contracts and promises prohibited him from talking about much of his time in the military and working for the government. But he could share something. If he made her understand the regrettable years from his past, he could salvage something of their future together.

If not . . . well, he did not want to think about that option.

He searched his brain for a logical way to start the conversation. When that failed, he went for blunt. "I don't talk about my marriage."

"What?" she asked without looking up from the documents in front of her.

"It was an absolute failure."

The papers rustled when her hand jerked. She pretended to keep reading, but he knew she concentrated on listening and nothing else. The pretense of her being relaxed failed when her neck straightened and eyes darted from the page to him and then back again.

"I'm not someone who fails at anything."

An electric charge filled the air and a new alertness came over her. She lowered the papers to her lap.

"Karen wanted this fairy-tale life with a man who always agreed with her, never yelled, and did not suffer from any faults. I was the wrong guy. I couldn't give her anything like that."

Lexy looked up at him with a searching gaze. "You wouldn't be able to give anyone those things."

"Uh, thanks."

"No human could live up to a standard with those prerequisites."

That sounded a slightly less insulting. "I guess so."

He wanted to pile up the blame and drop it on Karen's doorstep, but that was too easy. Whatever she needed, he was too young or too something to provide it. That was the added burden that fell on him whenever Lexy complained about their relationship and insisted he bore the brunt of the responsibility. He had failed before and knew about the fallout.

As a guy without a sense of normal when it came to a home life, he tried the best he could. Knowing how it *should* be was the problem. How *not* to be a husband was ingrained on him from an early age. The rest of the rules he made up as he went along. And despite all his efforts, he kept getting it all wrong with Lexy, the one woman with whom he had to get it right.

"Why did you marry her?" Lexy asked the question without any judgment.

He had asked the same one in his head a million times. Meeting Lexy, learning all about her, and sharing the days and nights by her side, he saw that the life he had with Karen was destined to fail. It took years and a whole bunch of aging and maturing to come to terms with that reality. But why he had plunged in in the first place and ever believed it could last with Karen, he did not know.

"I think the *idea* of marriage appealed to me. You come home to someone. No dating rituals. No games."

"That's sort of an idealized view."

He did not see it that way. "Seemed rational enough to me."

"So, guaranteed sex and a hot meal." Lexy chuckled.

"Both good things."

"Joint bank accounts and family picnics."

To a guy who never had any of that, it sounded pretty good. "That's a bit simplistic, but yeah."

She reached out and took his hand. "You wanted to belong."

"Don't girly it up."

She squeezed his fingers, and not in a sweet love gesture. She was trying to strangle the blood out of them.

"Hey!" He covered her hands with both of his to prevent

losing a finger or two. "All I mean is that I thought marriage was this thing I was supposed to do. I found a woman I cared about and did it."

"Cared? That's sort of a lukewarm reaction."

"Works for most guys."

The pressure on his hand eased up. Her touch went back to being gentle. "What about love?"

Talking about a woman he thought he once loved with a woman he actually loved is just not what he envisioned for his evening activities with Lexy. "What about it?"

"A very guy reaction."

Good thing he was a guy then. "I cared about her as much as I knew how to care for anyone at that point in my life."

"What does that mean?"

This theory came to him just before he proposed to Lexy. The romantic views of love never really moved onto his radar screen. He still was not convinced about the whole puppies-and-flowers routine. But he knew about fear now.

As a man who had dodged bullets for part of his life, loving a woman ranked as a much riskier proposition. Losing Lexy taught him about spinning out of control and being physically sick with panic.

He used his guy words to explain. "A man doesn't know shit about love until he falls for the right woman."

Her eyebrows lifted.

He seriously considered shaking her. "You, Lexy. I mean you."

"If you're thinking you might get lucky later . . ." she put her head on his shoulder. "You're gonna."

He decided right there and then that he needed to fess up to his past sins more often. "How lucky?"

"Depends on whether or not you keep talking."

Now there was an incentive. "I really liked Karen's dad. I know that doesn't explain anything, but I did. Sometimes I think I missed him more than Karen when the whole thing fell apart."

"Ah."

The sound rumbled against his arm. "Is that female code for something?"

"You were looking for a family."

There had to be some other topic—any other topic—they could discuss but this one. Hell, he'd be willing to eat a meal in the resort dining room if that meant the informal psychological study of his motives could end.

"Sounds like psychobabble to me," he muttered, hoping she'd get the hint.

"Maybe, but it's obvious psychobabble. You wanted a real father, and she came with that."

That was his Lexy, intuitive and clear. She analyzed the situation and came to a conclusion that made sense to her. With that done, maybe they could—

"That explains the marriage and, for the record, I'll be fine with us never talking about Karen again." He leaned down and kissed the tip of her nose. "Now, there was some talk about me getting lucky?"

Lexy lifted her head off his shoulder. "Not so fast."

His good mood crashed. "But you said—"

"We're not done."

His body certainly thought the talking portion of the program had ended. "Damn, woman."

"I appreciate you opening up and giving me a peek into what's happening in that big head of yours."

"Is this your idea of foreplay?"

"Everything you said explains the marriage, not the man."

He noticed how he did not get a single point or *atta boy* for running on about Karen. A woman should give a man credit for something that big.

"I'm the same man you agreed to marry."

"Stop ending the conversation by circling around it." Lexy's fingertips softened her rebuke. They danced over his shirt as her legs shifted on the bed. "There's so much more to your life, to you, that you refuse to share."

Would it kill the woman to accept half a story? Just once he wished she'd be satisfied with what he could say or wanted to say and leave it at that.

He thought about telling her that. Let her sit on the defensive for a while and see how much she liked it. But he wanted to have sex again some day, and he saw hope flicker in her eyes. Her mouth opened a little as if she were anticipating the next bit of news. The reactions were small but significant. He had to keep going until she reached whatever level of satisfaction she needed before she could wear his ring again. He sure hoped she got there soon.

"Some of the work I did is classified." He chose his words with careful precision.

"I'm not asking you to break the law."

She kind of was. "What are you asking?"

She had an answer ready and fired back. "What shaped you? Other than your family and your early marriage, what made Noah into Noah?"

"Gum and a lot of beer."

The punch landed on his forearm, but bounced off. "Anything else?"

He sighed. "You aren't going to let this drop?"

"You started the conversation. I'm just going along."

Right. Deciding to move forward meant telling the parts that sucked. The aspects of him that were not all that attractive or easy to explain.

"Noah?"

He tapped the back of his head against the headboard. On the fourth beat, he started talking. "After I got out of the military, I did some work for the Defense Intelligence Agency. Contract stuff. Most of it covert."

"There's an ominous name for a government agency."

"It's no worse or better than any other. It performs a service. Not one I always understand, but I followed orders."

Something sparked in those intelligent eyes. "What kind of orders?"

The kind no one wanted to receive. The kind that made you aware of which side of the law you walked on. "I did some work on men I knew while in the military."

She sat up, but stayed close, with an arm wrapped through his. "You managed to say a whole bunch of words that meant nothing."

"Impressive, huh?"

"Not really."

It was worth a shot. "These guys figured out that drug-running paid more than the military. That factor outweighed their integrity and the government benefits. They got lured, then got sloppy. Got in way over their heads and thought no one knew."

"You knew."

"The government knew."

"And?"

"I infiltrated and brought them in."

"Sounds like undercover work."

Some of the men called it disloyal. Noah knew acting was the right thing to do, but he negotiated his retirement after. Seeing decent young men go to hell and off to jail was not what he signed up to do. "Something like that."

"Can't imagine the men took your work and the results very well."

"I got that point when they shot at me." Outrage burned on her face, so he rushed to calm her down. "I'm fine."

"Are you?"

"I shot back. Believe me, I won that battle."

Her hand moved to cover his heart. "But you learned something."

"Yeah, to duck."

"You learned not to trust."

Women and their dramatics. "See, again, you're making this into a woman thing."

"How does a man see it?"

"I did my job."

"Do you always do your job?"

"Yes."

"Even if it involves Mexico or a parrot."

Not the most subtle dig for information, but he appreciated the effort. "The former arose out of a night of too much drinking with some buddies. It started in San Diego, then crossed the border. We were fine until that point. Some contract work with the Border Patrol led to the latter."

"Classified?"

And unimportant compared to what he had shared. "Mostly."

She leaned up and kissed him. "Thank you," she said in a whisper against his lips.

"For?"

"Trusting me with that information."

"Trust was never the issue." Not on his part. Her trusting him to tell her what was relevant did continue to be an issue for them, but he was not about to risk her goodwill by bringing that up.

"You could have told me about any of those incidents months ago and we would not be sitting here."

He still did not quite understand why he had to tell her

the information now. Why was talking about his past the litmus test? "It doesn't matter any more today than it did then, Lexy."

"It matters to me, but I don't want to fight with you."

Finally, they agreed on something. "That's a nice change."

Those fingers trailed down his chest to rest on his stomach. "Right now you have another job."

Looks as if it was time to go back to work. "Henderson?"

"No." Those fingers dipped lower to cup him. "Me."

Relief swamped him. Whatever pitfall waited in front of him, he had managed to step around it. This time.

"Well, if you insist." He swept the papers and files off the bed and onto the floor. Hell, he'd already be inside her if his arm had not fallen asleep from her laying on it.

"Oh, I definitely insist." Clicks sounded in the room as she lowered his zipper. "I may even insist on another round."

"Remind me to open up to you more often."

"Count on it."

Chapter Twenty-four

Lexy's body hummed and a song played on her lips the next morning at breakfast. She sort of missed the early morning hikes out in the fresh air, but Noah was making sleeping in worth her while. The fact the police made Tate cancel the outside activities helped her to go along with Noah's stay-in-bed-and-make-love mandate.

After just a few days of being with him, happiness flowed through her again, blocking out everything else. Now that he shared something with her despite his reluctance, she dared to hope. For the first time in months, she believed they had a chance to get past the secrets and make things work.

Shame the same thing could not be said about breakfast. She stared down at her white empty plate. Noah stood outside talking with Gray and Dex about some subject she was sure would tick her off. Maybe she could convince one of them to take her to a fast-food place for something greasy and edible.

"You're in a good mood," Marie said as she sidled up to the food bar and ladled a spoon full of brown slop into a bowl.

Well, she *was* feeling fine. She bet that would fade in

about two seconds, or however long Marie planned to stay and talk.

"I'm not happy about this breakfast." Whatever happened to toast?

"The choices are very healthy."

"Okay."

Lexy glanced over at Marie's leotard of the day. Hard to miss the outfit, since it was bright pink and yellow and stuck to her body like skin. If eating this food every day was what it took to have a waist that tiny and a butt that firm, Lexy resigned herself to a larger size. She vowed to never complain about gaining weight again.

"Every dish has been chosen to detoxify the body and promote optimal energy."

No wonder Noah found the resort spiel so annoying. "Not very tasty, though."

Marie stared at her as if she were a squashed bug on a windshield. What her husband, Tate, or any other man on the planet saw in this woman was a mystery. Okay, men appreciated *those*, but breasts were about the only things this woman had going for her and she had to buy those.

"Tate told me you understood food's function as fuel."

Lexy was pretty sure she heard bitterness behind the other woman's tone. "I do, but every now and then the idea of a doughnut sounds good."

Marie's mouth dropped open. "Do you know what sugar does to your body?"

Marie followed up the question with a full-body scan. Her gaze wandered up and down Lexy's frame. Lexy thought about shoving the woman's face into a big bowl of green soupy stuff.

"I don't overindulge."

"Hmmmm."

Clearly Marie disagreed. That was okay. The dislike was mutual.

"If you'll excuse me." Lexy grabbed her mug of green tea and walked over to sit at the nearest table. She never expected Marie to follow.

"May I?" Marie asked the question after she pulled out a chair and sat down.

"Uh, sure."

Lexy looked around for reinforcements. People occupied three other tables. Two older women waved with a welcoming smile, but they did not make a move to come over and say hello. She couldn't blame them. She avoided Marie whenever possible as well. Hard to do that now when she sat across the table eating brown paste.

"Where is Tate today?"

The spoon stopped halfway to Marie's mouth. "I am not aware of his schedule."

Uh, okay. "I meant that I haven't seen him around."

And since the scene in Henderson's room, Lexy wanted to make sure Tate had not accidentally shot off his foot or some other important body part. She also wanted to do a temperature check just to see if Tate engaged in a little pillow talk with Marie about the, to borrow his favorite word, incident.

"Since I miss the walks, I thought maybe he could show me a good, safe trail to try instead."

"I'm surprised your sidekick would allow that." Marie clanked the spoon on the side of her bowl.

Sidekick? "You mean Noah?"

"Of course."

"He'll love that nickname."

"He strikes me as a very possessive man." Marie got all breathy as she made that assessment. "There is something very attractive and reassuring about a man like him."

That was enough of that. "He has his moments."

"A woman would know that she'll be taken care of with a man like that."

Not exactly how she looked at her relationship with Noah, but whatever. "I actually can take care of myself. Half the time I end up watching over him."

Marie smacked the spoon on the side of the bowl again. The noise echoed into Lexy's brain. One more tap and she'd grab the thing and bend it like a pretzel.

"You're a very lucky woman. Not all men are like yours." Marie stared at the far wall. "Some wallow in laziness, expecting you to do everything for them."

That explained the husband. "But you were lucky enough to find someone just like him."

Marie snapped out of her stupor. "What?"

"Your husband."

"Oh, yes."

Not exactly a ringing endorsement for the woman's better half. "Does he work here?"

"No." Marie snapped out the answer. The only good news is that she finally dropped her spoon.

"Did I see your man outside?"

"His name is Noah." Marie just sat there, so Lexy continued. "He's talking to my brother."

"Oh, the other one." Marie nodded. "Not as impressive as your man, but close."

Instead of folding up the spoon, Lexy decided she should bend it around Marie's neck. Apparently the bony chick liked the idea of Noah being all protective. Well, she could forget it. Noah was taken. If Lexy had to kick the aerobics instructor's ass to make her understand that fact, she would.

"I would have thought the two of you would be back in San Diego by now."

"Soon." Lexy sipped on her tea. The hot liquid warmed her throat as it went down.

"I'm just saying that Tate has enough issues without having to play host to all of your friends."

Well, well, well. "They're all paying for their rooms, Marie."

"That's not really the point. Tate is under a great deal of pressure. His mood is short and he barely gets a minute away, what with the reporters and police and angry guests."

Lexy guessed that meant Tate didn't have time for Marie. Now there was a shame. "Tate strikes me as a savvy businessman. He likely cares more about the cash than having a few more guests, especially since some people left after the murder."

"But not you."

Lexy took that to mean Marie wanted them to leave. "Detective Sommerville insists that we stay on here for a few more days."

"Because you're a suspect."

"Because a man died in my room."

Marie sat back in her chair and folded her arms across her chest. The move pushed her breasts up and over the top of her leotard. "And why is that, Ms. Stuart?"

"Excuse me?"

"How did you know Charlie?

Charlie. Interesting. "I didn't."

"It's just us girls. You can tell me if you were enjoying some of the local talent before your boyfriend arrived."

Right. Because Lexy felt *that* close to Marie. "I'd never met Henderson before I saw him facedown on my carpet."

"I see."

Since the woman was intent on being rude and nosy, Lexy decided to join in. "How well did you know him?"

"Who?"

"Henderson. I believe you called him Charlie."

The sour expression on Marie's face was not from the food. "Our jobs rarely had us in the same place."

How the hell was that an answer to the question? "Surely you have employee meetings, get-togethers, that sort of thing."

"I can't stick around for all of those activities."

"Why?"

"My husband."

Nice of her to finally remember the poor cuckolded bastard. "I haven't met him."

"Why would you?"

The pretense of friendliness disappeared in a flash. "Do you have a problem with me, Marie? I get the impression you don't care for me very much."

Marie's chair scraped against the floor as she got to her feet. "I make it a policy not to get close to the guests."

A fabulous parting line. But suddenly Lexy did not want Marie to have the final word. "I guess you prefer the men who work here."

A flush of anger washed over Marie's face. She looked as if she was about to unload a verbal attack. Then she glanced over Lexy's head. Whatever she saw had her watching her words. "It will be a shame to see you leave, Ms. Stuart."

Noah got to the table just after Marie stormed off. "Something I said?"

"She's a scary woman."

"What did she want?" He leaned down for a firm but quick kiss before sitting beside Lexy.

"She doesn't like me."

"I find that hard to believe." He glanced at Marie's left-over food and pushed the bowl to the other side of the table.

As far as Lexy was concerned, it was not far enough. The stuff stank. "Apparently she does like you. Very much."

"Aren't I the lucky guy?"

"In the rankings, you are ahead of Gray."

"That makes sense. I see it that way, too." Noah took a long drink from her mug, then made a face. "What the hell is this?"

"Tea."

"Is coffee forbidden here, too?"

"I think so."

"Stupid-ass resort." He shoved the cup back in her direction.

Enough food talk. She had something bigger in mind. "I think she was sleeping with Henderson."

"*What?*"

"She called him Charlie."

"So?"

"I detected a tone. It was like she was warning me off the resort and men here."

Noah smiled. "And that means?"

"She's a busy lady."

"Is there anyone she isn't sleeping with?"

"Not that I can tell."

"So this husband. Any news on him?"

"Sounds like a lazy bum."

He traced his thumb over the mug handle. "How did you come up with that assessment?"

"The way she talked about how some men are lazy bums."

"I leave you alone for ten minutes and you get all the dirt," Noah said.

"I'm good."

"Yes, you are."

She glanced around the room. They now were one of two occupied tables. Appeared no one was rushing to breakfast today. "What's up with the boys?"

"Dex's talking with the Scanlon folks. Comparing notes

and that sort of thing." Noah reached over and touched her hair. "Thanks for getting them on board."

"I told you. No one at Scanlon wanted to believe you were involved. They kept tracing and kept coming back to you and the company. Giving them another lead was as much a relief for them as us." She twisted in her seat to face him, resting her feet on the bottom rungs of his chair.

"Between the Scanlon experts and Dex, they'll follow the trail and figure it out." His fingers toyed with her small loop earring. "That leaves us with one problem."

"Henderson."

"I say we start taking a closer look at Marie."

Lexy made a face. "Do we have to?"

"The sooner we solve this, the sooner we go home and eat real food."

"Well, when you put it like that . . ."

Chapter Twenty-five

"Why are you digging into this?" Detective Sommerville threw her ever-present notebook down on the bed.

Noah watched it bounce and then land on the same spot where he made love to Lexy earlier. He fought off the urge to grab the thing and start reading. But fight he did. The detective carried a gun and a nightstick. A man did not test a woman with weapons.

Noah did have to smile at the officer's furious tone. He knew they were overstepping with the suggestion about investigating Marie, but he insisted to Lexy that they try to do this the *right* way first. The undercover option would be available if they needed it later.

The detective tried again. "I ask a question. What's your interest in this?"

"I thought that would be obvious," he said. "We're trying to give you suspects who aren't us."

"Which is what makes me skeptical."

Lexy paced the small area in front of the door, sending sparks of energy flying in every direction. "We're trying to help, detective."

Last thing he needed was two fired-up women in the

room. "We're passing the information on. That's all. It's up to you what you do with it."

The detective leaned against the bathroom door. "Why assist now? You two were not exactly open and honest with me about your relationship to Henderson. Getting you to answer questions has been a challenge."

He could see where she came to that conclusion.

"Believe it or not, we're not bad people." The frown on Lexy's face matched her sharp tone. She wanted to do something that proved otherwise. "Most people like us."

The detective smiled. "I don't believe that for a second."

"They like her, not me," Noah added.

"That I can believe."

Lexy scoffed. "Talk about ungrateful."

If she kept this up, they'd both be in jail. Noah spun into damage-control mode. "I think what my fiancée is so delicately trying to say is that you may question our motives, but we're trying to help."

"Let me understand this." The detective tapped her pen against her open palm. "You've been snooping around, asking questions, doing computer searches, and otherwise making this investigation difficult for the actual police working on it."

"That pretty much sums it up," Lexy said.

"You've been poking around and causing trouble, and you call that helping?"

She wasn't exactly wrong, so he did not try to deny it. "We're trying to figure out why a man who trained at our company showed up dead on Lexy's floor."

"I thought you didn't know Mr. Henderson."

Lexy stopped pacing. "We know who he is. That's it."

"Quite a coincidence that you all ended up at the same resort." The detective reached for her notebook. Being without it seemed to make her twitchy.

"If this is where you accuse me of murder, save it." His patience for being accused of criminal acts had expired.

"You'd rather I believe that the aerobics instructor killed Mr. Henderson."

That was easy. "Yeah."

The detective flipped pages until she found a blank one. "What would be her motive?"

"Sex." It was the best motive around as far as Noah could see.

Lexy frowned at his description. "We think she was fooling around with him. She's trying to downplay the relationship, but there was one."

Noah flashed Lexy a questioning look, which she promptly ignored. It was quite a leap from Lexy's previous sense that she heard a "tone" in Marie's comment about Henderson to envisioning them all over each other.

"I thought she was seeing the resort's owner behind her husband's back."

Seemed Marie was not doing a good job of keeping her affairs quiet. Noah wondered if the woman even cared. "It's only one small back, but there appear to be several men behind it." Noah did not want to even think about Marie's behind or any other part.

"I'm not sure where she had all this sex, but somewhere," Lexy added.

"She has a small apartment on the grounds." The detective dropped that interesting bit of information as if it was not a big deal.

"Why?" Lexy asked before Noah could get the question out.

"Tate said all the employees got them. Had something to do with changing and showering." The detective turned to Lexy. "Did she admit this other affair to you?"

When biting her lips didn't help, Lexy fudged. "Almost."

"Oh, that's convincing," Noah said.

"I'll take that as a 'no.' " The detective wrote something down. Noah tried to catch it, but could not see it. "She has an alibi for Henderson's murder."

"What is it?" Noah asked.

"If I tell you, will you stop pretending to be a policeman?"

Noah shrugged. "Maybe."

"At least you didn't lie to me."

"But I thought about it." He considered a lot of things. Getting rid of the detective. Getting out of town. Finding a decent lunch.

All of those sounded good. Unfortunately, he knew the rest of the day would be spent doing something very specific. Figuring out Marie's tie to Henderson. Now that Lexy had the connection in her head, that's all she would talk about. If he ever wanted to have sex again, he had to resolve this first.

"She was at a party near the dining hall. Several people reported seeing her there." The detective scanned her notes. "Before that, she taught a class and then had a meeting with Tate. I didn't ask about the subject matter of that meeting, but I can guess."

"That didn't happen." Lexy's hands were moving almost as fast as her mouth.

Noah could see her mind turning. She mentally examined the pieces and saw that they did not fit together. And she was right.

"You think all of those people lied for Marie?" the detective asked.

"I don't know any guest who would cover for her. Most of them can't stand her." From the distaste in her tone, it was clear Lexy was included in that group. "That's not the issue."

"What is?"

He knew this part. "We were in the dining room with Tate."

"Noah's right. We sat there talking, and Marie was nowhere around." Lexy ended the comment with a smug smile.

The detective ignored the attitude. "Was she in the dining room?"

"No."

"No or you don't know?"

"I know," Lexy insisted. "Marie isn't exactly someone who enters a room quietly and blends into the wall. She comes in with a flourish and makes sure everyone sees her."

Noah let Lexy take the lead with this one. She was doing too well to interfere.

"Marie came into the party and made sure everyone knew she was there. She waltzed around, saying hello to everyone and hanging on Tate."

The detective nodded. "Those were the reports we got."

"But before that she was nowhere around. She taught the class and then I didn't see her until she walked into the party."

"How long in between?"

"Over an hour." Lexy looked to him for confirmation of her memory, then continued. "And when she did arrive, she was wearing a different leotard from the one she wore to class."

Silence filled the room as the detective scribbled down a few notes. Noah used the lull to study Lexy. Excitement pulsed off her. She thrived on analyzing information and selling her story. Whether marketing a program or describing her theory of a murder, she did it with intelligence and flair.

"No one on the staff mentioned a relationship between Marie and Henderson. She makes her connection to Tate clear. Any theories on why she would hide the other?"

Noah and Lexy shared a smile over the detective's change in attitude. Suddenly she wanted their help.

"To keep both men happy," Lexy suggested.

"You came up with that excuse a little too fast for my liking," he muttered because the idea called for muttering.

"My point is that Tate is the boss. He's her ticket to more money, prestige, and possibly her way out of a bad marriage."

"The marriage is bad?" the detective asked.

Noah thought the answer to that one was pretty obvious. "The serial adultery didn't give that away?"

"Cheating does not always mean the end to a marriage."

"It does for me." That was a nonstarter for Noah. Marriage meant fidelity. Lexy cheating on him would result in bloodshed. He could handle a lot from her. Never that.

Not that he ever expected to worry about that issue. Lexy had faults. Infidelity was not one of them.

"I can see your point about her wanting to keep Tate happy. You have to wonder what that meant to the other men in her life," the detective said, clearly warming to the topic and idea of Marie as something more than a cheating spouse.

"Sounds like motive to me." Lexy's interest in the topic mirrored the detective's.

"Why, detective, did you just admit that we might not be the killers?" Noah joked.

"I'm sure I didn't say that." The detective pocketed her notebook and pen. "Now let me make something clear."

"This sounds bad," Lexy mumbled under her breath.

"This is a police matter. You are not to get involved or get in the way."

"Meaning?" Noah asked.

"Stay away from Marie until we know the specifics of her relationship with Henderson and whether or not she's dangerous."

"She's an aerobics instructor. What is she going to do, throw a weight at me?" Lexy did not try to hide her sarcasm.

"A man is dead."

Noah had to give the detective credit for a strong comeback. "Good point."

"Stay away from Marie." The detective's threat hung in the air.

"We heard you the first time." He did not intend to comply, but he heard her.

"Are you going to obey?"

"I have trouble with the word 'obey,' " Noah said.

Lexy delivered a half-choke, half-laugh. "He's not kidding."

"Do you have trouble with the word 'jail,' Mr. Paxton?"

Big trouble. "You made your point."

"Good."

Chapter Twenty-six

Lexy exhaled in relief the minute after the detective left. "That went better that I thought it would."

"She's listening. That's something," Noah said.

"Does this mean we're letting the police handle the situation and we're backing out?"

"Of course not."

She knew he would say something like that. "Do we have a plan?"

"Yep."

Uh-oh. "Is this going to tick me off?"

"Yep."

A terrible thought popped into her mind. "Are you going to be the bait?"

"Sort of."

"Come up with another plan." One that did not put him near a potential murderess who also happened to be a woman on the prowl. She knew enough about Marie to know she was dangerous, whether or not she ever killed anyone. "Now."

"Too late."

"How can it be too late? The detective left a half hour ago."

"I already developed the plan." He tapped his finger against his temple. "In my head."

"It must be rather lonely up there."

Noah's sexy smile lost some of its wattage. "That's not very charming."

She knew she going to regret this as soon as she said it, but . . . "What's this brilliant idea of yours? And lay the whole thing out. I don't want half the plan."

"I'll give Marie a reason to believe we have some information directly from Henderson."

Yeah, regret. "I don't get it."

"It's a brilliant plan."

"I still don't know what it is."

"Watch a master at work." He cracked his knuckles.

She had never seen him do that before. She'd be happy never to see him do that again. "You?"

"Of course me."

"Maybe I should just call the company lawyer now and arrange for bail money."

"Not a bad idea."

The man was completely infuriating. "So when do we launch this piece of brilliance?"

"Depends."

"On anything in particular?"

"Does Marie teach a class today?"

Lexy hated this plan more every second.

"Well?" he asked.

She glanced around the room looking for her resort brochure. Noah had picked up the area. Folded this. Put that away. The place was a mess, but less cluttered now that everything had a place.

"Stop touching my stuff."

"But I like touching your stuff."

"You know what I mean."

"I didn't have a choice, since I couldn't find the bed."

"I don't know where anything is," she said, trying to hide the anger in her voice. "You messed up everything."

He did not take the bait.

"Where did you put all the paperwork?"

"On the desk."

Fighting held some appeal, but she abandoned the idea in favor of getting this follow-Marie-around plan done. The sooner Noah was away from that one, the better. Oh, she trusted him with Marie. He had a disclosure problem, but his zipper stayed up around other women. Still, Marie gave her the creeps.

Lexy pulled out the aerobics class schedule. "She teaches in two hours."

"Perfect."

"I still don't know why."

"I have plans." His hands went to his belt buckle.

"And you have to be naked to do them."

"Oh, yeah." He lowered his zipper.

"What are you doing?"

"Burning through the next two hours. Want to help me?"

She did.

A little less than two hours later the memory of the mind-blowing sex with Lexy still lingered in Noah's mind. Something about the idea of his going off to meet Marie made Lexy even more flexible than usual.

And since the sight of Marie turned him off to sex or anything related to sex, Noah was grateful he had just enjoyed a fix. Now it was showtime.

He walked into the aerobics studio. Finding Marie was not hard. She wore the brightest costume he had ever seen. The thing was tight and psychedelic pink and utterly annoying, but it served the purpose of getting her noticed. Noah figured that was her goal.

He did not have to go up to Marie. She came to him. "Mr. Paxton."

"Call me Noah."

Her smile turned feral. Not exactly a turn-on in Noah's book. Kind of made him feel like prey.

"I still can't let you sit in on a class."

Time to lay on the charm. "I apologize for interrupting. I needed to find Lexy."

At the mention of Lexy's name, Marie's smile took on a nasty edge. "She's not here."

"Damn. And I have good news for her."

"Something personal, perhaps?"

Did Marie just throw her hair back over her shoulder? "About the resort, actually."

"About what specifically, if I may ask."

That's exactly what he wanted her to do. The woman walked right into his trap, as he knew she would. "I just talked to the police about the murder . . ."

"And?"

"Well, I don't want to bother you. I can wait to talk to Lexy. You have a class."

Marie did not let him take a step away from her. She grabbed on to his forearm and started whispering. "I'd love to hear the news. After all, I worked with Charlie."

"Of course."

"What happened to him was horrible."

She certainly did not sound broken up by the guy's death. If the way she had her hand wrapped around Noah's arm and her body stuck to his side was any indication, two more minutes and she'd be climbing all over him.

"The police finally have a break in the case."

The color drained from her face. "What is it?"

"Are you okay?"

"I'm very happy about your news." She stumbled over the words.

She was thrilled. He could tell. Right.

"Apparently Henderson—or did you call him Charlie? You know I never used the man's first name."

She almost crawled out of her skin. Her cheeks looked ready to burst. "You mentioned something about the police?"

"Right." He patted her fingers where they dug into his skin. "Seems Henderson kept a diary."

"Charlie?"

"Yeah."

"Do the police have it?"

"No. They found some crumpled pages in with his employee uniforms. They figure he hid the diary itself and it contains information that could lead them to his killer."

"Do they know where this diary is?"

Since it didn't exist, no. But he bet she would tear the resort apart looking for it.

"That's the odd thing. His room was pretty empty when they went to check it out."

"He did not own a lot of things."

Interesting how she felt the need to mention that when she insisted to Lexy she barely knew the man. "They figure he stayed with someone else at the resort most of the time. The plan is to search his room, including ripping out the wall if they have to, and then start checking other employee rooms just in case some of Henderson's stuff is in one of those. The diary is somewhere."

"When?" Marie barked out the question.

The high-pitched sound grabbed the attention of most of the ladies in the room. All three of them. The stared at her, then scowled.

Lexy was right. Marie was not a woman other women liked.

"Later tonight sometime."

He had decided to make the time line as tight as possible. Better to trap Marie fast. She would teach her class and then start looking. Noah bet that's how this entire scene would unfold.

Dex was waiting near Henderson's apartment just in case. Gray took Marie's apartment as a lookout. Noah would follow her just in case she had another place to check that they did not know about. Between the three of them, they would see if Marie panicked and went searching for the nonexistent diary.

The goal was to make the woman crack. See if she did have a tie to Henderson and then poke at it. Once they had her on the run, they could work on that angle. Give Detective Sommerville whatever background she needed to finish the job.

"I would like to talk to the detectives. Maybe I have some information that could help."

"Did you know Henderson well?"

"No." She gave a quick glance around the room and saw her class lined up and ready to go. "Do you know exactly what time the police plan to come by?"

"Detective Sommerville was not that specific, but I got the impression that they'd be here around dinnertime. Something about getting search warrants and that sort of thing." He reached into his pocket with his free hand. "I do have her number—"

"That's not necessary."

Of course not. "Well, I'll let you go."

Marie did not take the hint. She continued to hold on to his arm. Noah figured it was less about making a pass and more about being lost in thought.

"Marie?"

She jerked back. "Sorry."

"Enjoy the exercise."

Chapter Twenty-seven

Marie ended the class forty-eight minutes later. She gave the women a quick apology for the short session and then ran out of the room. Noah knew because he watched the entire scene. Peeking in windows and hanging out in doorways were not his usual ways to spend a day, but he had to admit there was a certain energy that came from sneaking around like this.

Instead of sticking around to shower or chat with the ladies, Marie left. She grabbed her bag and headed across the parking lot to the back side of the resort's campus. To exactly where the employee apartments were located.

She did not stop or linger. She did not hide her trail, either. Following was pretty easy, since she did not look around. Didn't even stop to say hello to the two employees who tried to stop her to engage in conversation.

With so few people staying at the resort, nothing blocked her path. She could make her way around with little hardship. Hiding was not easy, either. He did a lot of ducking behind buildings and kept a decent distance between them just in case.

Less than fifteen minutes later, she stepped onto Henderson's porch. Noah glanced around, checking the area for Dex. Wherever his friend hid, he did it well. Noah could not see him, anywhere. That meant Marie could not see him either.

But Noah had a clear view of Marie. He hovered at the far side of the dome-shaped building next to the one that housed Henderson's apartment. The sun beat down on him. Even dressed in a light polo shirt, his skin melted from the heat. Damn, but dry heat was still heat.

She took one last quick look around. Unlike Dex and Gray, she did not have to resort to breaking in. That was a key she slid into the lock. For a woman with no interest in the crime, she sure did have access to the dead man's property.

When she slipped inside, Noah came around the building, crossed in front of another one, and made his way to Henderson's apartment. The sight that greeted him almost made him laugh. Sure made him smile.

She stood inside turning over drawers, throwing whatever wasn't nailed down onto the floor, and generally doing nothing to hide her noisy search. Wood crashed. Something that sounded like breaking glass came next.

If there were a diary in there, she would have found it. Since it was all a ruse, all she did was make a mess. And prove that she had something to hide in relation to Henderson.

The plan worked. Well, except for the part where he ordered Lexy to stay out of the way and she ignored him. Noah did not see Dex. He did see his wayward and stubborn fiancée. She did a not-so-great job of hiding at the opposite end of the row of apartment domes.

When he locked eyes on her, she stared right at him as if daring him to say something. She probably figured he'd stay quiet and accept her presence without question.

Wrong.

With one last look inside at Marie, who was ripping down the ceiling tiles one by one, Noah stalked over to

Lexy. He stepped right in front of her. Had to put his hand over her mouth when it looked as if she was going to squeal.

"What's with the screaming? You saw me coming to get you."

"I didn't expect you to be so angry."

She had to be kidding. "I told you to wait in the room."

"I ignored you."

He took in a huge breath. It was either that or lose control completely. "Why are you here?"

"To help."

"Are you trying to get killed?"

"Don't be dramatic." Her frown turned into a smile. "I was right about Marie, wasn't I?"

The self-satisfied look meant trouble. If Lexy got the idea that running around causing trouble was a positive thing, he'd spend the rest of her life trying to protect her from herself.

"You're missing the point." And he assumed that was on purpose.

"What is she doing in there? Sounds like major reconstruction."

Since Lexy was ignoring his fury and did not seem particularly in the mood for a lecture, he gave up. There would be time for yelling later.

He suspected she knew that his actions were limited at the moment. She had the upper hand and they both knew it. Kind of hard to tail someone and remain out of sight if you stood ten feet away screaming your head off.

"You're leaving." He did not waver.

"Why?"

She was going to be the death of him. He was convinced of that fact now. "Lexy, do not test me on this. It is not safe for you to be here."

"Or for you."

"That's different."

"Because you're a man?" She snorted at the idea.

"Because . . ." He actually did not have a good reason why it was different. Probably did have something to do with his sex and superior ability to hide, but Lexy would discount those like she did everything else.

"That's what I thought. Stop acting like a bully." She did not bother to hide the satisfaction on her face.

"You are totally out of control."

Lexy grabbed his arm and dragged him to the side of the building.

"What are you—"

"Shhhh." She threw a hand over his mouth. He was so surprised, he stopped talking.

She took one last peek around the corner before she let go of him. "Marie has left the building."

"What?" He watched Marie's tight butt scurry back across the parking lot. "Where is she going?"

"Looks like she's headed for the main resort buildings."

"To her apartment."

"Not much of a surprise that hers is a small room near the main conference center, huh? The only apartment near Tate's house. How convenient."

"I'm sure there's some explanation about it being closer to the exercise facilities."

"Sure."

"One of the benefits of boffing the boss, I guess."

"Let's get going."

Noah made sure they hung back. Him getting caught was one thing. Allowing Lexy to get picked off was a different story. Besides, they were out in the open again.

Instead of taking the right and heading back to the aerobics room, Marie took a left and headed for her apartment.

Talking to the detective earlier provided this lead. Noah

never would have expected a married woman with a house in town to keep a separate apartment at the resort. Went to show how he kept underestimating Marie. Just when he thought she could not get any lower, she dug a hole and crawled right in.

Marie did not stop, either. Her legs whipped back and forth until she reached the hidden beige staircase that led to the second-floor area above the conference center. She took the steps two at a time to get to the top.

"How the hell are we supposed to follow her up there?" Lexy stood with her hands on her hips and stared up at the small window next to Marie's front door.

Knowing Lexy, she planned to climb up on the roof and lower her body down to peek into Marie's windows. He did not mention the possibility for fear she would try it.

"Good question."

"You didn't make a plan for this?"

"Like what, a hot-air balloon?"

Lexy took a step forward. "We could be quiet and go up—"

"No." He held her arm just in case she decided to make a break for the stairs.

"You didn't even know what I was going to say."

"Yeah, I did. The answer is still no."

"Now what?"

She sounded disappointed that there wouldn't be a shoot-out or something more dramatic. "We've proven our point. Let's find Gray and let him know what's going on."

"What point?"

Was he the only one who understood the plan? "That Marie had something to hide relating to Henderson."

"Oh."

When Lexy continued to look disappointed, he tried again. "Did you think we would catch her in the act of doing something criminal?"

"I was hoping for a confession."

A little investigating and the woman went Special Ops on him. "The heat is making you insane."

She ignored his observation. "I didn't see Dex back at Henderson's apartment."

"Because *he* knows how to stay hidden."

"I saved you from being smack in sight when Marie came out of the apartment." Lexy hit the back of her hand against her other palm with a crack to prove her point. "You could be a little more grateful."

"I wouldn't have been out of position and in the open if I hadn't seen you standing there where you were not supposed to be."

"I don't see it that way at all."

"Of course you don't."

"I didn't agree to stay hidden. You've got the wrong woman if blind devotion is what you want."

"What I want is for you to exercise some common sense."

She rolled her eyes, a gesture she knew he hated. "Are we going to fight all day?"

"Apparently."

She pointed past him. "There's Gray."

He turned around and followed her gaze. "And there's Sommerville, Lindsay, and four other officers."

"That's bad."

"Well, it's not good."

Detective Sommerville stopped right in front of them. "Mr. Paxton. Ms. Stuart. I see you both ignored my directions. Again."

"We're just taking a walk."

"Right."

"We're going up." Detective Lindsay called out his plans, then headed up the stairs to Marie's apartment with the other officers.

"What's going on?" Lexy asked.

Gray answered her. "They're here to arrest Marie and search her apartment. The detective dragged me out from behind that building over here."

"I was afraid we'd accidentally shoot him."

"Would that really be an accident?" Noah asked.

Lexy saw the entire situation differently. "So you did listen to us."

"We were investigating Marie before you came to me with your theories."

"Sure," Lexy mumbled.

"We decided to move this afternoon instead of waiting as we wanted to do." The detective aimed her comments at Noah. "We figured you two would do something dangerous and potentially ruin our chances of catching Marie before she could destroy any more evidence. Our timetable shifted to prevent a full-scale disaster."

"More evidence?" Gray asked.

"Seems Tate is not so trusting of his employees. He has security cameras stationed outside their residences. Those cameras caught Marie cleaning out Henderson's apartment yesterday."

Gray looked impressed with Tate's business ingenuity. "Score one for Tate."

"The guy's a pig."

Noah agreed with Lexy's assessment. "Why didn't any of those cameras catch the murderer going into Lexy's room?"

"Apparently Tate is less concerned about the guests and their security. There are cameras on the grounds, but not as many and not as prominently placed."

"That's ridiculous," Lexy said.

"He said seeing the cameras scare the guests. If they see the security, they think they aren't safe."

"As opposed to having a murder on the grounds?" Gray asked.

Noah understood Tate's philosophy. Didn't like him one bit, but got where the man was coming from. The guy wasn't all that deep. He had one worry: money.

"He's always worried about his bottom line. Upset guests mean fewer bookings and less money coming in," Noah added when Lexy remained unconvinced.

"Well, the camera near Ms. Stuart's room caught a figure entering her room. A small figure, but that's all we could make out." No notepad this time. The detective knew this information without help.

"You thought it was me," Lexy said.

"It was a logical conclusion to check into your background and see."

The apartment door opened and Detective Lindsay marched Marie down the steps. He grinned like a fool until he saw the small crowd gathered at the bottom of the steps. Probably figured it was time to act like a serious professional and put on his police face.

Marie had no compunctions about making a little noise. She was complaining and swearing. She blamed Tate and Lexy. Called them both some choice names. By the time she reached the bottom of the staircase, a few guests and employees stood around watching the scene. None seemed concerned about Marie being in trouble.

Noah did not see Tate arrive until he walked up behind Lexy and started talking. "She killed Henderson."

They all turned and stared at him. The man looked terrible. Messed-up hair and a stain on his shirt. Not at all Tate's usual look. From the dark circles under his eyes, the poor bastard looked as if he had not slept in a month.

Detective Sommerville took a step to the left to block Tate's view of his girlfriend being dragged off in handcuffs. "Tate has been very helpful. He made the security tapes available. Provided some background information and cleared up Marie's alibi. Marie's fingerprints in Ms. Stuart's room did the rest. She tried to wipe off the lamp, but she missed others."

The next hour moved by in a haze. There were questions. Reporters arrived at the resort. Lexy tried to comfort Tate, and Gray went to bring Dex back from Henderson's apartment.

Just before she left, Detective Sommerville pulled Noah aside.

"Good detective work," he said.

"I told you we know how to solve crime here."

"You do. Sorry if I made that harder." As an apology, it sucked, but he did have to admit that the police were on top of this one.

"What's next for you?"

The personal question struck Noah as odd. "A few more days here to wrap up and make sure everything's been handled, then back to work."

She nodded in understanding. Noah thought she would walk off, but she seemed to be coming to a decision in her head.

"Is there something you want to say to me, detective?"

"No." This time she turned away.

"Okay."

"Actually." She faced him again with a look more serious than before. "What are you going to do about your other problem?"

He figured she meant his engagement to Lexy. "I'm making progress."

"You shouldn't fool around with blackmail. Get someone in law enforcement to help you."

Her verbal bomb exploded in his head. "What did you just say?"

"We reviewed your phone records. Saw your e-mails. You didn't erase the more objectionable ones."

It never dawned on him that they would pick through his private life. One of the reasons he wanted to turn this thing around and take the spotlight off Lexy was to make sure his private life stayed private.

"How do you—"

"Our experts agree that someone is trying to frame you from the inside. Someone with computer access and a grudge."

"Did you tie the blackmail to Henderson?"

"No. We weren't looking to fix your situation. I'm just saying that something bigger is happening to you. I'd watch my back."

Computers. Access. Very few people fell into that group. That feeling of dread from his old life settled in his stomach. It had been years since the churning stole over him. But it was back in full force.

"Do you still have the papers you took from Lexy's room on the night of the murder?" he asked.

"Of course."

"Can I come to the station get them."

"I don't think they'll tell you anything."

Lexy said Henderson's initial paperwork was in that stack in the police's possession. He gave biographical information and took some initial aptitude tests. Noah wanted to see them. He had a bad, bad feeling. He needed to disprove it before it settled in his head and refused to get out.

"I'll be there in a few hours."

The detective stayed quiet for a few seconds. "I'll be there. And Mr. Paxton?"

"Yeah?"

"Come alone."

Chapter Twenty-eight

Lexy, Dex, and Gray sat around one of the resort dining room tables waiting for Noah to return with a late dinner. He went off to find some pizza or any other food they could eat without choking. They had invited Tate to join them, but he declined.

The activity had died down, but adrenaline still flowed through the room. Most guests had retired to their rooms or were in the main lounge gossiping about everything that had happened that day.

Detective Lindsay came back after the initial arrest and confirmed that Marie had confessed. He had since gone again. It appeared that Marie saw Charlie Henderson, one of her boyfriends, go into Lexy's room and got jealous. The combination of Henderson being away in San Diego where Lexy lived and his skulking around Lexy's room sent her anger at potentially being jilted running.

"I still say that detective is hot," Gray said as he lounged back in his plastic chair.

Dex laughed off Gray's boast. "She wanted to shoot you. I picked up on her intolerance for you the second I got there."

"You missed the good parts."

"There were very few good parts about today," Lexy said.

Noah walked in the empty room. "You can say that again."

His angry frown seemed out of place in their big celebration. And he didn't have any food.

"What happened to dinner?" Gray asked.

Dex agreed. "I'm starving."

Lexy knew something was wrong. Noah was not giving any of them eye contact. When Detective Sommerville slipped into the room behind Noah, Lexy knew she was right.

"What's wrong?" She got up from her chair and went to Noah's side.

"Noah? What's going on?" Dex sounded as concerned as Lexy felt.

She turned her fury on the detective. "You can't possibly still think we had something to do with the murder."

"Lexy," Noah placed a gentle hand on her arm. "It's okay."

Gray nodded at the folder in Noah's hand. "What's that?"

Noah stared down at the paperwork. The stare was so vacant. So lost.

"This is the evidence that shows Dex was behind the Scanlon theft. How Dex used Henderson."

Gray returned his chair legs to flat ground. "What?"

Lexy was as stunned as Gray. "Noah, you can't be serious."

"What the hell are you talking about?" Dex's chair slammed to the floor as he rushed to stand up.

Noah dropped the file on the desk. "Henderson came to us to learn advanced combat skills and try out some computer work. He never got to me. Dex, here, got to him first. Put him to work on what Henderson thought were simulated tests."

"You're insane." Dex swore under his breath and did not stop until the detective took a step forward with her hand on that gun.

Noah started pointing. Anger spewed in every direction.

"You used the guy. You showed him how to get information and infiltrate systems. The fingerprints eventually lead back to him, but they belong to you."

Dex put up his hands in a defensive gesture. "Look, you've had a rough few days. Hell, you've had a rough time since Lexy dumped you, but don't lash out at me."

Lexy wanted to get to the truth before the situation got any more confusing. "Noah, what is going on?"

"Dex has been blackmailing me."

"What?" Gray and Lexy yelled the word at the same time.

How could that be possible? She and Noah agreed to be open. He talked about his past. Blackmail was not one of those things a guy forgot to mention. If someone had been threatening Noah, she would know. He would not continue to pretend a piece of his life did not exist even when she asked him directly.

But he did. The truth was on his face. He was not doing anything to hide his emotions. He unleashed them all on Dex.

The realization was one more blow. To go from being so euphoric and relieved one minute to being knocked over with shock the next wreaked havoc on her body. Her stomach kept spinning until she thought it would fly out of her body, and her heart throbbed with pain.

"Was the idea to get me out of the way so I wouldn't find out about the theft, or did you actually intend to set me up all along?" Noah did not try to hide the hurt and fury in his voice.

"There's got to be a mistake. Another setup." Gray said the words, but it did not sound as if he believed them.

"Exactly." Dex knocked his fist against the table. "It's my turn to be set up."

"The Scanlon folks say someone has been covering his computer tracks during the past few days and making new ones that lead away from Mr. Paxton and directly to Henderson. They traced the movements to southern Utah." The detective delivered her information from her position at the door.

"What blackmail?" Lexy shouted out the question that pinged around in her brain.

A fresh flash of pain moved in Noah's eyes. "E-mails about my background."

"Since when?" Gray asked.

That's what Lexy wanted to know. How long had this been going on?

"The fact I never received any payment terms threw me off." His dark cold eyes meet Dex's. "I kept waiting to hear what you wanted."

Dex's eyes darted around the room. "It wasn't me!"

"Could Henderson have been doing the computer work?" Gray asked the detective. He was fully engaged and thinking now.

"He was already dead when all of this happened," Noah said.

With that, Lexy's last hope at a reasonable explanation died.

The detective turned to Dex. "And the resort security cameras caught you going into Henderson's apartment right after Marie left this afternoon."

Lexy's heart fell to her knees. So many lies and so much deception. "Dex?"

"I was curious, Alexa. That's all." Dex was all but pleading now. "You know me. I wouldn't do this."

"You were missing in action during the entire time we followed Marie and the police arrested her," Gray pointed out.

"I stayed in position."

"I don't get it, Dex. Why?" Noah's voice broke on the question.

"You have it all wrong."

Noah's shoulders were stiff enough to crack. "You stole from Scanlon. One of our customers."

"I give up. There's no talking to you right now. I'm not saying another thing." Dex sat down and crossed his arms across his chest.

"I think you meant to frame Henderson and something happened. Maybe you figured if you needed to do this again, you wouldn't have Henderson to blame, so you used me. Made me your security. Tried to tie me up so I wouldn't be in a position to argue or cast blame."

Gray dropped his head between his hands. "I can't believe this."

Lexy's body went numb. She stood there, drained and empty. Dex almost ruined their company. She could see the hate in his eyes as Noah talked. Every word Noah said was pulled out of him on a note of pain, but they made sense.

Only the blackmail part did not compute. They had been through so much. She thought he finally understood how she felt about secrets. He promised, maybe not in so many words but by opening up and starting a discussion. Implicit in all of that was the guarantee that they had moved beyond this secretive behavior.

"You know what? I'm out of here." Dex got back up and started for the door.

The detective blocked his exit. "No, you're not."

"You can't hold me."

"I actually can. Scanlon is pressing charges. The California police have asked us to hold you."

The nightmare got worse and worse. Every thought in Lexy's head turned to mush.

"Noah, don't do this." Before Dex could touch Noah, the detective grabbed his hand and slapped a cuff on him.

"Mr. Paxton isn't doing anything. In fact, he's refused to

press charges against you. But I'm hoping he changes his mind." The detective nodded to Noah, who nodded back. "We'll be at the police station."

"I'll be down in a few minutes." Noah's voice, usually so loud and sure, sounded flat and emotionless.

The detective shoved Dex outside before any of them could react or Dex could complain.

The shock of the moment descended on the silent room.

The ripples were what nearly killed her. Noah being blackmailed. Noah not telling her.

"You okay?" Gray asked Noah.

Lexy knew the question should have come from her, but she did not have the voice to ask it.

"Not really." Noah did not sound any better than he looked.

She was so torn up inside. Standing next to Noah, she wanted to hold him. Tell him everything would be fine and that Dex's betrayal was not just one of the many he had suffered in his life.

But she could not manage any of that. All that ran through her mind was a lifetime of these moments. How many times would she sit there and find out some huge chunk of Noah's life by accident, or through a third party, or after the fact?

"Blackmail?" The word sounded strained even to her ears as she said it.

"It's a long story." The exhaustion was clear in Noah's voice.

"One you didn't see fit to tell me."

Noah waved her off. "Not now, Lexy."

His words lit a match to her temper. "Then when, Noah? Someone threatened you and you kept it quiet."

"It wasn't—"

"Do not tell me it was unimportant. You had been framed

for a theft. A man was killed practically in front of us. We finally open up about all of it and you still didn't think that a little piece of information about someone making your life miserable, someone blackmailing you, was important enough to share?"

"Not the sharing bullshit again." He rubbed his forehead.

"Again? The problem is still, not again."

"I made a call that I could handle it alone. I wanted to find out more information before I told you and Gray."

"You knew it wasn't us, right?" Gray rose to his feet until all three of them stood around the round table.

"Of course."

"Then what the hell was the problem with sharing?" She was screaming now. "This wasn't about a past that didn't matter. This was about our future. The here and now."

"I had it under control." Noah made the statement through clenched teeth.

"That is your excuse for everything."

"Lexy, maybe now isn't the best time." Gray reached out for her arm, but she shrugged it away.

She was far too angry, her nerves too on edge and jumpy, to be touched. "You just can't do it, can you?"

A red burn lit up Noah's cheeks. "What?"

"Tell me the whole story."

"You don't think that maybe, just maybe, you're blowing this situation out of proportion?" Noah's temper matched hers now.

"Okay, what information am I allowed to know about the man I'm sleeping with, Noah? The man I'm supposed to be marrying? What do you deem appropriate for me to know."

"I thought you broke off our engagement." His hit landed a solid blow.

"Smartest thing I ever did,"

"Christ, Lexy."

She heard Gray's muttering and ignored it. Her full focus was on Noah. That handsome face pulled tight with tension and the fists clenched into balls as he fought with his internal anger. He was the problem this time. There were no excuses like classified information or forgetfulness or even irrelevance. He hid a huge secret from her. One that threatened their safety and future.

And he still didn't get it. He never would.

An ache filled her body. She shook from head to foot. She couldn't do it. As horrible as the idea of walking away from him was, she could not live her life this way. Not anymore. The endless rounds of secrets. She had done that her whole life. He knew that. He just refused to accept it.

There could not be a future for them if he could not be honest about even his present. "I'm done, Noah."

"What does that mean?"

"I could figure out a way to accept that you needed to keep parts of your past to yourself. You convinced me that was okay. But this is different. This is you hiding things that affect me and that are happening as we speak."

"I can't battle you over this subject now."

"Not now or ever." She swallowed the tears that threatened to swamp her. "We're done."

"What?"

Gray shook his head. "Lexy, don't."

"You made your decision. Being in control and secretive is the most important thing to you. Even more important than I am."

"You're going to run again." Noah's voice stayed flat.

She shook her head. "No. I'm going home."

Chapter Twenty-nine

Lexy walked into her brother's corner office just before noon two weeks later. The floor-to-ceiling glass behind his cherry desk provided the perfect target in case she decided to throw him out the window. And she was considering that option.

She glanced out at the distant ocean as she plunked her portfolio down on his uncluttered desktop. "You summoned me."

Gray's hands froze on his computer keyboard, then he started typing again. "Yes, I did."

When she delivered an "ahem," he spun his chair around and faced her. "Care to tell me why you demanded an in-person appearance?"

"You wouldn't answer your phone."

Not that he was the only who got that treatment. She did not answer for anyone. "I've been busy."

"I stopped by your house and you pretended not to be home."

"Maybe I wasn't there." When Gray shot her a you've-got-to-be-kidding look, she tried again. "What, a woman can't have a social life?"

What she really wanted was to be left alone. She loved her brother, but knew his loyalty to both of them and friendship with Noah would compel him to lobby on Noah's behalf. She did want any part of that sort of pressure. Not when her body hovered on the verge of flying apart.

"You're telling me you're dating now?" Gray asked.

She wanted to say yes and end the conversation right there. "I have female friends."

"The bottom line is you were ignoring me."

"So you threatened to call a board meeting?" It was actually his vow to drag their parents over to her house for a long chat that got her up, in a suit, and over to the office.

"I needed you to come in today."

"Tell me what was so pressing that you had to mobilize the National Guard." She threw out her hands and felt her now too-loose skirt slip down on her hip. "What is so important? I'm here. Tell me."

He picked up his pen and laced it between his fingers. "And you brought along your nasty attitude, I see."

If he thought this was bad, he knew less about women than she thought. This version could talk business. Could function and answer a phone. The one who slept on her couch in order to avoid inadvertently inhaling Noah's scent in her bedroom was the one with the real problem.

"No more games, Gray. Why am I here?"

She preferred to be anywhere else. All those days without seeing Noah had taken a toll. Eating became an afterthought. Going out with friends did not even dawn on her as an option. Her mind wandered. Her heart felt as if someone grabbed it with two hands and squeezed until it exploded.

And all of that desperation came without seeing Noah. She dreaded the possibility of running into him in the hallway or anywhere else in the building. Emotional survival turned out to be a minute-to-minute ordeal. If she physically stood within touching distance of him, with her will weakened and mind scrambled, the rest of her might just wither into a dried-up piece of nothing and blow away.

"You look like hell." The comment came out as a fact. Gray did not sound upset or worried about it, either.

Like she needed that news bulletin. "I have work to do."

"Such as?"

Well, nothing. William had stepped in and taken over most of her work as she strained to function on at least a minimal level. "Client meetings. New proposals and plans. My company's business is booming."

"Interesting."

"You never thought so before." She went for snappy because that's how she felt in the inside, raw and sitting on the edge just waiting for someone to doubt her.

Gray tilted his head to the side and eyed her up. "Are you looking for a fight?"

Yes. "I'm not a child."

If she could verbally slap someone around for a few minutes, maybe something would ignite inside her and swallow up all that emptiness.

"You have work to do, sis." His phone rang, but he ignored it.

"Didn't I just say that?"

"What about this company and your responsibilities here?"

No way. "William is working on—"

"*You* have a PR campaign to develop and sell to Noah. That's your job. That was the deal."

Hearing his name sent a shiver rumbling around in her chest. "Still matchmaking, Gray?"

"Hell, no." Gray threw down his pen and came around his desk to lean against the front edge in front of her. "Believe it or not, I learned my lesson."

"Doesn't sound like it."

"Alexa."

"What?" She did not realize her hands had balled into fists until Gray took one into his palm.

"Christ, look at me."

She did. "What?"

"Are you okay?"

"I'm fine."

The stern businessman morphed into the concerned brother. His brows fell and his quick, rude responses fell away. "You're hiding again. Cutting yourself off."

Tiny pieces. Losing Noah crushed her heart into tiny pieces. She kept waiting for them to fall and crash to the floor.

"I'll survive." That she could stand up and form sentences was a bit of a miracle compared to the weepy mess that left Utah.

Gray dropped his hand. "That makes one of you."

The matchmaking crap reached up and smacked her in the face. Sure, Gray loved her and was trying to protect her. But he wanted her with Noah and never stopped pushing that agenda.

"I'm not interested in a reconciliation or being chased down, or any other scheme you're working on in that brain of yours." She tapped her finger against his forehead for emphasis.

"I told you. I'm sticking to the security business. Someone else can handle the dating business. It's a thankless job as far as I can tell."

Lexy knew the resulting silence would not last. Gray had something else to say. He *always* had some other point to make. That tic in his cheek meant the words were piling up in there just waiting to come out . . . and bite her.

Gray glanced at his expensive watch. "You have a meeting in five minutes."

And there it was. The Grayson Stuart bombshell.

"With?" But she knew the answer.

The only difference between this time and Gray's previous attempts to throw her back together with Noah was the absence of a gleam in Gray's eyes. Except for bursts of frustration, his affect remained flat.

"Didn't we go over this a minute ago? It's time to nail down the PR campaign. We need your ideas. You need Noah's input."

"Let me keep this simple." She picked up her portfolio. Almost knocked Gray in the head with the corner of it and wished for a second she had. "No."

"This isn't a request, Lexy."

What was left of her heart fell to the floor. "Excuse me?"

"The proposal we all worked out for this campaign months ago included a date by which you would get started. It's here. It passed, actually."

"Sorry, but I was dealing with a murder in another state."

"Yeah, and I was dealing with the fallout of having a criminal for a business partner."

Guilt flashed over her. She lost Noah, but Gray and Noah lost a good friend and partner. Dex killed something special when he bargained their trust for quick cash. A mutual business relationship that allowed Gray to find a few hours outside of the office fizzled. With Dex gone, Lexy wondered how Gray managed the workload and how he handled the emotional turmoil that came with that kind of a personal blow.

"I'm sorry about Dex."

Gray's cheeks hollowed as his skin pulled taut around his mouth. "Not important."

"Of course it is."

His phone started ringing again. The high-pitched sound rang in her ears, then seeped into her brain.

"Are you going to get that?" Hell, she almost reached for the thing.

"No."

"Someone keeps calling. Your assistant clearly thinks this person is important enough to put through to you." If he picked up the phone, she could walk out without too much argument.

"One of the benefits of being in charge is the ability to decide which calls I take. This one can go to voicemail."

"You don't know who it is."

"I don't care."

"In my office, we answer the phone." Back when she went in to the office.

"Good for you."

The fight sparked to life inside her. "You don't have to be a jackass. Or should I say a bigger jackass."

"Save the indignation, sis. It's not going to work." He waved her off. "The most pressing issue is the PR campaign. A lot of company resources and money have been invested. We need to get started. You've stalled long enough."

She wondered how stark and angry her brother would look with her portfolio stuffed down his throat.

Fine. Two could play at this game. It was not as if Gray was the only one with the family's controlling gene. "I'll have William call and make an appointment with Noah."

"William is busy."

"He works for me." For some reason the men in this office kept forgetting that little fact.

"Your company is on retainer to Stuart Enterprises."

She negotiated the deal. She knew the fine print. "Do not treat me like a contractor."

"I'm trying to treat you like a professional." Gray tucked his pen in his shirt pocket. "We have a contract. Hell, you're the one who insisted you needed a contract when dealing with family."

Because she feared her brother would be overly favorable to her despite her wanting to be treated like anyone else who did not own a piece of the company.

Boy, did she get that one wrong.

"That does not mean you own me or my employees," she insisted.

"I disagree. I've assigned William elsewhere."

"You did what?" She left a space between each word, spoke nice and slow, to make sure he understood her position on this matter.

"He's working on damage control after the Dex situation. The last thing I need is for clients to get word that our trainers and employees are not trustworthy. It's a potential disaster."

Since when did William listen to anyone but her? "William does what I tell him to do."

"We can argue about that later, but today he's not here. You are. You have intimate knowledge of the family business, not to mention a financial interest as a shareholder."

"This—me and Noah—is never going to happen, Gray. We're over. Not that it's your business, but there's no way to make the relationship work. Not when our priorities are so different."

"This is business, and you have four minutes to get to your meeting."

Her fingers ached from the death grip she had on the leather portfolio. "I can't believe Noah agreed to this."

"Noah is expecting William."

The news slapped at her. "Then he should get William."

Some small part of her figured that Noah stood behind this maneuver. Finding out he was as clueless to all this planning as she was should have been a relief. Instead, the realization hollowed her out even further.

Gray crossed one ankle over the other. "I want the best for this company, and that's you."

"Why should I?"

"Other than because your big brother asked?"

"Yeah. Other than that."

"Because if you really intend to move on, you should move on with dignity. Don't slink away from the family business this time. Stand up, stake your claim to what's yours, and do your job."

All good advice. When she was solidly back on her feet, she would work on that plan. Maybe in two or three years.

"Noah won't like it."

"Noah won't say anything."

The idea of a silent noncomplaining Noah struck her as odd. "Why?"

"Go see for yourself."

Chapter Thirty

Five minutes and a trip to the bathroom later, Lexy stood at the door to Noah's office. His assistant already told her to go in. No chitchat or girl talk like they used to do while she waited for Noah to finish a meeting or get off an important call.

This time, the older woman had taken one look at Lexy and nodded to her boss's door with a simple "he's in." Looked as if she was the bad guy in the situation. Again. Noah broke her heart and everyone sided with him. She had no idea how that kept happening.

With a deep inhale, she squared her shoulders and knocked on the door.

"Come in," came the muffled reply.

When she stepped into the large airy office, the one with the navy walls and furniture she picked out and arranged, memories assailed her from every direction, both fiery and comfortable. How they sat and talked as they ate lunch at his desk. How they made love on that same surface. Even the sweetest moments pricked her with pain as she remembered them.

Then she realized she was alone.

The door to the adjoining bathroom stood open. A sliver

of gray suit pants was visible in the light from the opening. "I just need a second, William."

Gray had not lied. Well, not about this. Noah really did expect a meeting with William.

"No rush," she said.

At the sound of her voice, Noah's head popped around the door frame. "Lexy?"

"I'm here for the meeting."

He stepped into the doorway wringing a crumpled towel in his hands. She figured she caught him in the middle of washing up.

"I see." That was all he said.

The towel remained wrapped over his fists, but she could see everything else about him. The mischievous spark that lit his eyes and so attracted her the first time she saw him years ago was gone. A deep frown marred his otherwise strong face and solid jaw. He looked tired. Sad.

Every emotion crushing her could be seen on his face. In his dull skin.

"What happened to William?" Noah asked in a tone as flat as his demeanor.

"Gray."

"What?"

Whatever scene Gray planned, he planned it alone. From Noah's frown, she could tell he was as in the dark about this situation as she was. "Gray insisted I take this meeting."

If possible, Noah's face fell even further. "Your brother's a stubborn ass."

"Do you expect me to disagree?"

"No."

"He insists he's not matchmaking."

Noah smacked his lips together. "And Gray never lies."

She had to smile at that. "Yeah, I know. I didn't get to

pick my sibling. Blame my parents. Gray is one more strike against them, I guess."

Noah motioned for her to take a seat in one of the mission-style chairs in front of his desk. "You may as well sit."

Was it possible he was even less enthusiastic about this situation than she was?

"Since I didn't know I was coming in today for this meeting, I don't have the specifics about the PR campaign." She didn't have anything. Only William got things done in the office right now. She was too busy mourning the loss of the man sitting at the desk in front of her.

"Did William pass my report to you?" Noah asked.

"Uh, no?"

Noah reached into the credenza behind him. "I wasn't sure what information you needed to set up the marketing and PR."

She had trouble getting up in the morning and he spent the same time making impressive files. Life sucked. She flipped through the folder he put in front of her, but did not see anything but a smear of black where the words should be.

"Then there's the added question about whether or not we should hold off and put some time and distance between the company and Dex's situation." Noah winced over his former friend's name.

She thought she heard a brief fumble in his voice as well. For a guy with a practiced serious look and determination to plow through the business in front of them, something terrible bubbled inside him. They were connected enough for her to know it. Feel it. To ache for him.

"I'm sorry about Dex." The comment came out as a whisper because resentment and pain backed up on her over Dex's actions.

And she was one step removed. She did not consider Dex

a best friend. Didn't spend hours with him. Trust him, work with him, and believe in him. She wondered what that sort of harsh betrayal did to a man like Noah. He lived by a strict code of right and wrong. His upbringing scarred him. In a way, warped him.

"He finally confessed. He set up Henderson and me." Noah broke eye contact and went back to his credenza. "I found some old marketing plans you put together for—"

The all-business attitude broke her will. She wanted to be strong and not care, but she was not that person. She loved him too much to play this odd role.

"Stop." The word came out as a whisper.

He swiveled back around. "Huh?"

"That's enough."

He had the nerve to look confused. "You lost me."

"What are we doing here?"

"Work." No compromise there. The word practically snapped out of him.

"We can't sit here and pretend nothing has gone on between us. The two of us trying to conduct business is ridiculous."

"You walked into *my* office. I'm trying to be professional about this. Trying to maintain some semblance of a regular meeting."

The coldness of his voice and actions killed her by inches. "We have too much history to act as if we don't."

He stared at her, not saying a word.

"What?" she asked.

"I'm just sitting here."

That was the worst part. He acted as if he did not care about her or anything she said. The only thing he let her see was a blank face and a stern expression. He treated perfect strangers with more warmth.

"What do you want from me, Lexy?"

Everything. That was the problem. She wanted him to put her first and not push her into an adult life filled with secrets and misplaced protectiveness. She had done that for too many years already.

"We have to figure out a way to work together," she said.

He rubbed a hand over his face. For a second, his rigid composure broke and she saw a brief glimpse of the compassionate, loving man who got treated her to a lavish dinner with champagne before getting down on one knee to propose. Then his face closed up again, leaving her standing on the outside looking in.

"You know what?" He tapped to his desk. "We can't. You were right to put William on this project."

So it was up to her to walk away and make herself scarce at the office. "We should be able to keep business separate from our personal relationship."

"That's not going to happen." His lips flattened. "There's a limit to what's possible."

The realistic and intelligent part of her agreed with his assessment. Some deeper dying part needed him to acknowledge that the situation was killing him the same way it was killing her.

She hit her fists against her knees in an attempt to bring all of her crazy thoughts back under control. "We care about each other."

His mouth dropped open. "Care? That's the word you're using to describe how you feel about me?"

She closed her eyes on a waved of pain. "I never denied loving you, Noah. That was never the issue."

"No. The problem was that you didn't love me enough."

His words flew at her out of nowhere and landed like a punch right to her stomach. The breath actually rushed out of her.

How in the world had he come up with such a wrong answer to what happened to them? This amounted to something more than a communications issue. "That's not true."

"Of course it is." He relaxed back in his chair even as his voice rose with anger. "Your love was conditional."

"No. Absolutely not." She wanted to scream the denial.

"You loved me only as long as I did what you wanted, when you wanted. When I broke with the plan you had in your head of how a fiancé should act, you left me."

He had the facts tangled and rearranged.

"I didn't—"

"You left me, Lexy. Not once, but twice." His voice trembled from the force of his words.

Their fights unfolded in her head in a very different way. She was trying to protect herself. To prove a point to him so that they could have a meaningful future together.

He gave her a sad smile. "You walked out of my life when I did something that disappointed you."

Once he started talking, emotion spewed out of him. From the tense way he held his body to the tight clench of his jaw, she could see how much the conversation cost him.

"You make me sound like a petulant child."

"You made me feel disposable."

The weight of his words crashed down on her head. "That's not how it was."

"It's exactly what happened." His eyes grew huge with a mix of fire and rage. "I blamed myself. I kept thinking if I changed, you would stop leaving me."

A sob rushed up her throat, but she choked it back. As she heard the words, she could almost see him work it all out in his mind. As the thoughts entered his head, he threw them at her. It was as if he did not realize how hurt he was until he started talking.

"We saw things differently. Things that didn't matter to

me, for whatever reason, mattered to you. When I didn't immediately see that, I got punished."

He made her sound so horrible. So little and petty. The more he spoke, the less sure of her position she became, but she rushed to defend her actions anyway. "The issue was trust."

"Did you ever really not trust me?" He shoved his chair back hard from the desk. "Really? Ask yourself."

She did not know if he wanted space or was just staving off the violence running through him. "My trust was not in question."

"Neither was mine. You had it from the beginning. I didn't question your parents or their odd behaviors. I supported you in your career and in therapy."

"Noah, come on. You wouldn't share any information with me. Then when you did, you still held back this huge secret about being blackmailed. After our deep discussion at the resort, you went back to acting the same way."

"So you walked out."

"I had to."

He stood up and turned his back to her. She could see his face in the window. Gone was the strong man who never broke down. Anguish, heartbreak. In that moment, she saw each emotion play across his face.

"No, Lexy. You chose to leave. You decided my love for you was not enough. That I couldn't change, or maybe that I wasn't worth the wait to see if I could."

She did not think her heart could splinter any more.

She was wrong.

"It sounds as if I'm not the only one who felt betrayed," she whispered the realization more to the room than to him.

"You're just now getting that?"

"You never said it before."

"Because I hoped I was wrong." He turned back to her with his mask of indifference firmly back in place. "You made it pretty clear how easy it is for you to leave me behind."

Her heart broke. This time, it broke for him. "It was never like that."

"It was only like that."

"You see everything in such black-and-white terms. Life is about gray."

"Not this. There's never been anything about my feelings for you that had to be hid in the shadows or explained or muted. Black-and-white. Love and trust or not." He visibly forced his fingers to unclench from the back of his chair. "You made your decision. I made mine. Unfortunately, we made different choices."

"You've thought about this a great deal."

"It's been a long two weeks." He looked down at his hands.

The longest and worst of her life. "What should I have done?"

"I don't understand what you're asking."

"You say I ran."

"That's not up for debate. I wasn't at that damn resort in Utah for a vacation."

He was right.

Her knees buckled, but she managed to stay on her feet. She failed to fight for him and refused to stick it out. The entire thing—the trip to Utah, the fights—all revolved around her needs. Her security depended on him acting a certain way. The demands she placed on him did not really have anything to do with him. They related to her and her anger at her parents. Yet she put it all on him.

It all made sense now. His history with Karen taught him to provide only happy news. His time in the military and government showed him how to separate out the parts of his life so he could handle them. His parents taught him that love came with a price.

And she broke his heart. That she had the power to do so stunned her, but watching him now, she knew. The man standing there, so firm and unbending, looking at her with hate in his eyes. She did this to him. Everything and everyone that came before her took him down one trail and she failed to help him see another.

The joking Noah turned back into that cold man everyone else saw when he started at Stuart Enterprises. He changed for her, maybe even for them, and earned the respect of every doubter. Now he had changed back to the cool operator who focused only on work and kept the softer side of himself locked away.

"I handled everything wrong." She knew that now. Felt it with bruising clarity down to her toes.

"You gave up."

"I didn't know what else to do." That was the truth. She kept running into walls. How many times could she bang into concrete before she got smart and walked around the wall?

"You could have changed me."

Whatever answer she expected, it was not that one. "What?"

"You taught me everything else, including how to love again without worrying about failure or . . ."

Then she taught him that love inevitably died. Her path to the wrong way stood out, so easy for her to trace. "And?"

"You could have cared enough to teach me to be the man you needed me to be."

Chapter Thirty-one

As soon as the words left his mouth, Noah wanted to catch them and drag them back. He could not go down this road with her. They did not understand each other. Watching her walk away from him a second time taught him what he always suspected was true. That he could not hold on to a woman like Lexy.

He eased his grip on the back of his chair. Much harder and he would puncture the leather. Not that he cared. Not that the office would be his much longer anyway. He could not stay here. Could not be this close to everything he ever wanted and not attain it.

As soon as he launched this new division, he would start to back out and rebuild his life elsewhere. He owed Gray and the Stuarts the guarantee to finish what he had started. They took a chance on him and accepted him without limits. Something more than his former fiancée ever did. He would repay that debt to the rest of the Stuart clan before he moved on.

"I'll call William and make an appointment to go over the plans." Hell, he would meet with anyone if that meant Lexy would get out of his office.

"No."

"What?" He looked at her then. Truly looked at her.

For a woman who finally made the break from him, she sure as hell did not appear happy about the fact. Her usually rosy cheeks now seemed hollowed out. She had lost weight. Fatigue pulled at her.

"Are you sick?" he asked, even though he did not want to care.

"Forget about William and the campaign and work." She dropped the portfolio she had been holding and stepped forward until she stood just on the other side of his desk.

If she came any closer, he would lose it. His temper wanted to rage until he inflicted as much hurt on her as she had on him. The only thing preventing him from unleashing was a thin barrier of decency.

"Noah."

He held up a hand to stop whatever she intended to say. "Don't do this."

"Noah, please."

He could not handle this confrontation. Not now. Not on zero sleep, and when his insides were rubbed raw. "I can't argue with you about this anymore."

"Then don't." Unshed tears shimmered in her eyes.

Not crying. He could not tolerate seeing her cry. "You should go."

"I want to stay."

What the hell was happening here? "Your signals are all over the place. Whatever you want from me, I can't give it to you."

She walked around the desk, to his safety zone, and brushed her palm down his arm.

He felt the gentle touch from the inside out. "What are you doing?"

"Talking to you."

"Do it from over there or by phone." He rubbed his forehead. "Look, I don't understand why you're doing—"

"Apologizing."

He shook his head to make sure he understood what she just said. "Did you just—"

"I'm sorry." She tugged on his arm until he turned to face her. "You're right."

His head started spinning. "About?"

"I abandoned you."

He had to be dreaming.

She lifted her hand to his cheek. Without thinking about it, he leaned in to her touch. The feel of her skin against his both soothed and burned him.

And her smell. That soft fragrance that scented her skin had played in his head every damn night since Utah. Now, with her standing just inches away, it filled his head until it possessed him.

"I don't understand." The whispered admission came out before he could stop it.

"That's my fault."

"Since when are you taking the blame for anything that's gone wrong between us?"

Her eyes blinked shut. When they opened again, the pain and sadness were there for him to see.

Since he walked out of the bathroom and saw her standing there, all he could think about was the hurt she inflicted on him. He gave her everything and she brushed it off and walked away. The roiling anger and frustration piled up inside him in the two weeks since they parted until he did not have room for anything else.

"I deserved that." She nodded her head when he started to talk. "No, I do. I was concerned with what I needed. I ignored your needs. I get that now."

"I only needed you. Ever."

"Past tense?"

He could not walk down this road again only to have her

turn around and leave him. "What do you want me to say, Lexy? I've never hid my feelings for you."

"Don't do it now."

But now was the one time he had to resist her. Just as he started to explain, she kissed him. A soft brush of her lips over his, but the caress was enough to burn through his resistance. Instead of pushing her away as he vowed to do every night as he sat alone in his house during the last two weeks, he pulled her close.

Fire raced through him as he grabbed her close and kissed her back. Lost in her scent and her mouth, he barely felt her arms come up to rest on his shoulders.

As the kiss went on, love and sorrow poured through him. But the feelings were not his, they were hers. He lifted his head. "What are we doing?"

"Starting over." She brushed her thumb over his lips. "I love you."

In the past, those words meant everything. Now they raised skepticism. Made his chest ache with uncertainty. "As you once told me, loving each other has never been the issue."

A small smile turned up the corners of her mouth as she studied his face. "Let me ask you this."

"What?"

"Can you try to let me in?"

"You were in." He said that over and over, but she refused to believe it.

"I mean emotionally. Telling me everything and not just what you think I need to know or can handle. An actual full sharing of our lives and fears, hopes, and dreams."

"I thought we were."

"I'm about to punch you."

He choked out a laugh. "That's romantic."

Her fingers speared into his hair in the way that always turned him weak and had him looking for a bed. Despite everything, this woman still held the power to bring him to his knees and make him reassess every promise he ever made to himself about staying in control.

"You still hold back, Noah. You love me, but treat me like you could lose me at any minute."

"Gee, I wonder why," he said in his driest tone.

This time she pinched him. "I'll take responsibility for my part of this."

"Which is?"

"Running when I should have stayed and fought for you."

She had never admitted that before. For the first time, she owned up to her propensity in her personal life to deal with facts straight on rather than try to whitewash reality. "That sounds about right."

"But you have to accept your part."

"Which was?"

"Pushing me into running."

His brain screamed out in denial. He wanted to explain for the hundredth time how his past did not matter, but he knew that was not true. He kept trying to sell the line, but no one bought it.

Sure, the details of his past were irrelevant to his life now. But who he was stemmed from those experiences, and the way he learned to deal with it all was keeping him from being with Lexy. He needed to own part of that. Even though he would rather blame her for not moving on, he had to take a second and wonder if he had really progressed as far as he always thought.

But there was a bigger issue at work here. "I can't worry that you'll walk out the door every single time I tick you off."

"I'd be walking a lot if that were the case."

"I'm serious." Dead serious. He could not think of anything more important than this point.

"So am I." She kissed his chin. "I'll make a deal with you."

The synapses in his brain continued to misfire as he struggled to keep up with her changing moods. "What?"

"You agree to live a little in the gray area. To not compartmentalize your life so I'm here." She pressed one hand against one shoulder and the opposite hand against the other. "And you're here."

The knot across his shoulders eased a bit. "And in return?"

"I'll stay and fight."

A lightness flooded through him. He could not identify the feeling, but for the first time in days he felt the weight crushing him into the ground lift. "Why does there have to be a fight?"

"Oh, with us there will be fighting." She pretended to frown, but her mouth kicked up in a smile. "No question."

Despite having her in his arms, he still did not understand what the hell was going on. Not really. Something had changed and he could not figure it out. "So, now what?"

"We start over."

"I have no idea what that means." He didn't. No clue.

"See, this is one of those times where being a bit less black-and-white would help you."

"So would you speaking English."

"Do you love me?"

There it was. She laid the gauntlet at his feet. He could play it safe and walk away before she did.

But he fell into the happiness pulsing from her instead. "Yes."

"Can you forgive me for hurting you?"

That one was harder. The very male part of her wanted to tell her to screw off and leave him alone. He promised himself that was what he would say if this opportunity ever arose again. But he did not count on the feel of her skin and the look of love in her eyes. He certainly did not realize his heart could heal with hope.

"Never again, Lexy."

"Promise." She said the word so fast that he almost didn't catch it.

But he believed her. Dope that he was, he let the happiness bubbling out of her infect him, too. She finally understood that she had caused some damage.

Now he had to take responsibility for his part of this mess. He roped his arms around her waist and pulled her so tight against him that she had to look up to see him. "Can you forgive me?"

"If you're willing to try to change and understand why I need you to."

Her parents and upbringing shaped her more than he realized until right that minute. He kept things close and quiet because he wanted to forget. She wanted openness because she never wanted to live in secret again. He got it now. And the fact they worked it out before it was too late sent all those doubts and all that anger rushing out of him.

"We're talking about a mutual thing." He understood that now. It would take both of them working and changing to make this work. If they failed, he would lose everything. So he vowed not to fail.

"A very mutual thing." She nibbled on his neck and his doubts vanished.

Laughter swelled inside of him. "Now, when you say start over . . ."

Her kisses trailed up to ear. "Yeah?"

"How much of a start are we talking about?"

She pulled back and smiled up at him with all the wonder and love he ever wanted or needed. "I figure it will take us six months to plan the wedding."

He picked her up until her feet dangled off the floor. Then he kissed her. Packed in there was the promise of a life together. Together they were better than they were apart.

"And time for therapy," she said when they rose for air.

"What?"

"Just some counseling to help us start off right."

"You're ruining my good mood." But she wasn't. If Lexy needed them to work through everything with someone else, he would do it.

He doubted they would need much coaching. Now that they tasted life without each other, they'd fight to leave it behind forever.

"What do I get in exchange for going to this counseling?"

"A fiancée and a PR manager."

All the broken pieces inside him healed. "I like the way you multitask."

She wiggled her eyebrows. "Tough talk for a man who's still wearing his pants."

"Damn, I love you."

The confession earned him another kiss. "I love you, too."

His mind moved on to the makeup portion of the day. "Did you lock the door?"

"Of course."

"Then let's try a little multisomething."

She laughed until he dragged her to the floor, then she moaned. Yeah, they were understanding each other just fine. He knew they would forever.

Have you read the newest Shannon McKenna book?
ULTIMATE WEAPON is in stores now!

Tam cupped her tea in both hands and inhaled the steam as she studied his face. She didn't like to admit it to herself, but it was taking more energy than she'd expected to withstand the gale force of this man's sex appeal. Erin had not been kidding.

For some reason, Tam had been expecting a generic male underwear model sort of good looks. Which was unfair. Erin was married to Connor, after all, and even Tam could appreciate his craggy, fierce good looks. Even in her most virulent, man-repelled moods.

But still. She was utterly unprepared for . . . well, him.

Lethal. It was the first word that came to mind, even though it embarrassed her. He was so solid, so hard looking. Dynamic, and yet calm and focused. Nothing soft about him, except for the gloss of that thick brush of black hair. She wanted to touch it, just to see if it really was as soft as mink. Gypsy dark eyes, inky brows and lashes. The planes and angles of his face were starkly masculine, arrogantly sensual, but that smile was pure temptation. She'd considered herself impervious to men's lures, so why was she marveling at the lines carved into his cheeks when he grinned, or that blinding flash of teeth against his dark skin? *Get a fucking grip, Steele. This is unacceptable.*

His face looked hard-used for a rich business consultant.

There were bumps on his slightly crooked nose, a white diagonal scar sliced through one thick, slashing eyebrow, and subtler scars that only a trained eye accustomed to evaluating the effects of cosmetic surgery could catch. And the hands, of course. He'd fought, in his life. Fought hard. Won, more often than not, judging from his vibe.

And what a vibe. It blasted out of him, full force. It was out of human range, a frequency that only a fucked-up freakoid with a weird, checkered past like hers could perceive. But so different from the danger waves that had throbbed out of the sicko madmen she'd had the misfortune to get close to before, like Novak, Georg, Drago Stengl. Their vibration had been a miasma of rot that made her tissues recoil.

Not so with Janos. In him, the danger was blended like a cocktail with seductive, predatory male sexual energy that assaulted her at every level. It silently said, beneath the smooth veneer of perfect gentlemanly courtesy, that he wanted to fuck her, left, right, up, down, and sideways. And that it would be well worth her while.

She didn't doubt it. But she wasn't going to listen, not even with her nerves jangling, her skin prickling, her heart thudding. Back off, boyo. This was business, and that was how it was going to stay.

"You're not what you try to appear," she said. "You are charming and flirtatious and inscrutable, Mr. Janos, but tiny details betray you. Your hands should be soft, from handling nothing heavier than a pen and a computer mouse, but yours are scarred and callused. And your face. Your nose has been broken. Several times it wasn't set. You can't blame the martial arts club. If it happened during sparring, why would a rich, image conscious businessman neglect to get his nose set? Of course, he would not."

"I did not see the point of—"

"So it happened when you were a boy," she went on

smoothly. "No one set your nose then, either, which implies poverty, neglect, or both. I'm thinking an urban environment, judging from your basic vibe. And those scars on your face, the tiny one above your lip, the one cutting through your eyebrow, the one on your forehead that you almost hide with your hair, it makes me wonder what other scars you hide with the beautiful six thousand Euro suit you're wearing. You've had laser treatments, dermabrassion, but the ghosts always remain."

"I'm glad you like the suit," he said blandly.

"You're no country boy," she went on. "But you're not from Rome. You don't have the accent of the Roman periphery. Your Italian has a Roman cadence, but to my ear, it is a studied one, not a native one. You grew up somewhere else, speaking something else, and learned your perfect Italian later. And you grew up rough. Very rough."

He stared back at her, frozen into stillness. His eyes were chips of black, opaque glass. "Go on," he said.

She set down the teacup, threaded her fingers together and rode the swirling current deeper into wild speculation. She felt like she was drifting on a boat into a night-dark cave of mysteries, and only the currents of air, the echoes, the flutter of distant bats' wings could hint at its true vastness. It was dangerous. And . . . exciting.

She pondered his stark face for a moment, and went on. "You are a ladies' man, and your charm is slick, practiced. You are accustomed to controlling women with sex, but unlike other men with that ability, your ego does not rest on it—although your looks and your body would entitle you to—"

"Thank you," he murmured.

"I am not complimenting you," she said, her voice impatient. "This is an analysis, Janos. Not flattery. Not flirting."

"Forgive me," he said, after a brief, startled pause. "Please, continue to invade my pathetic defenses. By all means, cut deeper to reveal my wretched, naked, cringing inner self. Feel free."

She did not acknowledge his sarcasm. "Sex is a tool for you," she said. "But when a tactic of seduction does not achieve its goal, you just change tactics without getting your pride hurt and try again, and again, and again. This suggests a lack of machismo not normal in a man from any culture I know—particularly not one who professes to have grown up in Italy. Italian men aren't known for their humility, or their self-control. This coolness, this calculation regarding sex is a trait I associate with high-end sex professionals."

His gaze flickered.

She pounced. "Ah. I've hit a sore spot," she murmured. "Have you ever been a gigolo, Mr. Janos? Do you have a more colorful past than you lead people to believe? Some dirty, dangerous secrets of your own?"

He stared at her. His eyes burned.

"Tell me something, Janos," she whispered. "Can you make your cock hard on command?"

His mouth was a hard, flat line. "Yes," he said. "But in your vicinity, no effort is necessary."

"What a lovely sentiment. Should I be gratified?"

"Reach under the table, and take the measure of your future gratification right now," he said.

"Oh, my." She pretended to be scandalized. "The veneer of the perfect gentleman is cracking."

"You should not wonder at it, since you shattered it yourself with an ice pick. See what lurks beneath the veneer. Go on, feel it. It's yours for the asking. I do not think you will be disappointed."

She stared at him, her heart pumping. The game had slipped out of her control and taken on its own life. She realized that she was tempted to do exactly as he invited. To grasp his cock, test his heat, the hardness. Feel the vital energy of him pulsing against her hand.

Make sure to catch
THE MANE ATTRACTION by Shelly Laurenston,
out this month from Brava . . .

Sissy Mae turned over and buried her head back in the pillows, trying her best to block out the sunlight. Since she'd never been a morning person, Sissy always kept the blinds in her room at the Kingston Arms Hotel closed. Why she didn't do that last night, she had no idea.

Well, it didn't matter. She was too exhausted to care at this point. Exhausted and in pain. Her throat was sore and raw, and her head throbbed. It felt like her brain was rattling around inside her skull.

It had to have been that last sip of tequila. The one where she clearly remembered saying to herself, "Well, I shouldn't waste it."

Unfortunately, that was the last thing she really remembered.

No, she wouldn't be getting up anytime soon if she could help it. And to prove it, she buried her face deeper into the pillow. It felt good to do that, so she did it again. In some bizarre way, the action helped her headache—she'd never call it a hangover out loud—so she did it again. Then she rubbed her head against the pillow.

It was that scent. She wanted that scent on her. A very shifter thing to do and one she'd never really be able to explain to a full-human without getting that telltale "ewww" response.

As her brain began to slowly process whose smell this could possibly be, she felt the bed dip and a heavy weight rest against her side.

"Baby?" a deliciously low voice said. "You awake? I need you, baby."

Sissy's eyes snapped open, but she immediately closed them again when bright sunlight brutally seared her brain right inside her skull.

"Mitchell?"

"Yeah," he purred, nuzzling her chin, her ear. "You up for more of me, baby? 'Cause we are so not done."

Not caring how much the light hurt, Sissy slammed her hands against Mitch's chest and pushed him off while scrambling back until her shoulders hit the headboard. Using both hands, she held the sheet under her chin.

"What the hell is going on?"

"What's wrong, baby?"

She stared at him in horror. "Mitchell Shaw, tell me you didn't!"

"Didn't what?" He crawled across the bed toward her. "Didn't turn you inside out and work you like you've never been worked before? Well, if you're asking me to be honest, I guess I'd have to say—"

"Don't." One hand released the sheet she had such a grip on to halt his words. "Not another word."

"Don't be that way, baby."

"And stop calling me that!"

He took hold of the sheet and began to pull it away from her. "Don't be shy, baby. We have no secrets now."

This wasn't happening! This wasn't happening! She was fully dressed!

Wait. She was fully dressed.

Sissy stared down at the clean white T-shirt and white sweatpants. She clearly smelled Ronnie's scent. These were Ronnie's clothes. Had to be. Sissy never wore white. She had a tendency to get food on clothes within seconds. And something told her it was Ronnie who'd put the damn things on Sissy in the first place.

"You are so hot, baby."

Slowly, she looked up at Mitch, and forcing herself to look past her hangover, she could see he was fighting hard not to laugh out loud.

"You. Big. Haired. *Bastard!*"

Sissy launched herself onto Mitch, knocking him off the bed and onto the floor. She punched and slapped at his face, and he held off her blows with those sides of ham he called arms. And it didn't help that he was hysterically laughing the whole time.

"I hate you, Mitchell Shaw! I hate you!"

"You *love* me, sweet cheeks! Admit it!"

"One day," she told him between blows, "you're gonna meet me in hell! And I'm gonna kick your big, white ass!"

"Last night you told me it was the best ass!"

"Shut up!"

He grabbed her wrists and turned, putting her on her back with him between her legs. "Are you going to keep fighting me, or you going to admit I'm your lord and savior?"

"Blasphemer!"

"That's what the priests all said."

"I should tell my daddy to kick your ass."

"He's on vacation. With your mother. Remember?"

And like that . . . all the fight went out of her. "She's gone? Really and truly?"

"Really and truly." He leaned in and kissed her nose. "Now are you going to keep fighting me, or are we going to get some breakfast?"

"Breakfast, you evil bastard. But this will not be forgotten."

Grinning, Mitch released her wrists and easily got to his feet. He reached down and grabbed Sissy's hand, pulling her up.

"You sure you feel okay?" He still held her hand. "I was just messing with your head."

"It was mean." And she shrugged. "Of course, when I think about it, I have to appreciate the evil of it."

He moved closer. "So you're not mad at me?"

"I should be—" Sissy looked up into Mitch's handsome face, and her words died in her throat when she saw something there she didn't see very often—maybe because she'd never really looked before. She saw desire. Pure, clear. It was there on his face and the way he stared at her lips.

Keep an eye out for
MIDNIGHT SINS by Cynthia Eden,
coming next month from Brava . . .

"You don't need to get out," Cara said when Todd braked at her house. Her voice sounded higher and sharper than she'd intended. "I'll be fine now." She thought about thanking him for the ride, then discarded the idea.

Yes, she knew the guy had been doing his job when he questioned her, but she wasn't going to overlook the fact that he'd been one serious jerk.

Being in the car with him had unnerved her. They'd originally gone to the police station in a patrol car. She'd sat in the back. Like any good criminal.

The confines of Todd's corvette were far too intimate. The leather seat felt soft and sleek beneath her, and with the windows rolled up, the scent of leather and man filled the car's interior.

Cara reached for the door handle.

"Wait."

Her fingers curled into a fist at the command, her fingernails biting into her palm. She glanced at him and found his stare trained on her.

The car was cloaked with shadows, but she could still see his eyes. The strong lines of his face. Cara licked her lips. "What?"

"You feel it, don't you?" A whisper that felt like a caress against her skin.

She shook her head. "I don't know what you're talking about." She could lie, too.

His lips quirked, just a bit. With a flick of his fingers, he unhooked his seat belt and leaned toward her. "There's something here."

The promise of hot, wild sex. Of power and magic rushing into her body and making her scream with pleasure.

But she'd given that up because after the burn of fiery release, she hated the ashes of cold reality.

The reality that a man wouldn't love a demon, no matter how enticing her physical trappings.

His hand lifted, reached for her.

Her fingers flew out and locked around his wrist in a fierce grip.

Silence. Then he said, "I just wanted to touch you."

He sounded sincere, *but* . . . "I thought you just wanted to send me to jail."

He didn't deny her words. Didn't fight her hold. Good thing, too, because the way she was feeling, Cara would have shown him just how strong a succubus could be.

Instead, his gaze dropped to her lips. "I wonder," he spoke with words little more than a growl. "Do you taste as good as you smell?"

The dam pheromones. "It's not me that you want." The admission was hard.

"Ah, baby, but I'm going to have to disagree." He was close, so close that she could feel the light brush of his breath against her face.

"You don't understand—"

He kissed her. A soft, fast press of his lips against hers.

Cara's fingers tightened around him as desire began to heat her blood.

"Not enough." His lips were just above hers. "I need another taste . . ."

And she wanted more.